CW01647366

ACCEL·WORLD 27

THE FOURTH ACCELERATION

REKI KAWAHARA

ILLUSTRATION BY **HIMA**

DESIGN BY **bee-pee**

GODDESS OF THE DAWN USHAS
ABANDONED PRINCESS BARI
"I-I'm sorry about that! I definitely didn't contact you on purpose. It was more like I had too much momentum…"

ARCHANGEL METATRON
OHIRUME AMATERASU
QUEEN MOTHER
OF THE WEST XIWANGMU

"Do you wish me to lull you to sleep?
So like a child, hmm?"

ARCHANGEL METATRON

True form of the Archangel who lives in the deepest level of the Shiba Park Underground Labyrinth, one of the four Great Dungeons in the Accelerated World. Treats Silver Crow like her servant.

"Chrysocyoooooon!"
UROCYON
Visitor from Dread Drive 2047.
Drive Linker, self-proclaimed
Unifiers' raiding party leader.
Nickname: Primal Fang.

"I *will* show that I can do a quadruple flip."
RISA TSUKIORI
Ninth-grade gymnast specializing in the vault. Seriously injured in the middle of a vault performance during the national championship on July 21, 2047, and is hospitalized, still unconscious.

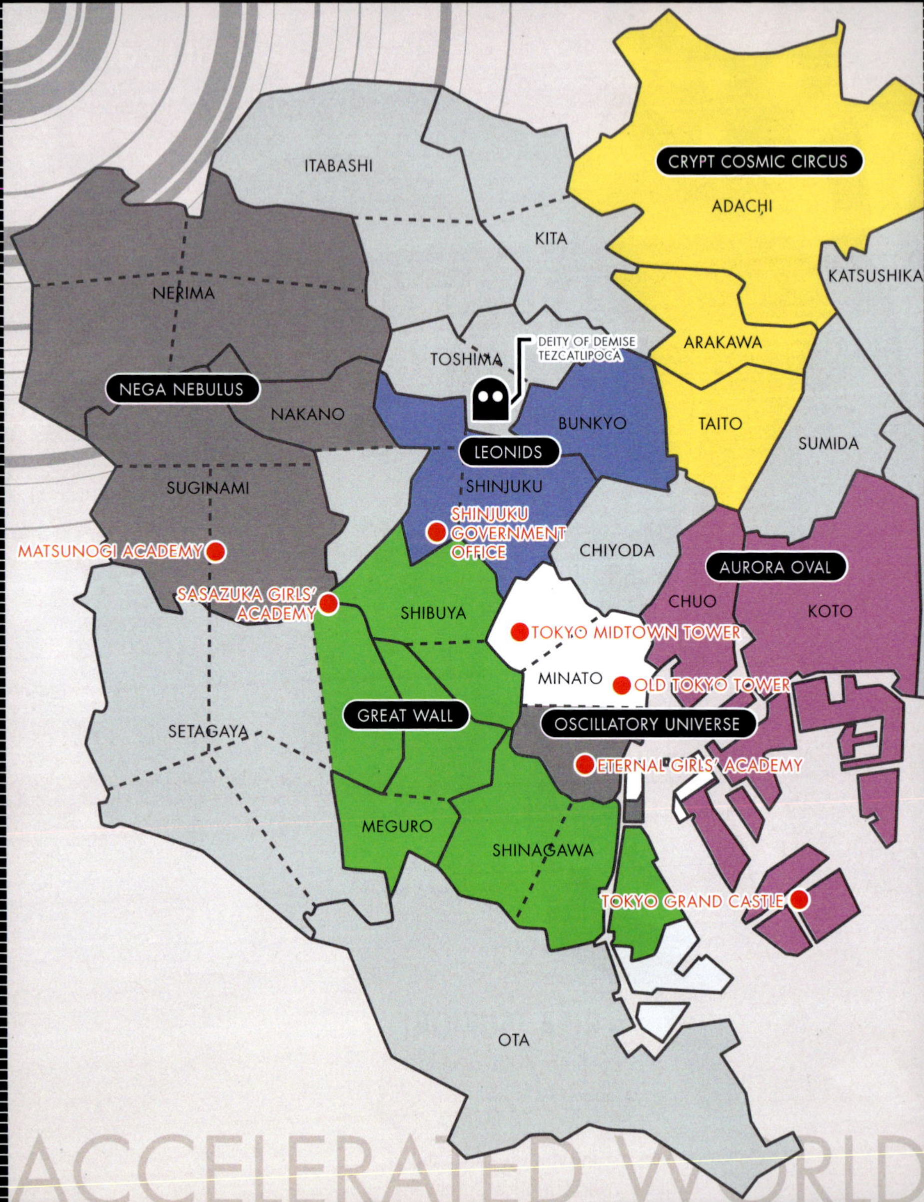

ACCELERATED WORLD MAP Ver. 4.1

Exercitus

A joint army of small and midsize Legions formed with the objective of crushing Tezcatlipoca — their name means "army" in Latin. The central groups are the powerful midsize Legions Night Owls, Ovest, and Cold Brew, with many small Legions and solo Linkers joining them. Their membership is in excess of five hundred, and immediately after formation, they became the largest force in the Accelerated World.

Deity of Demise, Tezcatlipoca

Giant Super–class Enemy over one hundred meters tall that appeared from inside the Sun God Inti. Its confirmed methods of attack are Toxcatl, gravitational waves released from its right hand; Miccailhuitontli, incandescent flames released from its left; and Level Drain. According to the White King, its power surpasses that of the Four Saints and the Four Gods combined.

ACCEL WORLD 27

THE FOURTH ACCELERATION

Reki Kawahara
Illustrations: HIMA
Design: bee-pee

YEN ON
New York

■ Kuroyukihime = Umesato Junior High School student council vice president. A "machine child" produced by parents who were researchers at Kamura, she had her brain overwritten with someone's soul. Her duel avatar is the Black King, Black Lotus.
■ Haruyuki = Haruyuki Arita. Grade eight at Umesato Junior High School. He left his "parent" Kuroyukihime and joined Oscillatory Universe. His duel avatar is Silver Crow.
■ Chiyuri = Chiyuri Kurashima. Haruyuki's childhood friend. As a Burst Linker, she possesses the extremely rare ability to go back in time and is active as the Black Legion's healer. Her duel avatar is Lime Bell.
■ Takumu = Takumu Mayuzumi. A boy Haruyuki and Chiyuri have known since childhood. When he had level seven in his sights, he was sent back down to level four because of Tezcatlipoca's Level Drain. His duel avatar is Cyan Pile.
■ Fuko = Fuko Kurasaki. One of the Four Elements. Rules wind. Taught Haruyuki about the Incarnate System. Her duel avatar is Sky Raker.
■ Uiui = Utai Shinomiya. One of the Four Elements. Rules fire. Grade four student in the elementary division of Matsunogi Academy. Uses the advanced curse removal command "Purify." Her duel avatar is Ardor Maiden.
■ Centaurea Sentry = Seri Suzukawa. The Third Chrome Disaster and one of the strongest players in the Accelerated World. Taught Haruyuki Omega style Whole Blade.
■ Rose Milady = Tsubomi Koshika. Ranked third of the Seven Dwarves, the White Legion's executive, but is fighting together with Haruyuki for the time being in order to save Megumi Wakamiya.
■ Ivory Tower = Identity unknown. Ranked fourth of the Seven Dwarves, full proxy of the White King. Also the true identity of Black Vise, vice president of the Acceleration Research Society.
■ Graphite Edge = Identity unknown. Burst Linker who belonged to the old Nega Nebulus. One of the Four Elements. His identity is still shrouded in mystery.
■ White Cosmos = Identity unknown. Master of the White Legion Oscillatory Universe. Also known as Transient Eternity. Kuroyukihime's older sister and "parent."

■ Neurolinker = A portable Internet terminal that connects with the brain via a wireless quantum connection and enhances all five senses with images, sounds, and other stimuli.
■ Brain Burst 2039 = Trial No. 2. Neurolinker application sent to Haruyuki by Kuroyukihime. Viewed as mainly a fighting game with Enemy hunting.
■ Accel Assault 2038 = Trial No. 1. High-speed shooting, one-on-one. A separate Accelerated World from Brain Burst, which declined because it was filled with excessive fighting.
■ Cosmos Corrupt 2040 = Trial No. 3. Hack-and-slash, mainly fighting Enemies. A separate Accelerated World from Brain Burst, which declined because it was filled with excessive harmony.
■ Duel avatar = Player's virtual self operated when fighting in Brain Burst.
■ Legion = Groups composed of many duel avatars with the objective of expanding occupied areas and securing rights. There are seven main Legions, each led by one of the Seven Kings of Pure Color.
■ Normal Duel Field = The field where normal Brain Burst battles (one-on-one) are carried out. Although the specs do possess elements of reality, the system is essentially on the level of an old-school fighting game.
■ Unlimited Neutral Field = Field for high-level players where only duel avatars at level four and up are allowed. The game system is of a wholly different order than that of the Normal Duel Field, and the level of freedom in this field beats out even the next-generation VRMMO.

■ Movement Control System = System in charge of avatar control. Normally, this system handles all avatar movement.
■ Image Control System = System in which the player creates a strong image in their mind to operate the avatar. The mechanism is very different from the normal movement control system, and very few players can use it. Key component of the Incarnate System.
■ Incarnate System = Technique allowing players to interfere with the Brain Burst program's Image Control System to bring about a reality outside the game's framework. Also referred to as "overwriting" game phenomena.

■ ISS kit = Abbreviation for "IS mode study kit." ("IS mode" is "Incarnate System mode.") The kit allows any duel avatar who uses it to make use of the Incarnate System. While using it, a red "eye" is attached to some part of the avatar, and a black aura overlay—the staple of Incarnate attacks—is emitted from the eye.

■ Seven Arcs = The seven strongest Enhanced Armaments in the Accelerated World. They are the greatsword Impulse, the staff Tempest, the large shield Strife, the crown/scepter Luminary, the straight sword Infinity, the full-body armor Destiny, and the Fluctuating Light (form unknown).

■ Mental-Scar Shell = The emotional scars that are the foundation of a duel avatar (mental scars created from trauma in early childhood)—this is the shell enveloping them. Children with exceptionally hard and thick "shells" are said to produce metal-color duel avatars.

■ Artificial metal color = Refers to a metal-color avatar that is not generated naturally from the subject's mental scars, but rather produced artificially by a third party through the thickening of the Mental-Scar Shell.

■ Unlimited EK = Abbreviation for Unlimited Enemy Kill. The subject avatar is killed by a powerful Enemy in the Unlimited Neutral Field, and after they regenerate once more after a fixed period of time, they are killed again by that Enemy, falling into an infinite hell.

▶▶▶ACCEL·WORLD

Duel Avatar and Enemy List

Black Legion: Nega Nebulus

Provisional Master: Black Lotus (Kuroyukihime)

Provisional Submaster: Scarlet Rain (Yuniko Kozuki)

Four Elements
- Wind: Sky Raker (Fuko Kurasaki)
- Fire: Ardor Maiden (Utai Shinomiya)
- Water: Aqua Current (Akira Himi)

- Lime Bell (Chiyuri Kurashima)
- Cyan Pile (Takumu Mayuzumi)
- Chocolat Puppeter (Shihoko Nago)
- Mint Mitten (Satomi Mito)
- Plum Flipper (Yume Yuruki)
- Magenta Scissor (Rui Odagiri)
- Trilead Tetroxide
- Centaurea Sentry (Seri Suzukawa)

Triplex
- No. 1: Blood Leopard (Mihaya Kakeya)
- No. 2: Cassis Moose
- No. 3: Thistle Porcupine

- Blaze Heart
- Peach Parasol
- Ochre Prison
- Mustard Salticid
- Lavender Downer
- Iodine Sterilizer

Temporarily transferred from Great Wall
- Ash Roller (Rin Kusakabe)
- Bush Utan
- Olive Grab

Blue Legion: Leonids

Master: Blue Knight

Dualis
- Cobalt Blade (Koto Takanouchi)
- Manganese Blade (Yuki Takanouchi)

- Frost Horn
- Tourmaline Shell
- Cerulean Runner

Green Legion: Great Wall

Master: Green Grandé

Six Armors
- First seat: Graphite Edge
- Second seat: Viridian Decurion
- Third seat: Iron Pound
- Fourth seat: Lignum Vitae
- Fifth seat: Suntan Chafer
- Sixth seat: ???

- Jade Jailer

Yellow Legion: Crypt Cosmic Circus

Master: Yellow Radio

- Lemon Pierrette
- Sax Loader

Purple Legion: Aurora Oval

Master: Purple Thorn

- Aster Vine

ACCEL·WORLD

White Legion: Oscillatory Universe

Master: White Cosmos

Seven Dwarves
- No. 1: Platinum Cavalier (Tomochika Kyobu)
- No. 2: Snow Fairy (Nanako Juholt)
- No. 3: Rose Milady (Tsubomi Koshika)
- No. 4: Ivory Tower
- No. 5: ???
- No. 6: Cypress Reaper (Airi Sagisu)
- No. 7: Glacier Behemoth (Rioh Koshimizu)

- Shadow Cloaker
- Orchid Oracle (Megumi Wakamiya)
- Silver Crow (Haruyuki Arita)

Acceleration Research Society

- Black Vise
- Argon Array
- Dusk Taker (Seiji Nomi)
- Rust Jigsaw
- Sulfur Pot
- Wolfram Cerberus (Armor of Catastrophe, Mark II)

Computation and Martial Arts Research Club

- Aluminum Valkyrie (Chiaki Chigira)
- Orange Raptor (Yuko Hori)
- Violet Dancer (Kurumi Kuruma)
- Iris Alice (Lilya Usachova)

Exercitus

Gallant Hawks
- Zelkova Verger
- Taupe Cape

Ovest
- Cotton Marten

Affiliation unknown

- Avocado Avoider
- Nickel Doll
- Sand Duct
- Crimson Kingbolt
- Lagoon Dolphin (Ruka Asato)
- Coral Merrow (Mana Itosu)
- Tin Writer

Enemies

Four Saints
- Archangel Metatron (Shiba Park Underground Labyrinth)
- Ohirume Amaterasu (Tokyo Station Underground Labyrinth)
- Goddess of the Dawn Ushas (Shinjuku Government Building Underground Labyrinth)
- Queen Mother of the West Xiwangmu (Tokyo Dome Underground Labyrinth)

Four Gods of the Four Gates
- East gate: Seiryu
- West gate: Byakko
- South gate: Suzaku
- North gate: Genbu

Eight Divines of the Shrine of the Eight Divines
- ???

Highest-ranking Beings
- Goddess Nyx (Yoyogi Park Underground Labyrinth)
- Abandoned Princess Bari (National Stadium Underground Labyrinth)
- Storm King Rudra (Tokyo Big Site Underground Labyrinth)

God-class Enemies
- Sun God Inti (Deity of Demise Tezcatlipoca)

THE FOURTH ACCELERATION

1

Exactly how many hours—how many days—had passed? Zelkova Verger, a Burst Linker from the small Legion Gallant Hawks, stood rooted to the spot in a half-lit, colorless world.

His avatar was uncomfortably transparent, and the outlines of the rocky mountains that rose up all around him were also nothing more than a smoky haze. The only thing clearly visible to him was the cluster of six small digital numerals decreasing soundlessly in the middle of his field of view. This timer was counting down the sixty minutes to his regeneration. When it reached zero, he would be revived and take on solid form once again in the Unlimited Neutral Field.

He'd died accidentally a couple times before on Enemy hunts with Legion members, and he'd then cursed the absurdly long wait to be brought back to life. Now, however, his heart was filled with the exact opposite feeling—the desire for his regeneration to come even a minute, even a second later, the wish for time to simply stop.

Because Zelkova Verger was currently trapped in a situation every Burst Linker lived in true fear of, the ultimate peril—Unlimited Enemy Kill. And it was no run-of-the-mill Enemy killing him repeatedly and instantaneously every time he returned from the dead. This Enemy was more powerful than even the Four Gods, the Super-class Enemies that guarded the four Castle gates. This was the most powerful and most destructive creature in the history of the Accelerated World, the Deity of Demise, Tezcatlipoca.

Actually...maybe this is it. Maybe I can't escape death—total point loss.

Zelkova closed his eyes and clenched his teeth in bitter resignation.

I probably underestimated this game Brain Burst. I happened to get a duel avatar with a good balance between offense and defense, I got lucky with good comrades and a good game space. So I made it to level six without any real crises, no real tight spots to speak of. Although it did take a while to get here. But I sort of assumed I'd keep going up and up. The Accelerated World's not so cushy as that, though.

I mean, I went all the way to Suginami 'cause I wanted to show off to my "parent," Taupe Cape, to look cool. The most unserious of motivations, for real. When I got my butt handed to me by Silver Crow, I should've realized I was full of myself; it was all my own stupid pride.

But I didn't. I talked Taupe and the rest of the Legion into joining the massive joint army Exercitus and challenging Tezcatlipoca. Sure, I wanted to believe in the manifesto in the invitation mail, all the excitement and hype. But I could've realized what they were talking about was seriously dangerous and not gone any further. The way Itabashi's midsize Legion Helix did.

So if I lose all my points here, it's my own stupid fault. But...

Zelkova looked around slowly as he reproached himself for his own role in this tragedy.

About a hundred meters away, a terrifyingly enormous human-shaped silhouette soared up into the sky. He could only see it as a black shadow, since he was a ghost at the moment, but he knew that it was the Deity of Demise, Tezcatlipoca, itself, motionless because it had slaughtered all of the Burst Linkers within its aggro range. But when even a single person within that range regenerated, it would instantly leap into motion once more.

At the foot of the gigantic shadow, he could see the flickering of countless three-dimensional icons patterned after small flames. All were the death markers of Burst Linkers who had joined in the mission to subjugate Tezcatlipoca. The truly fearsome thing was that a quarter or so of the more than three hundred markers that had been there in the immediate aftermath of the annihilation of the subjugation team had already disappeared. In other words, seventy or eighty Burst Linkers had lost all of their points and been permanently banished from the Accelerated World during the week—around 170 hours—since the team had fallen into the Unlimited EK state.

This, too, however, was perhaps only to be expected. The number of points a Burst Linker lost when killed by an Enemy in the Unlimited Neutral Field was fixed at ten, so the number of points lost in an Unlimited EK of 170 hours was basically 1,700. If a player had only just leveled up or made a large purchase at the shop, they could easily have had not even a thousand points remaining in their account.

Fortunately—well, he wasn't sure about that part, but anyway—Zelkova Verger had been squirreling his points away for months, gunning for level seven, so he had a stock of around 2,100. Even after a week of Unlimited EK chipping away at that stock, he still had a surplus of 400-ish. Which meant that if he kept regenerating and dying like this, he would face a total point loss in forty hours.

He regretted setting his automatic disconnect safety, a must when diving into the Unlimited Neutral Field, to sixty minutes of real-world time. He could make excuses and say he'd had to because that was what was in the Exercitus mission plan, and that would have been true. But if he'd ignored that instruction and set his safety to ten minutes—no, one minute—he would have burst out long ago.

But there was no sense in regret or what-ifs at this point. The fact was that in forty hours, Zelkova would no longer be a Burst Linker. He had more or less made his peace with that, although the feeling was a somewhat desperate one. But there was just one thing that he couldn't accept.

The small, colorless flame that flickered a mere three meters from his own death marker. If he hadn't been dead, it would have appeared to be a warm gray with a hint of purple to it, the death marker of his parent and the leader of the Gallant Hawks, Taupe Cape.

A grade below him at junior high school in the real world, she was more the cautious type, and she hadn't been particularly interested in taking part in this joint subjugation mission. Zelkova and fellow Legion member Dim, aka Rubidium Cooler, had talked her into it, and the entire Legion had joined Exercitus. So it wasn't Taupe's fault that they were in this situation. Most likely, Dim and their other comrades had lost all their points long ago, and Zelkova himself only had forty hours left to live. At the very least, however, he wanted to make sure Taupe survived. Given her personality, it might have been too much for her to revive the Legion on her own, but even still, he wanted her to continue living as a Burst Linker.

While he earnestly tried to maintain his thought clock speed, despite the fear, despair, and lack of sleep that pushed it ever downward, Zelkova Verger prayed with all his heart.

Please… Someone, rescue Taupe from this certain death. I don't care what happens to me. Take Taupe's marker and get it out of Tezcatlipoca's range…

But, of course, there was no one to hear this prayer.

The countdown in the center of his field of view continued its relentless march toward zero. Only five minutes and thirty seconds left until his nth regeneration.

Abruptly, the inky black giant stirred soundlessly, a hundred meters before him.

While the two hundred and some dozen ghostly Burst Linkers bound to this spot had initially died at basically the same time, over the course of being repeatedly resurrected and killed, the timing of their individual regenerations had grown more and more out of sync, so that now there was a gap of about five minutes among them. The earliest group had started to return from the dead, prompting Tezcatlipoca to move once more.

Ahead of Zelkova, the tiny fires—the death markers—flashed into bright bonfires one after the other and transformed into human-shaped shadows. The reborn feet of these shadows had no sooner touched the ground than they were dashing away, trying to distance themselves from the jet-black giant.

In the center of the scattering Burst Linkers, the god of the end raised its right foot up high and brought it down with a thunderous roar.

Zelkova was still dead, so he couldn't hear the sound, but shock waves rippled outward from the monumental foot, cracking and shattering the supposedly indestructible ground, and mercilessly swallowed up the fugitives. Their feet kicked out from under them, they pitched forward, and before their bodies could touch the ground, they burst and scattered one after the other. Not one of those Burst Linkers could withstand the force of even a single footstep, despite the fact that the majority of them would have been level-five or level-six veterans.

Even still, the ones who managed to flee the farthest had gained more than twenty meters of ground in those seconds before they died. If they kept hammering away at escape like this, they would eventually make it out of Tezcatlipoca's attack range. Zelkova himself had thought so in the beginning.

The next group regenerated and similarly attempted escape. The god of the end raised not its foot but its right hand this time. A black ring floated up above its open palm, and an inky sphere shot forth like a bullet of concentrated darkness.

The dense mass dug into the ground, as if it were made of butter, as it swelled to enormous sizes and churned violently. The fleeing Burst Linkers were instantly and helplessly sucked toward this wild vortex and broke into pieces that scattered in all directions the moment they touched the sphere.

This was one of Tezcatlipoca's special attacks, Toxcatl. Gravitational waves radiated from its palm and flattened its targets, or it generated a micro black hole at a random location, sucked the target in, and crushed them. The latter was the more terrifying, ruthlessly resetting the meager distance the Burst Linkers had desperately put between themselves and the giant every time they regenerated. The only way to escape from the Deity of Demise, Tezcatlipoca, was to use a teleportation-type ability or to fly like Silver Crow. This was the conclusion Zelkova Verger had come to over the course of his week in the Unlimited EK.

Naturally, neither he nor Taupe Cape had any such ability. The lone hope left to him was that someone—with luck, someone from the seven Great Legions—would come to their rescue.

But he was well aware that there was hope and then there were pipe dreams. The group Exercitus had been born of a determination to overthrow the current system of control via the seven Great Legions. Their objective was to muster the combined forces of the midsize and small Legions, defeat Tezcatlipoca, and petition the Seven Kings of Pure Color for an apology and reparations for all the damage they'd done up to that point. The seven Great Legions would lose a vast sum of points and their territories, and the hegemony of the Seven Kings, ongoing since the dawn of the Accelerated World, would be overturned.

He still thought the stated aspirations of the instigators of Exercitus were the correct course of action. But they and the more than five hundred people who agreed with them had misjudged the threat of Tezcatlipoca.

The key part of their strategy had been to sink the Enemy in water up to the neck in an Ocean stage, where the sea reached depths of eighty meters, and then freeze that water to render the creature unable to use the majority of its attacks. They had succeeded in this for less than five full minutes. Before the order to begin the actual attack could be given, Tezcatlipoca had exploded the ice apart with its fiery special attack, Miccailhuitontli, and the incredible heat this generated instantly evaporated Zelkova and the others in position on the thick ice.

For a while after he fell into the Unlimited EK, he blamed the people who came up with this plan, but three or four days of EK wore away these feelings, along with his burst points. If the leaders of the core Legions—Ovest, Cold Brew, Gouen, and Night Owls—had fled, his anger might have lasted a little longer. But they had been pulverized together with Toshima Ecomuse Town, the high-rise building that served as the command center for the mission, by the long-range blast wave emitted from Tezcatlipoca's mouth, and they had joined him as ghosts bound to the location of their death.

When he thought about it with a cooler head, the possibility of help arriving would have significantly increased if even one of the leaders had managed to escape. But the current time in the real world was past seven in the evening. Given that the majority of Burst Linkers were in elementary or junior high school, with even the oldest among them only in grade ten, this was pretty much suppertime if they were living in an average household. It was one thing if they'd made their excuses to their families, as the Exercitus attack participants had, but it would have not been a simple thing for most Burst Linkers to immediately dive into the Unlimited Neutral Field after getting the call. Even if they shoveled down the rest of their supper and did the bare minimum in preparation, they still wouldn't be able to dive until seven thirty at the earliest.

Assuming that help did come at that time, twenty minutes from now in the real world was 20,000 minutes from now—330 hours, give or take. If nothing changed about this Unlimited EK, the math said that he would lose another 3,300 points before anyone arrived. While he and Taupe would obviously have lost all their points by then, the carnage would most likely expand to include more than half of the two hundred and some Burst Linkers still surviving.

But the fact of the matter here was that help wasn't coming, no matter how many hundreds of hours they waited. Exercitus was a powerful group formed to overthrow the seven Great Legions. Their initial objective might have been to crush Tezcatlipoca and obtain the incredible bounty it would offer, but their future sights were set on a direct confrontation with the seven Great Legions. The Kings no doubt picked up on that, and if they were the sort of friendly souls who would expose themselves to the risk of total point loss to come to the rescue of the people who were trying to kick them off their thrones, they could never have reached level nine to start with.

No one was coming to save them.

No matter which way he looked at it, this was the only conclusion he could come to. As he digested this fact yet again, Zelkova stared at the timer counting down.

Time left until regeneration, ten seconds...five...three, two, one. Zero.

At the same time as the six digits turned into white flames and vanished, his avatar ghost was yanked back to directly above his death marker. The materialization that started with the tips of his fingers was complete in the blink of an eye, and his restored feet gripped the earth again, felt it tremble beneath him.

When he lifted his face, the dark-red giant a hundred meters ahead of him was in the process of ponderously turning its bulky body, massive enough to stand shoulder to shoulder with the surrounding rocky mountains—Higashi Ikebukuro skyscrapers in the real world. Its target was not Zelkova or the nearby Burst Linkers popping back into existence, but rather a group of about ten people on the opposite side of the giant, making a break toward Sunshine City.

It took about ten seconds for Tezcatlipoca to annihilate them and turn back in the opposite direction again. If Zelkova turned and started running as fast as he could right that second, even a heavyweight avatar like him could probably put fifty meters or so between himself and the colossal Enemy. But it would have been nothing more than useless flailing. He was certain to be hit with Toxcatl again and be yanked back to the giant's feet before he could manage to make it out of the attack zone. This Enemy's job was likely not to simply kill Burst Linkers once and move on, but to keep on killing them until they lost all their points, no matter the stage attributes.

Around 40 percent of the Burst Linkers who regenerated around him turned and started running, but the other 60 percent stood helplessly rooted to the spot like Zelkova. In another two days, there would probably be no one still trying to survive. Although by that time, he would be out of points.

He was too tired for his brain to work properly. *I could take a nap until my next regeneration after I die. But I'm maybe too hungry to actually sleep...* Thinking these absent thoughts, he waited for Tezcatlipoca to turn around.

"Zel!" a voice shouted from his immediate right.

He shifted his gaze from the giant Enemy and saw Taupe Cape, who had regenerated a few seconds after he did, standing there with a tense look on her face.

She'd also been steadily accumulating points for a while now, and she wasn't the type to waste them in the shop, so she should have had even more in reserve than he did. But it was a fact that total point loss came closer with every passing second, and they could panic all they wanted, but there was nothing they could do about it. She had to have known that as well.

But she whirled around before he could say anything and began to run at full speed. "This way!" she cried.

With no other choice, he chased after her. Her course cut around to the left, rather than in a straight line away from Tezcatlipoca like those of the other regenerated players. Getting away from the group would indeed lower their chances of being targeted, but the attack ranges for Toxcatl and Miccailhuitontli were simply too large, the blast wave too far-reaching. Any distance they could gain by running was basically a tolerance error.

Zelkova chased intently after the purple-gray cape armor fluttering before him as he opened his mouth to call out and try to stop her. But again, her sharp voice interrupted him.

"Zel!" she shouted, throwing an arm out to point at something. "Let's take this thing down!"

He looked and found a black pill bug–like crustacean crawling along the base of a large rock. But while a pill bug was small, this thing was more than a meter long. He was pretty sure it was an Eboniluce, a Lesser-class Enemy with minimal attack power and no annoying special abilities. But it rolled up its entire body at the slightest jab, and its armor was as tough as ebonite, which meant that physical attacks had limited effect, as did heat, cold, and electricity.

Thus, in order to defeat one of them, you had to do enough damage on that initial hit to cause it to die instantly. But Zelkova and Taupe had both only just regenerated, and their special attack gauges were empty. Their opponent might have been a Lesser class, but it was still an Enemy. Even if they both hit the weak point of its head at the same time, its health gauge wouldn't even drop 20 percent.

Kkkrrrrrraaaar! Came a ponderous roar from behind him to the left, like the thunderous rumbling of a mountain. After slaughtering the group that was fleeing in the direction of Sunshine City, Tezcatlipoca had turned around and was now beginning its attack on this side. In less than five seconds, one of its three special attacks would pour down on them, and crush, cook, or obliterate Zelkova and his comrades.

Even so, Taupe didn't stop.

It couldn't have been that she simply wanted to take out her frustration on the Eboniluce. And now that he was thinking about it, this was the first time since the start of the Unlimited EK that he'd seen any Enemies within a range reachable on foot after regenerating. He wasn't sure what Taupe's aim was, but this was probably the first and last Enemy to pop up near them. In which case, he had to have faith in his comrade—his "parent"—and give this everything he had. He was sure that Silver Crow would never stop racking his brain for a millisecond, even in a hopeless situation like this.

See more, take a broader view like he does...

The eyes he'd had fixed on the Eboniluce grew almost too big and caught sight of something he hadn't been able to see before.

"Taupe!" he yelled. "The rock!"

Taupe Cape responded immediately, just as she was about to go around to the head end of the Eboniluce.

The massive pill bug was sluggishly crawling along the base of a rock that looked to be about five meters across. If this was a Scorched Earth stage, it would have been porous like pumice, but fortunately, this was a nature-type, earth-affiliated, neutral Demon Stone stage. The large stone Zelkova and Taupe leapt onto shone with a greenish luster, and simply touching it, he could feel how dense it was.

If the rock had been half—no, even a third—buried in the ground, the two of them alone wouldn't have been able to move it a millimeter. But the thick bedrock was exposed in this area, and the massive rock was simply resting on top of it.

"Hngh… Aaah!" Zelkova howled as he pressed his right shoulder up against the rock and pushed.

An ominous roar sounded behind him, like thousands of motors whirring into operation. Miccailhuitontli had slammed into the ground and generated a micro black hole. Once the power of its gravity began to pull on this stone, they would have no chance of moving it in the opposite direction.

"Hnnnnngh!" Taupe Cape let out a groan the likes of which he had never heard before, pushing on the rock with her hands and head.

Zelkova also mustered up the last of the fuel he had, his consciousness 70 percent worn away, and pushed with everything he had.

He felt the pull of the black hole on his back just as the rock wobbled and pitched forward slowly, as if to toy with them. Before the Eboniluce crawling along the base on the other side had time to curl up into a ball, the massive rock crushed it. He heard a horrible squelching sound, and the Enemy turned to dust rather anticlimactically.

A message informing him of the points he'd gained was displayed in his field of view. This bump delayed their descent into total point loss the slightest bit, but Taupe's intention had likely not been to stave off the inevitable for the briefest of instants.

And then a gravitational force yanked mercilessly on his entire body, so powerfully he was surprised it didn't lift the surface of the ground itself. But rather than resisting this force, he looked back, threw his right hand out determinedly, pressed it to the ground, and shouted, "Monolithic Wall!"

His special attack gauge had been fully charged by the destruction of the Eboniluce, and now it dropped 70 percent as a reddish-brown slab shot straight up from the bedrock before his eyes. This was his level-five special attack, a monolith of a wall reaching a thickness of ten centimeters and a height and breadth of two meters. With no offensive power, the technique was for defense only, and it was highly resistant to every attack type except fire. Its unique feature was that it absolutely would not move from the spot in which it was generated unless the supporting surface itself was destroyed.

Zelkova poked his face out from behind the wall he'd produced, and the shock that hit him was so powerful, he worried it would shatter his face mask. His health gauge dropped nearly 30 percent, but his descent into the black hole was just barely stopped.

Taupe Cape slammed into his back. Her body flipped over, unable to withstand the intense gravity, and just as she was on the verge of rolling out from behind the wall, he grabbed on to her arm and yanked her back. Dust and sand and rocks flowed past like a river to either side of them.

"Thanks! Don't let go!" Taupe Cape cried, her voice pained.

As instructed, he wrapped his arms around the small avatar from behind and held on tightly. He'd never been this close to Taupe Cape in the Accelerated World before, much less in the real world.

Thinking about it, he didn't even know the reason why Taupe decided to make him her "child." Their only point of contact was the handicraft club they belonged to at school. But the girl members mostly sewed and knit, while the boy members focused on woodworking, so they basically never talked to each other. The only thing resembling a conversation they'd had before he became a Burst Linker was when he helped her look for the embroidery needle she'd dropped.

Alone with a younger girl after school in the craft studio, Zelkova hadn't known what to do with himself, so he'd gone on and on about his congenital night blindness and how he'd enhanced his ability to see in the dark since he was a baby with a Neurolinker and special contact lenses. Taupe must've chosen him as her child because she'd learned by chance that day that he met the first condition to become a Burst Linker—continually wearing a Neurolinker since immediately after birth.

He wanted to talk with her more. He wanted to tell her about himself, about his own guess as to why he'd ended up with a tree guardian, Zelkova Verger, as his duel avatar. And he wanted her to tell him about herself, about her convictions as a Burst Linker, her objectives as Legion Master. It had been a year and a half since they became parent and child, and yet this was the first time he had seriously felt this.

His instantaneous thoughts couldn't have been transmitted through their armor, but Taupe made a movement like the smallest of nods and cried out in a hoarse voice.

"Mole Hole!"

This technique name was unfamiliar to Zelkova. He watched as semitransparent, four-footed creatures glowing with a purple light leapt forward from her hands and began to dig furiously at the surface of the ground in front of them. For a second, he thought they were enormous mice, but judging from their stout bodies and their shovel-like front paws, they were probably moles. After all, that's what "mole" meant in English, and Taupe had told him before that her color name meant the shade of a mole's fur in French.

The semitransparent moles dug up the supposedly indestructible earth with surprising force and disappeared into an opening the size of a manhole.

Abruptly, he heard a dull *thrrk* and a hard *crack* at the same time. The *thrrk* was the sound of the Monolithic Wall supporting them breaking and bending in the middle. And the *crack* was the sound of his armor fracturing, unable to withstand the pressure.

"Zel, once your armor breaks off, jump into the hole!" Taupe cried, and his eyes flew open in surprise.

The hole was about sixty centimeters across. Heavyweight Zelkova had a shoulder span of nearly eighty centimeters, so he would absolutely get stuck if he tried to jump into it in other circumstances. But with the armor around his shoulders and hips shattered in the gravity of the micro black hole, and with his avatar body exposed, he should have been just barely able to pass through the opening.

How long, exactly, had Taupe been cooking up this strategy?

She'd waited intently until the weakest class of Enemy popped up nearby, defeated it to charge up their special attack gauges, opened a hole in the ground with Mole Hole, used Tezcatlipoca's Toxcatl to smash his armor, and finally had him leap into the hole. Each of these steps was far more difficult to carry out than finding an embroidery needle in a dark craft studio, and yet Taupe had managed to successfully execute four of the five.

But one serious issue remained.

"Taupe, can the two of us fit in here?!" he cried.

"It'll be fine! You first, Zel!" Taupe responded without a moment's hesitation. Almost like she had expected him to ask the question.

He heard an even louder *crack* as the armor on his back and left arm shattered. The gravity of the black hole grew endlessly stronger and tried to plunge the two of them into an inky darkness. Monolithic Wall had only barely stopped that process, but it continued to bend under the pressure and would likely break apart entirely in the next ten seconds.

Zelkova wasted a too-precious second in thought and made up his mind.

Without a word, he grabbed Taupe's waist and lifted her off the ground.

"Z-Zel?!" she yelped.

He ignored her and took a step forward, fighting the overwhelming gravity. Cracks raced across his armor, and pieces peeled away. The damage reached his naked avatar body, and his health gauge started to drop rapidly, but he ignored this and put all of his strength into moving his right leg.

"Unh. Ah. Aaaaaaaaah!" Letting loose with a scream unlike any sound he'd ever made in any duel, he took another step forward and lifted Taupe up high.

"No!! Zel, you can't!" she half screamed, struggling to free herself.

Although he wanted to thank her for everything, he didn't even have the extra strength left needed to move his mouth. Holding his breath and gritting his teeth, he threw her into the Mole Hole. He caught a rock tumbling along like a beach ball, in thrall to the gravitational pull, and mustered up the very last of his power to shove it into the hole and make a cover.

He didn't know whether or not this would save Taupe Cape. The Change came over the Unlimited Neutral Field once every week or so, and all damage to the world was reset when the stage attributes changed. While there was a real possibility that the Mole Hole would disappear and Taupe would be spat out, if the hole could make it through the Change…

As Zelkova used up the last drop of his mental focus, his feet peeled away from the ground. At basically the same time, Monolithic Wall shattered into pieces and transformed into countless atoms.

Wrapped in ephemeral, shining particles, Zelkova Verger fell into the roaring vortex of the black hole.

2

"Trial Number Two service ends today! Any of you wanna disappear, you go right ahead. Anyone sticks around, and we'll give you your final notice. This game's official version, the name's Dread Drive 2047!!"

Haruyuki Arita heard every word of this loud declaration, but he needed a few seconds to understand its meaning.

Trial No. 2 was the Accelerated World, formally known as Brain Burst 2039, the battleground and lived-in space for Haruyuki and the other Burst Linkers. Just as the name indicated, Brain Burst began service in 2039 and had continued over eight years into the present. And this guy was saying that today was the end…?

Slightly dizzy, Haruyuki blinked his eyes repeatedly beneath Silver Crow's mirrored goggles.

To his right and left, the reddish-brown large rocks particular to the Wasteland stage covered the ground, almost endless in number. The model for this stage was apparently a picturesque area in the United States' Colorado Plateau known as Monument Valley, but he very much did not have the brain space to take in the scenery at the moment.

Haruyuki and Chiyuri Kurashima, who had dived with him, were standing shoulder to shoulder on the roof of the mixed-use skyscraper Toshima Ecomuse Town, which housed the Toshima Ward office in the real world. To the north side of the building they looked down from was the large intersection where Green Street and Arterial Road No. 81 met, and a strangely shaped statue rose right in the middle of it.

Two cylindrical pillars stretched up vertically and fused together about forty meters off the ground to become one thick pillar. Another twenty meters up, this pillar was severed horizontally, leaving the cross section exposed. The stone statue looked almost as though everything above the waist of an enormous sculpture of a human figure had been destroyed.

Actually, it didn't merely look like that. This was exactly what it was. The statue was the remains of the Super-class Enemy, the Deity of Demise, Tezcatlipoca, which destroyed itself after plunging the Accelerated World into total chaos.

But this was absolutely not the end of that chaos.

From inside the crumbling Tezcatlipoca, a swirling red elliptical light—a portal—had appeared, and through it, ten unknown Burst Linkers had stepped into the Unlimited Neutral Field. The one who had declared that "service ends today" was on the far right. A small male-type wearing a blue mask and suit with a design reminiscent of a canine creature.

"...Dread Drive 2047..." Haruyuki murmured, almost silently, and then it hit him.

If Brain Burst 2039 was the name of a different world and a different game, then these ten people were not Burst Linkers. They should be called "Drive Linkers," and they were, in the truest sense of the word, visitors—no, invaders.

"Give final notice...?" Chiyuri muttered next to him, her voice hoarse. "They think they can do anything, just the ten of them?"

Below the Drive Linkers lined up along one edge of the stone statue, the area was dotted with fiftyish Burst Linkers and about the same number of death markers. The members of Exercitus, the joint army launched through a merger of a number of small and midsize Legions in order to subjugate Tezcatlipoca. There had likely been more than three hundred of them at the start of the subjugation mission, but they had been trampled down by Tezcatlipoca before Haruyuki and Chiyuri arrived, and two-thirds—more than two hundred army members—had been pushed to a total point loss.

In terms of the number of people sacrificed at one time, this was without a doubt the largest tragedy in the history of the Accelerated World. The majority of responsibility lay with Haruyuki, who had destroyed the "egg" that was the Sun God Inti, awakening Tezcatlipoca. He felt his heart being crushed in his chest at the mere thought of it, but giving in to despair now would solve nothing.

The issue was, just as Chiyuri said, what these ten people were planning to do.

He very much doubted that the words "end of service" were to be taken literally. Because while this was an unprecedented situation, what with the portal to another world/game and with the red hexagons embedded in the sky of the stage, the fact was that Haruyuki and the others were still there, inside Brain Burst 2039.

Nevertheless, a part of him did think that this was maybe the beginning of the end. Snow Fairy, aka Sleepy, the second of Oscillatory Universe's Seven Dwarves, had once told him on the Highest Level.

The end can no longer be avoided. The question is only how we Burst Linkers will end. Will we finish our time in pain, humiliation, and despair like the Assault Linkers and the Corrupt Linkers? Or...?

What if the end that Fairy was referring to was this very situation? Was today—July 27, 2047—really the day that Brain Burst service ended after eight years? Had the ten Drive Linkers' messengers come to spread this message far and wide?

Haruyuki somehow managed to process this much in his half-paralyzed brain, when the blue-masked Drive Linker shouted down once again from the edge of the stone statue.

"If you're not gonna get out, then we're assuming you're ready to tango with us! I mean, a Linker's always up for a little dancing, am I right?!"

He pointed at the survivors on the ground with his right hand.

"I'm gonna eat up every last bit of that pride of yours! Say hello to the captain of DD2047's Unifiers' shock corps…Urocyon!"

"We're not a shock corps. There's only ten of us," the witch in the wide-brimmed hat sitting in the air behind him retorted coolly.

"Shut up!" Blue Mask barked, kicking at the edge of the statue to drop down through the air.

While the top half had been destroyed, Tezcatlipoca had been a powerful presence on the landscape, standing shoulder to shoulder with the skyscrapers around it, and the top of its remains still stood sixty meters above the ground. Even a high ranker couldn't survive a drop from this height without cushioning the impact somehow.

But the blue-masked Drive Linker Urocyon did not run vertically down the wall like Blood Leopard did with her Constant Full Run ability, nor did he descend slowly as Centaurea Sentry's Feather Fall ability allowed her to do, nor did he spread his wings like Silver Crow's Flight. He simply plunged toward the ground in a straight line, yanked down by gravity. *Ka-wham!* He slammed into the hard earth.

The shock wave reached even the roof of Ecomuse Town a hundred meters off horizontally and two hundred meters away perpendicularly, albeit faintly, and Haruyuki instinctively assumed that Blue Mask was dead.

But a heartbeat later, a blue shadow shot out of the cloud of dirt and dust puffing up into the air, whirled around as though inertia had no grip on him, and closed in on the nearest Exercitus survivors.

"Huh?" Chiyuri gasped. "He's not even hurt?!"

Haruyuki was equally surprised. He couldn't see the Drive

Linker's health gauge, but he couldn't pick up on any kind of injury from the impossibly nimble movements of the invader.

The survivor he'd set his sights on, a green-type midsize avatar, abruptly threw his arms up, as if yanked out of a dream, brought his hands neatly together in front of his body, and took on a completely defensive posture. The thick armor of his forearms fused to produce a pentagonal shield.

Even if this green-type was level four and had only just gained entry to the Unlimited Neutral Field, breaking that shield with simply a physical attack would have been difficult. If Haruyuki watched the Drive Linker's reaction, he should be able to get some small sense of the abilities and power of Blue Mask and thus of the other Drive Linkers.

He felt bad for using as guinea pigs the Burst Linkers who had managed to somehow survive Tezcatlipoca's savage attack, but there were currently more than fifty Exercitus survivors, and basically the same number of dead about to regenerate. Even if, in the worst case, Blue Mask had the power of a King, he wouldn't be able to take all of those Burst Linkers out in a single blow.

My focus here has to be on careful observation of the situation, so I can report back in accurate detail to Kuroyukihime and my comrades in Nega Nebulus, Haruyuki told himself, and then remembered that he was no longer a member of Nega Nebulus. His virtual heart throbbed painfully, but he ignored it and widened his eyes intently.

Blue Mask, aka Urocyon, closed in on the green-type avatar from head-on, whirled around in midair, and launched a backward roundhouse kick with all his force riding on it. The movement was almost frighteningly smooth, master-level, but it was nonetheless a simple blow with no extra bells or whistles.

Haruyuki could practically see the kick repelled by the thick shield and Urocyon flipping back in midair before being knocked flying by a counterattack.

However.

The very instant Urocyon's foot touched the green shield, there was a flash of blue, and the five-centimeter-thick shield shattered like it was made of candy. And the roundhouse kick didn't stop there—it pulverized both of the green-type's sturdy arms and dug deeply into the chest armor beyond them.

Kakrrrrnk! Even Haruyuki, far up in the sky above, heard the sickening crunch as the green avatar's torso broke into countless fragments.

"...No way...," Chiyuri murmured, stunned.

Urocyon was already leaping over the death marker that had appeared at his feet and running toward a new target, a red-type avatar with large guns equipped in his swollen arms.

This avatar chose to attack rather than to defend. He turned the palms of his hands toward Urocyon to send jets of bright-red flames from the barrels that were three centimeters across.

He fired repeatedly over the span of two seconds, with the flaming bullets shooting out at seemingly impossible speed. Urocyon ran in a zigzag pattern to dodge the first four shots, but the fifth hit him squarely in his left femur.

The skintight blue suit was quite thin and very much did not look equipped with enough defensive power to withstand a thirty-millimeter shell. Haruyuki wouldn't have been surprised if the Drive Linker's entire leg had been blown away. And yet the fat bullet merely generated blue sparks and a dull metallic *clunk* before rebounding back and disappearing somewhere behind Blue Mask.

Haruyuki was absolutely astonished, and he was far away from the action, watching from a safe place. So he had no trouble understanding why the red avatar froze in place for nearly two seconds.

Those two seconds were a bounty for Urocyon.

Closing the distance between himself and the red linker in a single leap, he threw his right hand out in an overhand punch. He didn't so much as try to disguise the advance motion for this very obvious blow.

Recovering from the mental shock of his futile attack, the

red-type attempted to block the punch with his rough left hand. His palm, equipped with the barrel of a gun, was both thicker and larger than that of the green-type, who had so recently fallen.

But Haruyuki still shouted reflexively, "Don't! You have to dodge!"

However, his voice, coming from a rooftop nearly two hundred meters in the air, couldn't possibly have reached the avatar on the ground below.

The instant the red-type's raised hand touched Urocyon's fist, it scattered in all directions, as though the attack had turned his hand into some kind of viscous liquid. The fist kept shooting forward to dig into the red avatar's, like it was made of butter, plunging deep into his thorax from the shoulder.

Kakrrrrnk! The red avatar's upper body exploded into dust.

The events that followed could not have been called a battle, by any definition of that word.

During the weeks of internal time in Unlimited EK, the Exercitus survivors had no doubt experienced unimaginable terror and despair. They'd also likely not had anything like proper sleep, but they nevertheless flew at Urocyon one after the other to avenge their slaughtered comrades.

But the Drive Linker easily evaded or pulverized the punches and kicks, swords, and hammers that rained down on him from all sides, and with a single counterattack, transformed more than one Burst Linker into tiny particles. He didn't even try to avoid the bullets and lasers that rained down in long-range attacks, instead repelling them with his entire body.

This was no longer a fighting game or a Battle Royale game. It was an unparalleled action game with a lone hero mowing down the enemy army. Haruyuki's conviction of only a few minutes earlier that Urocyon wouldn't be able to defeat the more than fifty survivors remaining was dramatically shaken.

When the twelfth—no, thirteenth—Burst Linker had been transformed into a death marker, a cry he couldn't hold back slipped from his mouth. "...Stop..."

"Haru," Chiyuri next to him murmured, perhaps hearing his cracked voice.

He'd been convinced she would stop him, but the words that followed were the exact opposite.

"I'll come with."

"...Okay." If he were honest with himself, he would've preferred that she wait here, but Chiyuri was not the type to have accepted that option.

The reason they had dived into the Unlimited Neutral Field in the first place was to check on the well-being of Chiyuri's friend in the midsize Legion Ovest, Cotton Marten, and they still didn't know if she was all right. There was a definite possibility that she had been driven to total point loss long before they arrived in this place. Even so, given that she might have been among the survivors or the death markers on the ground, if Haruyuki was going to go down there, then Chiyuri was absolutely going to go with him.

"But don't do anything reckless," he said, giving her a warning at least, and Chiyuri nodded firmly.

He thought for another second, then gave her two more instructions before wrapping his arm around Lime Bell's waist. After getting a solid hold on her, he put his foot on the natural stone wall that wrapped around the roof. Right before he jumped, he shot a glance at the stone statue rising up to the rear of the battlefield.

The nine Drive Linkers showed no sign of moving. The long-haired boy in the red suit in position in the middle of them stood tall, with his arms crossed in front of his chest, but the other eight were sitting on the edge of the statue, leaning against one another, or even lying down farther back.

Suddenly, Haruyuki got the faintest feeling that something was off. But no matter how he strained his eyes, he couldn't see what it might have been.

"What's wrong?" Chiyuri asked, and Haruyuki shook his head slightly.

"Oh… It's nothing. Let's go." Without waiting for her reply, he kicked at the stone wall and leapt into the air.

Although the full-speed flight from his condo to this place had used up a fair bit of the special attack gauge he'd charged right after they dived, his gauge still had about 40 percent left. This was not a comfortable margin to be charging into battle with, but he didn't have time to go around smashing objects.

He spread the wings on his back the bare minimum necessary and descended at a sharp angle to at least not use up what remained of his gauge with flight. He put on the brakes on the south side of the Higashi Ikebukuro Intersection and let Chiyuri down. After confirming out of the corner of his eye that she'd actually made it safely, he set his sights on the center of the battlefield and charged forward at super-low altitude, practically crawling along the ground.

He slipped past the feet of the members of Exercitus who had formed a large circle, and saw red and yellow lights flashing intermittently on the other side of the clouds of dust rising into the air.

While it went against his own policy of not launching a surprise attack against a new opponent, even more people could be sacrificed during the time it took for him to land and introduce himself. Making up his mind, he gave his wings just a moment of thrust.

Bwaan! Haruyuki shot through the dust clouds and grasped the situation ahead of him in 0.1 seconds.

The first thing he saw was a large blue-type avatar swinging a massive oak tree with both hands. He had seen this figure before—Covelline Miner, a member of the midsize Legion Cold Brew based in the Kita Ward. And in front of Covelline, with his back turned to Haruyuki, was the vanguard of the ten Drive Linker invaders from another world, Urocyon.

Just as his name suggested, Covelline Miner was a Burst Linker whose purpose in life was using his single pickax to dig up mountains in the Unlimited Neutral Field and unearth rare metals and gems. Given this, it might seem that he would be skilled at fighting, and indeed, every so often, his tunnels hit an Enemy nest. He even had a story about crushing a worm-type Wild-class Enemy on his own. Or so Takumu had told Haruyuki once.

Covelline was most likely one of those Burst Linkers who focused all their energy on one aspect of their avatar, devoting all his training to the piercing power of his pickax. No matter how tough Urocyon's suit was, it seemed unlikely that he would be able to avoid damage from a blow with all the power of Covelline's raison d'être riding on it.

But the Drive Linker merely raised his right hand again in an artless motion.

The instant Covelline's pickax pierced it, Silver Crow would beat down on Urocyon's wide-open back with the most powerful close-range attack he had, Spiral Kick. Making this instantaneous decision, Haruyuki flipped around and thrust his right foot straight out.

The tip of the pickax touched Urocyon's hand. Blue sparks rained down, the pickax gouged into the palm of that hand—no. This pickax had penetrated even the armor of a Wild-class Enemy, and yet the moment it touched Urocyon's palm, it bent like a needle and then shattered. The pieces quickly melted into a shower of sparks.

"...!!"

Stunned as he was, Haruyuki nevertheless tried to complete his surprise attack bearing the full weight of his strength.

His Spiral Kick was a serious technique, powerful enough to shatter the super-heavy armor of Glacier Behemoth, aka Habakkuk. As long as the blow landed, it was impossible for the target to defend against it and get away scot-free.

He adjusted the thrust in his wings and was about to spin his whole body around like a drill, when in an almost nonchalant motion, Urocyon threw up his left hand to the rear, into the path of Haruyuki's kick. His position and timing were impeccable; it was like he had eyes in the back of his head. It was too late for Haruyuki to shift the aim of his Spiral Kick.

This won't stop me! Back or hand, I'm going through it! he shouted in his head. And then he spotted it.

An extremely faint blue light enveloping Urocyon's hand. And this was no mere light effect. It had to have been…

"Laser…" He didn't know if he actually said the word out loud or if it merely echoed as a prayer in his head.

Instantly, a pale halation brightened the edges of his field of view, a by-product of his efforts to muster up the strongest image he possibly could.

Before he could finish shouting the attack name, his right leg and Urocyon's left hand made contact.

Skreeeeeek! Together with a strange metallic screeching, blue and gold light twisted and swirled like living creatures.

The feedback that came to him through the toes of his right foot was an unbelievable hardness. Not the hardness of nature that metal or stone might possess, but the hardness of unshakable confidence, a firmness of will. Or to put it another way—Incarnate.

Gritting his teeth, Haruyuki reversed the thrust in his wings. Using the force from Urocyon's hand knocking him away, he somersaulted backward and came to stand on the ground in a spot nearly ten meters away.

"…"

He slowly let out the breath he'd been holding and half folded the metal fins on his back as he glanced down at his own right leg.

A single crack, thinner than a strand of spider's silk, ran through the armor over the tips of his toes. The injury was slight enough that it had no impact on his health gauge, but if that conflict had continued another five—no, three—seconds, his foot could have been shattered. And if he'd been even half a second later in mustering up his Incarnate power, he would have been a death marker right about now.

It was essentially a miracle that he'd managed it in time despite having never before tried to manifest an Incarnate technique with his foot, he thought, as he looked out at the scene before him.

Covelline Miner stood stiffly rooted to the spot, gripping in both hands the shaft of his pickax—more than a weapon, a part of his own self—which had been shattered by Urocyon's bare hand.

The avatar in the blue suit standing in front of him, however, had already relaxed his posture, as if he'd lost interest in the enemy before him. He slowly turned around, and since Haruyuki had attacked the Drive Linker, he could now see the still fully charged health gauge displayed above his head.

Urocyon's mask had looked doglike from afar, but now that Haruyuki was facing him up close, he could see that it had a prominent snout and sharp triangular ears, making it seem more like a fox than like a dog. The material of his suit seemed to be rubber and metal fused together, and it clearly revealed the lines of the sinewy muscles covering his small, muscular body. Although the suit looked, at most, two or three millimeters thick, the place where the cannon had hit it was not even discolored, much less damaged.

Haruyuki finally understood why.

Urocyon had the Incarnate System activated constantly while attacking and defending, even in that very moment. The fact that his overlay was barely visible was no doubt because his imagination had been perfectly optimized.

The Incarnate overlay was due to overflowing excess signals being processed as a light effect when the user's imagination passed through the BB system's image control. But Urocyon activated only the bare minimum Incarnate required for the shortest time necessary, so there was almost no signal overflow. The basic principle of Incarnate still stood, however: The only thing that could resist Incarnate was Incarnate. So no matter how powerful an opponent's attack, it couldn't so much as scratch Urocyon, and no matter how thick that opponent's armor might have been, he could shatter it with a single punch.

Haruyuki widened his stance and braced himself with the foot that had narrowly evaded real damage.

"Well, well. So finally someone who can use Psion shows up," Urocyon said, bending his neck from side to side. The blue fox mask only covered his face from the nose up, and Haruyuki could see that his mouth was human, but his skin and his lips were a mechanical gray. "I was real shocked, disappointed even, that my esteemed elders are actually just a bunch of stupid newbs who don't know the first thing about fighting. But I guess not all of you are, huh?"

While the words themselves were challenging, Haruyuki could feel the very real relief in Urocyon's voice. Taken aback, he asked the very obvious question in response. "...What's 'Saion'?"

"Psionic power, obviously. Supernatural abilities. Wait. Do you BB warriors not call it that?" Urocyon said, raising his right hand.

Reflexively, Haruyuki braced himself, but the Drive Linker merely lifted his index finger. At the end of it sat a blue light—overlay—flickering like a flame.

Haruyuki also turned the index finger of his right hand to the sky and focused his imagination. It took him a half second longer than Urocyon, but soon a platinum light shone there, a glittering silver star.

Behind Urocyon, Covelline Miner had at some point retreated more than ten meters, while the other survivors had formed a large circle around Haruyuki and Urocyon and were now silently watching over the proceedings.

Maintaining the light at the tip of his finger, Haruyuki responded to Urocyon's question. "We call this power 'will,' the Incarnate System."

"Will, huh? Makes sense. Looks like the principle's the same anyway." Nodding, Urocyon quenched his overlay and put a hand on his hip. "So, where'd they dig you up from anyway?"

Haruyuki felt something off in Urocyon's casually challenging attitude, the same feeling he'd had looking over at the Drive Linkers lined up on the stone statue, and he suddenly realized what it was.

Urocyon and the other nine Drive Linkers weren't radiating the crushing force—the information pressure particular to high rankers. Was it because they were visitors from another game, or was there some other reason?

No. This isn't the time to be worrying about that.

Haruyuki lowered his hand and double-checked his Legion membership in his head before identifying himself. "...Silver Crow, member of the Legion Oscillatory Universe."

"Oscillatory... Dang. Fluctuating space-time? That's some name. I don't hate it, though." Urocyon grinned pleasantly, brought his other hand up to his opposite hip, and whirled around to take in the crowd.

Perhaps at their mental limits at last, the survivors didn't so much as twitch at the glare directed at them. This was no wonder. They had taken on the Deity of Demise, Tezcatlipoca, met with defeat, and then experienced several weeks of Unlimited EK. Most likely, they had run in a frenzied panic every time they regenerated on the hour to try to gain some distance, only to be dragged back by the gravitational attack Toxcatl, a tale of endless penance on par with the Greek myth of Sisyphus.

And just when Tezcatlipoca was suddenly destroyed and they thought they were finally free of this endless hell, mysterious intruders showed up and began a fresh slaughter. The leaders of Exercitus couldn't have possibly foreseen this, and they could be proud of any resistance they were able to put up, even if it was for only a minute or two, given they were up against Urocyon now, who made free use of Incarnate.

Which was why he couldn't let any more of them be sacrificed. Given that he was a member of Oscillatory Universe, the most authoritarian of the seven Great Legions, and that Exercitus rejected that authority, they might have been unlikely bedfellows, but when faced with external enemies invading the Accelerated World—BB2039 itself—they were all the same Burst Linkers.

"...Urocyon. What exactly is your objective—desire?" Haruyuki asked, as he earnestly pushed down the many emotions swirling in his heart.

The smile disappeared from the face of the Drive Linker in blue as he replied, "Whoa, whoa. Way to kill the mood, dude. We've been waiting for this day—the moment when our worlds got hooked up—for months now. We figured you'd have, like, the fiercest BB warriors lined up to jump us. But these losers are half-dead, and they can't even use Psion. And then *finally* someone who's got a little fight in him shows, but he won't shut the hell up about—"

"H-hang on," Haruyuki interjected, stunned. "You were waiting for the moment our worlds connected? So then you all knew this was going to happen?"

"Natch." Urocyon nodded firmly. "There was the whole system message when we hit level nine."

"...!!"

Haruyuki inhaled sharply.

The fact that the Drive Linkers before him were level niners was also a surprise, but the issue was more serious than that.

Back when he'd only just become a Burst Linker, Kuroyukihime had told him that a system message had appeared when she reached level nine and informed her of three things: Five wins against level-nine Burst Linkers were required to reach level ten; if two level-nine Burst Linkers fought each other, the loser would immediately lose all their burst points and have Brain Burst forcibly uninstalled; and anyone who reached level ten would meet the developer—the creator of the Accelerated World—and be informed of the true reason for the existence of the game known as Brain Burst 2039.

But it seemed that the players of Dread Drive 2047 received a different message when they became level nine. He keenly wanted to know each and every word of that message, but the

Drive Linker likely wouldn't tell him if he asked, given the situation.

Instead, he made sure he kept standing tall, so as not to show any weakness as he spoke. "We didn't get any message from the system. And the Burst Linkers you say are half-dead, well..."

He pointed at the stone statue rising behind him to the right—the lower half of Tezcatlipoca.

"They really are half-dead because they were just fighting this Super-class Enemy. If you're into beating up people who basically can't fight back, if you're satisfied with battles where you have the overwhelming advantage, then go ahead and do your worst."

"..."

Even after Haruyuki finished speaking, Urocyon stayed silent, his mouth turned down into a frown. Finally, after nearly ten seconds had passed, he said, sounding disgusted, "*Tch*! You're talking like we're taking candy from babies or something. But listen, man, we got our own stuff, too, all right?"

"Your own stuff?" Haruyuki parroted.

"I don't gotta tell you everything from one to ten," Urocyon snapped. "But, well, smacking down folks who're already on death's doorstep isn't exactly my jam. So...Silver Crow, right? I'll give you a chance."

"A chance?" Haruyuki frowned. "What kind of chance?"

"A chance to prove you're not full of it," the Drive Linker responded. "If what you're saying's true, then once these fighters are back to full strength, they'll be able to put up a real fight, yeah?"

"...Yeah."

In point of fact, unless they knew both of the first-stage Incarnate techniques Attack Power Expansion and Armor Strength Expansion, the Exercitus survivors could never have defeated Urocyon, even if they all attacked him together. But if they got a decent rest to recover, they would, at the very least, be able to act more strategically instead of randomly attacking.

"Woh-kay." Urocyon snapped out his index finger. "In that

case, you gotta show us you mean business. If I win one-on-one against you, then—hold up. What level are you?"

"...Six," Haruyuki said slowly.

"Whoa, seriously?" Urocyon rolled his eyes and shrugged somewhat theatrically. "Ugh, fine. If you can stay alive for five minutes, we'll let you and these other kids get out of here."

Haruyuki couldn't help but feel a fire spring up inside him at the condescension in the other fighter's voice. He was sorely tempted to ask what would happen if *he* won, but he bit his tongue to keep the question inside his mouth. The conditions Urocyon was offering were the best he was going to get in the current situation. He wouldn't be able to live with himself if his obstinacy caused Urocyon to change his mind and make the fight until death.

He took a deep breath and nodded. "...Fine."

Urocyon grinned a second time before lobbing an unexpected question his way. "You got any cool nicknames?"

"..."

The breath he had started to take caught in the back of his throat, and he very nearly choked.

Even Silver Crow, still far from a high ranker, had what could be called nicknames. The one that likely rang truest for the members of Exercitus was "Betrayer," but to give that name now would make it sound a little too much like he was trying to play the villain. And Urocyon would have no clue as to the meaning of the title of "Antidote King," bestowed on him by the Red Legion's Iodine Sterilizer, so he overcame his embarrassment to give the Drive Linker a nickname that was appropriately nickname-ish.

"...Speed Star."

"Oh-ho!" Urocyon said, without any hint of poking fun, and waved his hand to the side. "Woh-kay! All you out there! The champion for BB2039, 'Speed Star' Silver Crow and the champion for DD2047, me—'Primal Fang' Urocyon—are going head-to-head! Don't go tagging yourself in or anything stupid!"

Instantly, a quiet stir ran through the survivors watching from a distance.

The members of Exercitus no doubt had a hard time accepting Haruyuki, a member of Oscillatory Universe, as their champion. But even if any of them could use Incarnate, Haruyuki found it hard to believe that they could have mustered up any real imagination at the moment, worn down as they were from weeks of Unlimited EK.

Several of the survivors apparently reached the same conclusion and called out to their neighboring comrades to fall back. Now that he was thinking about it, they could have escaped through the portal in Sunshine City now that Tezcatlipoca was no longer binding them to the spot. But perhaps they'd refused to abandon their comrades still on regeneration standby; he didn't see anyone attempt to flee to the real world.

Once the survivors were all outside of the intersection, Urocyon clapped his hands together loudly. "Yeaaah. Looks like we finally got a real challenger."

"Is Dread Drive 2047 a one-on-one fighting game like Brain Burst?" Haruyuki asked reflexively, in response. The reason he was curious was that the already shuttered Trial No. 1, aka Accel Assault 2038, had been a high-speed, 3D shooting game, and No. 3, aka Cosmos Corrupt 2040, had been a hack-and-slash, both totally different genres from BB2039.

"A fighter?" Urocyon blinked eyes that emitted a pale-blue light before turning his palms up in front of him. "It's maybe got fighter-y bits, but DD's something else. It's like… I dunno, hard to nutshell it. If I had to say, it's a MOBA with dashes of 3D shooter, fighter, and hack-and-slash, maybe?"

"…!"

MOBA stood for "multi-player online battle arena," a game genre mixing action RPG with real-time strategy that had spread and garnered popularity starting around the 2010s. And what the Drive Linker was saying was that despite the fact that MOBA itself was cross-genre, elements of shooters, fighters, and hack-and-slash had been further added.

Haruyuki could not picture at all the kind of game that would have resulted from this mishmash. But what bothered him about that description was that the three additional elements Urocyon named were the genres of AA, BB, and CC, respectively. Almost like he was saying Dread Drive 2047 was the actual, complete game, founded upon the three trials…

"But no need to get all up in the deets if we're just going one-on-one. We start throwing punches, and the one left standing—no, if you're still alive in five minutes, you win." Urocyon shrugged casually, perhaps misunderstanding Haruyuki's silence.

While he hadn't been worried about the rules of the other game, it was true that this was the only thing that mattered at the moment. "Got it," he replied briefly, and raised both of his arms, stepped forward with his left foot, and pulled his right back.

Like his mirror image, Urocyon put his right foot forward and readied himself. In boxing, this was a southpaw stance, but it would have been premature to decide from this alone that the Drive Linker was left-handed.

Either way, defense was his top priority. But even if Urocyon's attack was mere punches and kicks, he wouldn't be able to defend against them without using Incarnate. Which meant that for the next five minutes, he would have to continuously maintain his Laser Sword image.

I can do this.

When he copied Haruyuki's Range Expansion Incarnate technique Laser Lance, "Basher" Platinum Cavalier, first of Oscillatory Universe's Seven Dwarves, had calmly told him that he could maintain a copy of "simple techniques" like Haruyuki's own light beam series for days.

Yes. Even for a first-stage Incarnate technique, Laser Sword was one of the simplest possible. This simplicity, making it so that Cavalier could easily reproduce the technique, could be an advantage now.

When Haruyuki cloaked his hands in silver overlay with no advance movement, Urocyon also brought up blue phosphorescence, as if he'd been waiting for him to be ready. Haruyuki's light was brighter, but that merely meant his was less optimized.

How long exactly had it taken Urocyon to get this kind of fine control over his imagination? Haruyuki nearly cried in admiration. But the battle was starting.

Bwwn! The air shook, and Urocyon instantly closed the distance between them. With speed such that his entire avatar was nothing more than flowing blue lines, he shot out with two rights in a row, super-high-speed jabs that would beat Great Wall's boxing Linker, Iron Pound, at his own game.

But after surviving Platinum Cavalier's divinely fast Femto-style slicing attack, Haruyuki was just barely able to react in time. He guarded against the rapid-fire punches coming in at slightly different angles with the armor on the back of his left hand and arm. Blue and silver sparks scattered, and the impact shook him to the core of his avatar body. Both fighters were knocked back over a meter from the repulsive force of their Incarnates making contact.

Haruyuki's Laser Sword was not an armor strength expansion Incarnate technique, but Urocyon's right jab wasn't actually an Incarnate technique, just a normal technique enhanced with Incarnate power. Thanks to that, he was able to defend against the attack somehow, but if his opponent were to use Incarnate for real, he probably wouldn't be able to completely protect himself from it with his overlay alone.

Which was why he couldn't focus solely on defense if he was going to survive these five minutes. While Urocyon was taking these preliminary test shots, he had to make him eat an Incarnate technique with more power than his opponent imagined he had. Even if a fatal blow was out of the question, he had to at least destroy an arm or a leg…

His mind racing, Haruyuki tightened his guard in preparation for the next attack.

"Cerdocyon!" Urocyon shouted as he launched a right hook to the body.

It's too fast. After this thought flashed through his mind, he felt a shiver of fear cold enough to freeze his spine.

Point zero one of a second later, this fear became reality.

The aura in Urocyon's left hand transformed into the head of a transparent blue animal and flew ferociously toward him. Bearing a strong resemblance to his mask, the animal head opened wide a maw filled with sharp fangs and tried to bite into Haruyuki's side.

Instantly judging that defense was impossible, Haruyuki leapt back and desperately twisted his body to the side.

Krnch! A disgusting sensation raced through his entire body, followed by an incandescent pain. The blue animal head slipped to his rear, droplets of red light dripping from its closed mouth, and disappeared.

"Hngh!" Groaning, Haruyuki put even more space between himself and Urocyon. When he glanced down, he found a large hole in the armor on his right side, and a deep bite taken out of his naked avatar body. His armor cross section was smooth, like it had been polished, and he was 90 percent certain that the fox head had been no ordinary special attack.

"...Was that 'Psion,' too?" he asked, to confirm his suspicion, and a bold smile rode up on Urocyon's face.

"Yep. And I'll tell you just this once, as a special treat. Cerdocyon's a crab-eating fox in South America." He pulled his left hand back and readied himself in the southpaw stance once more. "You got any Psion Arts, you can go ahead and use 'em. This isn't the kinda sitch where you gotta save your special treats for later, yeah?"

"..."

Haruyuki nodded wordlessly and also readied himself. He had learned two things from this round. One was that even Urocyon, who seemed to have perfect control of Psion—Incarnate power—also needed to shout the technique name when activating it. And the other was that the Drive Linker didn't show any fear of the dark side of Incarnate.

He was curious if this was because Urocyon simply didn't care or because he had overcome that dark side, but any further questions would seem like he was trying to kill time. He checked and saw that he had 90 percent of his health gauge left still and played one of his trump cards—he vibrated the wings on his back at full power.

Three of the five metal fins on either side were folded up, so he couldn't produce even half of his normal thrust, but he was still able to go from dead stop to mad dash, causing Urocyon's reaction to be delayed the tiniest amount.

He first pulled his right hand back, and then as he thrust it forward, he shouted, "Laser Sword!"

The overlay he'd been maintaining the whole time stretched out into a silver blade. Urocyon reinforced the aura in his arms as he tried to throw up a cross guard.

Just as the Incarnate sword extending from his right hand was on the verge of making contact with Urocyon's aura, he stretched out the five fingers of his left hand he had readied on his hip and called out another technique name.

"Laser Lance!"

Skreenk! A metallic sound rang out as Urocyon's arms blocked the sword of his right hand.

Whunk! A heavy sound accompanied the direct hit the Incarnate lance extending from his left hand made against Urocyon's right flank.

Haruyuki had been convinced his lance pierced the Drive Linker's side, but the health gauge above Urocyon's head did not drop. He looked down to find a thick aura concentrated on Urocyon's side, stopping the tip of his Laser Lance.

He can do that, *too?*

Haruyuki was awed by Urocyon's control of the aura—overlay—for defense, when he'd thought it was nothing more than a light effect incidental to the Incarnate technique.

Judging from the game's name of Dread Drive 2047, Urocyon and his friends would have had to have been given the program in January of this year or later. In fact, before the fight started, he said that they'd been waiting months for the two worlds to be connected—not years.

So then that meant all the Drive Linkers including Urocyon had shorter battle histories than Haruyuki, who became a Burst Linker in October of last year. Naturally, it was possible that they had him beat on accumulated accelerated time, but even still, how on earth did Urocyon obtain this kind of technique in less than a year of real time?

Brushing away a shiver of terror, Haruyuki focused all of his mental powers in his hands.

The key to the Incarnate System was changing the world through overwriting it; in other words, through the imagination. Laser Sword and Laser Lance were manifestations of the image of going further, ever further; momentary increases in range and force, just as the "light" of the name suggested. They were never geared toward prolonged conflict. Not to mention that this was the first time he'd ever activated both sword and lance simultaneously.

But if his Incarnate disappeared without breaking Urocyon's defenses, then one of his arms—or if he really fumbled, his head—could be carried away in the counterattack.

The blue aura that repelled Haruyuki's Incarnate had communicated only an overwhelming hardness on first contact with it, but now he felt a supple tenaciousness in addition to that. *Almost like a wild animal...* It wasn't only Urocyon's appearance that made him think this.

This aura could repel thirty-millimeter rounds. He wouldn't be able to pierce it with force alone. He had to polish and hone his blade of light to the ultimate hardness, thinness, sharpness. But he'd never once drilled with a technique like that—

Actually, he had.

While it had been with a different sword, Haruyuki had soberly trained to cut that which could not be cut right up until that very day. Omega-style Whole Blade handed down to him directly by "Ruthless" Centaurea Sentry, a technique that was impossible to defend against. Whole Blade found the smallest point—the "minuscule" that was in an object, no matter how hard or big it might have been—and cut it with the "maximum" force.

Haruyuki had become Centaurea's student so that he could learn how to use Lucid Blade, the sword-type Enhanced Armament he'd obtained as his level-six bonus. But a sword was a sword, a blade a blade. It should have been possible to use the Omega technique even with the Laser Sword, an imaginary blade that had no physical form.

It had already been five seconds since this standoff began. The aura lodged in Urocyon's arms and side didn't so much as flicker as it continued to fend off the Incarnate sword and lance. But Haruyuki's own imagination would only last another three seconds. If he was going to do it, it had to be now.

At the same time as he extinguished the Laser Lance of his left hand, he set another image onto the silver overlay stretching out from his right hand, the image of a hard, thin, sharp sword. Previously, he would have had to invest a lot of energy and time to picture a color and shape, but the hours he'd spent with his beloved Lucid Blade had become a fixed muscle memory carved into his body, into his soul.

Wheen! The immaterial Laser Sword shrank down to less than a fifth of its thickness, the hard blade carving out a perfectly straight line—a Light Sword.

"…!"

Urocyon reacted with lightning reflexes and opened his mouth wide, perhaps intending to utter some technique name.

But before he could, Haruyuki tore into the blue aura with his shining white blade, albeit by the smallest amount.

He'd only dug into it by mere millimeters when the aura rapidly increased in hardness and tried to repel his blade. But the fact that the aura was hard meant it had definite form. If it was a hard armor attached to the suit rather than an undefined, rubber-like aura, then he could find the minuscule in it.

The instant he felt the Incarnate blade and the aura armor come into contact at a single point, Haruyuki mustered up all of the mental power that remained to him and prayed.

Extreme!!

Krshk. The Light Sword slipped straight down.

But he could no longer maintain the image, and the sword flickered and then disappeared.

He used the physical strength of his right leg and the thrust of his wings to jump back, and once he'd gotten more than five meters away, he let out the breath he'd been holding.

Here, at last, he saw the results of the blow that he'd poured all of his knowledge and technique into.

One of the arms that Urocyon held stationary and wrapped in his thin blue aura crossed in front of him, the right arm that had defended against the Light Sword soundlessly split in two midway between wrist and elbow.

Thd! The hand that bounced against the ground didn't shatter into fragments of light like a Burst Linker's severed limb, but was instead enveloped in blue flames and instantly burned up.

The extremely thin line of a blade was also carved into his remaining arm, but the cut was apparently not deep enough to sever the hand. Haruyuki's plan had been to cut off both of Urocyon's arms and also do damage to his torso if luck was on his side. But the Omega-style Light Sword he'd staked everything on had taken nothing more than a single arm. And if his opponent was the sort of person to lose the will to fight over a thing like that, he wouldn't be the captain of a raiding party.

Haruyuki had basically used up all of his Incarnate power, but he still had to keep going somehow until time was up. Although how would he even know when five minutes was up anyway…?

"…I get it," Urocyon said, lowering his arms and gazing at the stump of his right. "So this is Incarnate… The principle looks the same as DD's Psion Arts, but application's different, huh? Got a little secret spice in there that brings the heat."

A gray tongue shot out of his mouth and licked the cross section. This couldn't have told him anything, but he nonetheless smiled like everything made sense to him now as he turned his eyes to the northern sky.

"How many seconds left, Complicator?"

His voice wasn't particularly loud, and yet from the top of the stone statue towering over the intersection, a voice with a somehow mechanical edge to it came in response.

"You were the one who decided on this condition. You could at least calculate the time yourself." And then after a short pause, "One hundred twenty seconds left."

"Roger! Lemme know when we hit zero." Urocyon turned his face back and stared hard at Haruyuki. "Now, these last two minutes, I'm going full throttle. Keep up with me, Silver Crow."

He had no sooner made this statement than he was turning his intact left arm and his severed right arm up high toward the sky. He threw his sinewy body back, opened his mouth below his fox mask, and shouted, "Chrysocyoooooon!"

The cry of the technique name was bold, like some anime hero's. Haruyuki did feel the desire to stay and watch what happened, but he had no leeway for intelligence gathering at the moment.

As he dashed forward, he quickly called out, "Equip Lucid Blade!!" Instantly, a pool of light condensed on his left hip to produce a slender longsword.

This was his second trump card. Urocyon wouldn't expect him to summon a real sword after going out of his way to create a sword with Incarnate. He gripped the hilt in his right hand and the scabbard in his left, and he sank down low.

A flaming blue aura rose up from all over Urocyon, but Haruyuki ignored this and drew his sword to launch a surprise attack. He had confirmed that the Drive Linker's Incarnate—no, Psion armor—could be cut with the "extreme." And even if that aura was made up of real flames, Lucid Blade had been enhanced to nullify heat damage, so those flames couldn't touch it.

Urocyon still had both arms thrown up into the air, and Haruyuki slid his blade toward the Drive Linker's defenseless right flank. Focusing the small amount of mental stamina he'd recovered during their conversation, he prepared to use Gou the instant the tip touched the aura armor.

But before he could, he was hit with an impact like the air itself had exploded, and the figure of Urocyon was erased.

No, it hadn't been erased. Haruyuki just barely caught sight of a blue afterimage in one edge of his field of view. Directly above him.

Yanking his sword back with everything he had, he threw his head back.

A dark, black figure floated in a sky tiled with crimson hexagons. For an instant, Haruyuki thought it was a flight ability, but that wasn't it. Urocyon had *jumped* from a standing position to an incredible altitude, probably more than twenty meters.

Arms and legs splayed, the silhouette that dropped toward him now was clearly a different shape from only a few seconds ago. The arms had already been a little long for the body, but now they were even longer and more muscular. The waist was constricted almost abnormally, while the thighs of both legs were swollen, albeit with the legs lean and compact from the knees down. And a tail stretched out from the backside, looking like blue flames.

Lycanth.

The word flashed through Haruyuki's mind at the same time as Urocyon curled into himself, instantly increasing the speed of his descent.

Haruyuki did a backflip to try and dodge the blue-black mass of the werewolf hurtling toward him. But while he was still in the air, Urocyon threw his legs out and kicked at the air.

It was unbelievable, but unmistakable. Haruyuki saw a ring-shaped flash of light kick back from the empty space, and the angle of Urocyon's descent shifted sharply. Onto a collision course with Haruyuki.

He could use his wings to increase the skip distance, but Urocyon would no doubt kick at the air again to precisely target his new position. In which case…

Haruyuki fully deployed the ten metal fins on his back, spread out the still-equipped Enhanced Armament Metatron Wings, and vibrated them all at full power. The enormous thrust powerfully accelerated his avatar not to the side, but up—straight for the descending Urocyon.

He didn't know whether the Drive Linker expected something like this or was caught off guard. But either way, Urocyon spread his contracted limbs and used the air resistance to decelerate as he concentrated the burning blue aura in his arms.

His intact left hand grew to nearly twice its original size, claws like lethal weapons stretching out from his fingertips, sharp tips glinting. Including the aura enveloping them, the claws looked to have a reach close to thirty centimeters. A single swipe would no doubt tear off a limb or remove his head. And the right hand that Haruyuki had severed was reproduced with an aura of the same size.

If Urocyon swung arms that massive in midair, his body should spin in the opposite direction in reaction. But Haruyuki immediately discarded this idea.

Just as he'd expected, Urocyon stepped on empty space, upside-down, and using this nothing as a foothold, he swung both arms simultaneously.

Glaring at the ten claws carving out a blue V in the air as they shot toward him, Haruyuki shouted, *Light Speed!!*

Once more, he didn't know if the technique name had actually come from his mouth or if it had only echoed in his mind. But the silver wings on his back responded to his will and generated a thrust so powerful that the metal armor of his own body creaked.

The distance between the two fighters rapidly approached zero. Claws shrouded in blue flames closed in on his helmet.

If he let fear in for even the merest fraction of a second, his acceleration would slow, and those claws would make mincemeat of his head. He beat back reason and common sense with the fire burning in his heart, and he pushed himself to go even faster.

Zzt! He heard a scraping sound like an arc discharge, and the claws grazed the sides of his helmet and slipped off to the rear.

Urocyon's head was right before his eyes. Mere seconds earlier, it had been a human face wearing a fox mask, but now it was completely animal.

"Graaaaar!" the Drive Linker roared ferociously, his sharp teeth bared.

"Aaaaaah!" Haruyuki also let out a cry from the depths of his stomach and slammed his head with everything he had into the werewolf's snout.

He didn't have the time to activate his special attack Head Butt, but even if he had, it wouldn't have worked against Urocyon's Incarnate technique level defenses. His sole hope was that the image of the second-stage Incarnate technique Light Speed would overwrite those defenses.

His face gets crushed or my head goes flying! One or the other!

A dizzying impact and flash of light. Even his own health gauge disappeared in the pure white halation of his field of view.

Haruyuki braced himself for the death message YOU ARE DEAD to pop up there.

But a second later, the world took on color again, and his health gauge was displayed once more. The quantum circuits for his brain in the Main Visualizer—the Brain Burst central server—had apparently malfunctioned due to the powerful impact, albeit only for a moment.

His health gauge had dropped more than 70 percent, but he was still alive.

In the center of his recovered field of view, he saw the werewolf reeling, head back and growing distant. Haruyuki was also falling, similarly reeling. He wanted to follow up with an attack using Lucid Blade, but he could no longer move any of his limbs or the wings on his back. There was more than a minute left until time was up, though. If Urocyon recovered first and counterattacked, it was all over.

He had just one card left to play.

Scraping together what little remained of his mental strength, he prayed intently, *Chiyu, now!!*

There was no way this thought could reach her, and yet a green light flashed in the right corner of his view. A vivid lime-green beam of light shot forth from a gap in the rocky mountains standing to the northeast of the battlefield, and stretched out in a straight line.

Its target was neither Haruyuki nor Urocyon but was the thing that had once been the left leg of the gray statue in the center of the intersection—the Deity of Demise, Tezcatlipoca.

Right before they'd descended from Ecomuse Town, Haruyuki had asked three things of Chiyuri. One was to absolutely not do anything reckless. The second was, if the battle turned into a free-for-all, to find Cotton Marten among the survivors and leave through the Sunshine City portal. And the third was an instruction that envisioned a situation where Haruyuki and the blue Drive Linker ended up fighting one-on-one.

I'll do whatever it takes to create an opening of ten seconds. When I do, you cast Citron Call on the remains of Tezcatlipoca.

Chiyuri was carrying out that final instruction. In which case, Haruyuki also had to keep his own promise.

Before him, the plummeting Urocyon shuddered violently as he quickly regained consciousness, and then yanked his lolling head up. He was still a werewolf, and the aura encasing his claws was also still there.

The beast's eyes narrowed suspiciously for a mere heartbeat and then flew open wide. He'd seen the green light cutting across the red landscape and realized that it meant something critical.

Given that Urocyon could move by kicking at the air itself, he would probably be able to get to Chiyuri in five seconds or less.

"Raaah!" the werewolf howled and pulled back his legs in preparation for a jump.

Haruyuki tried to turn his sword on him. But his right hand was numb, and it was all he could do to keep hanging on to the hilt of his beloved blade.

At Urocyon's feet, the compressed air shuddered in a ring shape.

Crow! Use my wings!

Abruptly, a voice—no, a mind—flashed like lightning and shot through the core of his own mind. At the same time, he felt a faint warmth spring up in the wings on his back, not Silver Crow's metallic fins but the Enhanced Armament Metatron Wings attached to the upper part of his shoulder blades.

This modest energy changed into instantaneous power, and Haruyuki cried out in a hoarse voice, "Ektenia!!"

His right wing became a beam of dazzling light that carved a large arc in the sky as it streaked out to attack Urocyon.

But the Drive Linker showed no signs of panic. He stayed tense, in position, and then kicked at the air at the last possible second.

Just when Haruyuki thought Urocyon had evaded him, and when Urocyon no doubt also thought that he had dodged the blow, the beam of light turned at an impossibly sharp angle and shot through the werewolf's left shoulder.

Ektenia changed the Metatron Wings into beams of light, a fixed attack of the Enhanced Armament itself and not an Incarnate technique. So for a second, Haruyuki feared that it would not pierce Urocyon's Incarnate defenses and would instead be ripped apart like a piece of paper. But while the ribbon of light extending from Haruyuki's back did bend in the impact, it was not destroyed.

Showers of sparks flying, Ektenia and Urocyon froze together at a single point in space.

Skreeenk! There was a sound like space itself shattering, and then both were thrown back with incredible force.

Unable to absorb the blowback from the ribbon of light, Haruyuki dropped in a tailspin. Thirty seconds remained until his five minutes were up, but this time, his energy was well and truly spent.

Chiyu, it's up to you now.

Sending up one last silent prayer, Haruyuki crashed into the ground and rolled along the surface for an indeterminate amount of time before finally coming to a stop. His health gauge was at 10 percent.

Desperately clinging to consciousness and pushing back the darkness that tried to swallow him up, Haruyuki somehow managed to turn his head. The stone statue rising up forty meters ahead of him was enveloped in a faint green light. The nine Drive Linkers encamped on the top of it should have noticed the change, but they were in Haruyuki's blind spot, and he couldn't see them.

Citron Call, the special attack of Chiyuri—Watch Witch, aka Lime Bell—had the fearsome power to rewind time or lasting status changes. She had activated Mode I here to rewind time. Normally, she used this to recover her comrades' health or special attack gauges, or to heal damage. She had never turned this power on an Enemy.

But she had once used this technique to take back the burst points stolen from Blood Leopard by the God Seiryu. Which meant that she had changed the status of a Super-class Enemy, albeit indirectly, and in that case, maybe she could also have an effect on Tezcatlipoca, given that it was the same category of Enemy. Or so Haruyuki thought.

Naturally, his aim was not Tezcatlipoca's recovery. True, if the Enemy was revived, the Drive Linkers would also be gone, but it was hard to say which threat was worse. Not to mention that to completely revive a creature this enormous, Chiyuri would need a support squad as big as or even bigger than the team formed to attack the Sun God Inti.

What Haruyuki had planned was not recovery but repair—to rewind the level of destruction just a bit.

Countless lumps of small and large rocks sat at the foot of the stone statue. A green light wrapped around 20 percent of them, and just as he noticed this, the rocks danced up into the sky, in defiance of the law of gravity. They glued themselves to the upper cross section of the statue with a dull clattering noise, and the cracks between them vanished instantly.

"Dammit! What the hell?!" came an understandably panicked cry, together with the sound of slight footsteps. The blue werewolf was racing animal-like along the east side of the intersection toward the source of the green light. He no doubt intended to stop Chiyuri, but he was too late.

While Urocyon was still in the middle of the intersection, the light of Citron Call flickered and disappeared. Chiyuri's special attack gauge was empty. The issue was whether Haruyuki's plan had succeeded or not. And in order to find that out, he needed to take a look at the top of the stone statue, but he was still too weak to stand up, much less fly. Still, he pushed on the ground with a trembling hand and somehow managed to sit up.

Keen, keen, doooong. The metallic ring of clear chimes poured down on him from nowhere in particular, followed by a flat voice.

"Five minutes have passed, Fang."

Instantly, Urocyon slid to a screeching halt as he raced along on all fours. The werewolf stood up on two legs, and the aura emanating from it became a bright-blue pillar of flames, which melted into the air and disappeared.

Once again small-statured and wearing a blue mask, the Drive Linker bent his neck from right to left and back again in a stretch before looking up at the red sky.

Haruyuki also turned his gaze upward to find a human figure dancing down soundlessly from the top of the stone statue.

Unlike Urocyon's uncontrolled leap, this was a leisurely descent at a fixed speed, reminiscent of Centaurea Sentry's Feather Fall ability, but Haruyuki felt something off in the way the cloak swung around the body. It seemed like rather than the speed of descent being controlled, the flow of time was slower around only this person.

Abruptly, the cloak flapped loudly, and the person dropped the last three or so meters at a normal speed to land on the ground.

They cut a strange figure. Two meters tall, but strangely slender, and completely covered from neck to toe by the black cloak. Only their head was exposed, but that head was bizarre—a machine. Brass gears and flywheels whirled and spun with a faint *klak klak*, packed into a silver frame. It resembled Elinvar Governor of Prominence's Steel faction, but this head had far and away more moving parts.

The gear avatar looked around with a face that had neither eyes, nose, nor mouth, and then began to walk, the hem of their black cloak flapping. The Exercitus survivors stared from where they stood around the edges of the intersection, their number increased now to about seventy, thanks to the ongoing regenerations. But the avatar let their gaze slide over them like a breeze blowing past as they cut across the large intersection and came to stand in front of Urocyon.

"Honestly," they sighed, their voice tinged with a mechanical vibration. "It's truly shocking that you can't even take care of a single level six using such flashy Psion."

Here, Haruyuki finally realized that the gear avatar was who Urocyon had called out to in order to find out the time remaining, the person he'd called "Complicator." Haruyuki knew that "complicate" was English for making something more complex or worse, and there was no doubt that the design of that head was the most complicated of any avatar he'd seen in the Accelerated World.

"Hmph," Urocyon snorted, in a very obviously sarcastic manner. He jerked the thumb of his left hand toward the statue. "That light beam, it was some kind of healing or reversing power, yeah? What happened up top?"

"The rocks came flying up from the ground and buried the portal," the gear avatar replied. "We tried to destroy them, but even with Steel's punch, we couldn't break them."

"For real?" Urocyon replied with genuine surprise. "So what happened to the others?"

"Force made the decision they should return to DD before the portal was completely buried. While small, there is nevertheless a possibility that we will be locked up here."

The instant he heard these words, Haruyuki let out the breath he'd been holding. This was precisely what he'd been aiming for when he'd asked Chiyuri to use Citron Call to rewind time for the statue. He'd hypothesized that if they could rebuild two meters of the crumbling rocky mass, then maybe the red portal the Drive Linkers had come through would be buried. In which case, they would probably choose to return to the DD world.

His plan had more or less been a success, but he did wonder why Complicator had chosen to remain on this side.

Urocyon bluntly lobbed that very question at them. "So how come you didn't go back, Wheel?"

"It's your fault, Fang," Complicator replied coolly. "You asked me to tell you when the count reached zero, yes? I despise changes to a schedule once it's been set."

"Oh, right, yeah. Sorry 'bout that." Urocyon waved the stump of his right arm apologetically and glanced at the statue once more. "Well, if we smash up that pile of rocks, the portal should show again."

"I don't know about that." Complicator shrugged in sheer exasperation. "Although the situation is such that we have no choice but to try."

Abruptly, a resolute voice rang out across the field. "I'm not letting you do that!"

The Drive Linkers whirled around, and Haruyuki said, groaning, "Why did you show yourself?!"

But it was already too late.

Marching forcefully toward them from the east side of the

intersection was an F-type avatar with a large bell-shaped Enhanced Armament on her left arm and a wide-brimmed triangular hat on her head—Lime Bell.

When she stopped more or less in front of Urocyon and Complicator, who had their backs turned to Haruyuki, Lime Bell/ Chiyuri threw the head of her small avatar back and shouted again.

"I mean, what is your guys' deal even! Giving us our final notice? Coming in here and talking like you're all that! If you're gonna duel, the rule is bright, fun, and polite!"

"..."

The Drive Linkers appeared to be stunned into silence.

Haruyuki was similarly at a loss for words. Even among Burst Linkers, politeness and manners were expected only in a normal duel. If they encountered each other in the Unlimited Neutral Field, they would instantly and without question start in on slaughtering. Not to mention that Urocyon and Complicator were invaders from another world, and the Burst Linkers should really have just been glad they even gave their names first.

Haruyuki's thoughts were interrupted by a voice as cold as ice.

"Fun duel? What kind of nonsense...? This is no longer a game, miss. It's a fight for survival." It was Complicator who spoke. The flywheels on their head clicking away, they glared at Chiyuri. "If we win, your world will disappear. If you win, our world will disappear. This is the immutable rule decided on by whoever created and maintains the two games. We have no interest in losing DD2047, and you all don't intend to abandon BB2039, I assume. In which case, all that remains is for us to fight, yes?"

Their polite tone reminded Haruyuki of Glacier Behemoth, aka Rioh Koshimizu, but the mechanical edge erased any note of humanity. The question of whether they were really a Linker flitted through his mind, but the instant he digested Complicator's words in his own way, that doubt flew out of his head.

"...!"

He drew a sharp breath, still slumped down on the ground.

If you win, our world will disappear. He had nearly let that go in one ear and out the other, but this was the most important piece of information yet. Urocyon had only said that today was the end of service for Trial No. 2, but the end was equally possible for Dread Drive 2047. If Haruyuki and the other Burst Linkers met some kind of victory condition, then it would be DD2047 that disappeared.

Most likely, this was the "stuff" that Urocyon had danced around earlier. Even this warmongering, bestial fighter with unfathomable power hesitated to give voice to the annihilation of DD. In which case, the possibility of Haruyuki and the Burst Linkers coming out of this victorious was not zero. In fact, he would bet that Urocyon and his team had also estimated that they had a 20 or 30 percent chance.

But only they had been told how the Burst Linkers could win. He had to do whatever it took to get that information out of them. He forced his leaden legs to push against the ground and staggered to his feet.

Ahead of him, Chiyuri was overwhelmed for an instant, but then held her head higher to respond boldly, "...Even so! You could at least talk to us first. If we shared all of the information we have without hiding anything, we might be able to find a way where no one's game has to go anywhere!"

"I bet all the players of the long-gone Accel Assault and Cosmos Corrupt would've loooooved to know this mysterious way of yours," Urocyon muttered in a strained voice. He put his left hand on his hip before apparently realizing he had no pocket there and letting it drop once more. "You. Name?"

Chiyuri hesitated for a second and then replied, "...Lime Bell."

"Uh-huuuuh. So do all you BBers got a color in your name?" Urocyon nodded in understanding. "Listen up, Lime Bell. You're free to be all sunshine and flowers and hope in vain however much you want. But don't go pushing that on us. Before we went through that portal, we talked about it so much, our tongues practically fell out. If you're such a pacifist, then cover your eyes, plug your ears, and go sit in a corner somewhere."

"How do you know my hope's in vain?!" Chiyuri cried, her voice even more courageous.

"Oh, I know," Urocyon spat in response, before raising his left hand nonchalantly. The film of an aura wrapped around his fist instantly grew thicker and flashed up like flames.

Chiyuri still hadn't learned how to use the Incarnate system. Or more precisely, she had provided backup for Haruyuki and Takumu with the overlay generated by the bell of her left arm exactly once when they were trying to dig a hole in an indestructible wall with their Incarnate techniques after infiltrating the headquarters of the Acceleration Research Society in Minato Area No. 3 of the Accelerated World. But she'd passed out at the same time as the light disappeared, and she hadn't done any particular Incarnate training since.

Which was why if she were jabbed in the head or the torso with Urocyon's Incarnate-enhanced fist, she would die instantly.

"...Stop!" Haruyuki cried hoarsely, desperately forcing his noncompliant legs to move.

Perhaps noticing his approach, Urocyon turned his head back the slightest bit and said, "Don't get the wrong idea, Silver Crow. I told you I'd let you go if you survived for five minutes. Roar Ring."

He opened the hand he held at shoulder height and then clenched it shut once more, sucking the swirling flames inside his fist.

The action looked like nothing big, but Haruyuki saw the intensity with which the Drive Linker clenched his hand and twisted the air—no, space itself.

Before he had time to even cry out, the ultra-compressed aura exploded with a roar reminiscent of the howls of several hundred wild animals and became a ring of blue light, which instantly expanded.

Standing next to Urocyon, the tall Complicator merely staggered slightly when touched by the ring of light, but Chiyuri before them was knocked high up into the air like a rag doll.

"Bell!" Haruyuki started to rush to Chiyuri's side, but he was unable to dodge the ring of light as it grew at unbelievable speed. He was hit with a pressure powerful enough to crush the metallic armor covering his body, and his back slammed into the ground once more.

A second later, dozens of cries echoed from all directions all at once. Urocyon's ring of light—the aura impact wave—had crossed the sixty- or seventy-meter radius of the Higashi-Ikebukuro Intersection to reach the edge and mow down the Exercitus survivors.

Curiously, his health gauge didn't decrease after being hit with this intense impact. Even Lime Bell, who had been up close and dead center, seemed to have not taken any significant damage, although she had been knocked backward onto the ground. Most likely, the technique was a nonfatal one, deliberately fine-tuned by Urocyon to be that way. He had used his imagination to retain the collision power of the attack while reducing the offensive force to nearly zero, a far more difficult task than amplifying that force.

"Silver Crow, all you jerks out there, you should thank Lime Bell." After showing them his overwhelming power, Urocyon lowered his left hand and said, as if to push the point home, "This shrimp's guts bought you another day of real time. We'll leave the portal buried until July twenty-eighth at twelve midnight."

"Are you certain, Fang?" Complicator asked, a note of concern in their voice. "Drill's definitely going to snap if you make a promise like that without consulting anyone."

"I'll deal with that then, Wheel." Urocyon turned to look at his comrade. "And you said you got something you wanna check out in this world anyway, yeah?"

"Well, that is true… But please discuss with me in advance the next time you are going to decide something." Shrugging, as if to say they were used to his shenanigans, Complicator turned their head all the way around. Without so much as a glance at Silver Crow and Lime Bell on the ground nearby, they began to walk in the direction of Otowa Street that stretched out to the southeast from the intersection.

"Okay, but you don't get to just pick where we go without the whole discussing part!" Cursing, Urocyon chased after him.

Haruyuki knew he needed to get at least a hint of what the condition for victory in this war might have been, but it was all he could do to lift his head mere centimeters. He opened his eyes wide and focused intently to at least try to see where the two Drive Linkers were going.

Black cloak flapping as they walked, Complicator spoke in a somehow languid voice, "Rattrapante."

Haruyuki had never heard this word before, but he was at least sure that it was a technique name. Because the small gears attached to either side of Complicator's head flashed with a golden light—most likely, an Incarnate overlay.

The instant this flash reached his eye lenses, something strange (curious??) rose up before him—the semitransparent dial of a clock. But there was only one hand. Actually, no. There were two hands of exactly the same length, sitting on top of each other at the twelve position.

Tic tic tic tic... The two hands began to move simultaneously. But soon enough, the movement of one slowed. It did a full sweep in one second, but then it was two seconds a circuit, then three... And then it stopped with a faint *tic*.

Instantly, Haruyuki felt like he was sliding into unconsciousness and blinked his eye lenses several times.

At some point, the phantom clock had vanished. And Urocyon and Complicator, walking along some ten meters away, had also disappeared like smoke.

3

It took nearly thirty seconds for Haruyuki to manage to pull himself to his feet somehow. His duel avatar did not get tired in the same sense as his real-world self. He felt pain if his avatar body was injured, and his movement was limited if he lost a limb, but lactic acid did not build up in his muscles, nor did his glycogen dry up.

So he should have been able to stand up if he wanted to. Or at least, this is what he told himself repeatedly, but the limbs of the supposedly lightweight Silver Crow were heavy as lead. Unable to muster up any strength at all, he eventually had to get an assist from his Metatron Wings in order to peel himself off the ground.

While he sat cross-legged, taking deep breaths, sensation finally returned to his half-paralyzed limbs, and he at last yanked himself to his feet.

He first headed for Chiyuri, lying at the base of the statue. She looked more or less intact, but she was flat on her back and not moving a muscle. He wondered if she had lost consciousness, but when he drew near, she raised her right hand ten or so centimeters off the ground.

"Haru," she said weakly. "Help me up…"

"Yep." He bent over and grabbed her hand with his left. He himself was far from full strength, but he gave a hearty "heeyah" and pulled her up.

Although she staggered for a second once upright again, she managed to get her feet under her with Haruyuki's hand as support. She shook her head several times before saying, "Thanks. I'm okay now."

He let go of her hand, and she sighed at length.

"...They were pretty strong, huh?"

"Yeah," he agreed slowly. "And it didn't seem like they were even going all out..."

"And, like, how did they disappear?" she demanded. "You saw that clock thing from a second before they vanished, right?"

"Uh-huh," he assented.

Most likely, the phantom two-handed clock and the disappearance of the Drive Linkers were due to this Incarnate technique—Psion Arts—called Rattrapante that Complicator had used. But as to what specific effect it had, he still couldn't say even now, several minutes after he'd been hit with it.

"Probably some kind of perception-inhibiting technique," he said, after looking up at the gray stone statue towering above them on their left. "At any rate, let's go look for Cotton Marten. Can you move?"

"Yeah. I'm good," she replied. "I still can't entirely feel my legs, but if we're just walking..."

"Same. That Incarnate technique Urocyon used maybe didn't just have a knockback effect but a stun effect, too." Gritting his teeth all over again at the unfathomable strength of the Drive Linkers, Haruyuki swept his gaze around to both sides.

Three great valleys stretched out from the large intersection to the north, southeast, and northwest. The valleys to the north and southeast were Otowa Street in the real world, and the northwestern valley was Green Boulevard. Over half of the Exercitus survivors mowed down by Urocyon's Psion Arts were apparently also recovering from a stunned condition and leaning on one another as they started to assemble on Green Boulevard.

When Haruyuki hesitated, Chiyuri took a step forward and said, "Let's go."

He nodded wordlessly and started walking toward the northwest. He was "Betrayer" to Exercitus, but none of them were likely to try to fight him in this situation.

And there were a lot of them. Coming together in twos and threes at the mouth of the valley, the survivors numbered at least seventy on a rough count. Additionally, nearly thirty death markers still dotted the intersection.

But two or three times this number had likely been assembled when the mission to attack Tezcatlipoca began. Meaning that the number of Burst Linkers driven to total point loss in this place was, at minimum, a hundred people, and at maximum, two hundred. Most likely, the majority of the survivors had lost forever friends and comrades…and maybe "parents" and "children."

The chances that Cotton Marten had survived definitely were not high, but Chiyuri walked forward courageously nonetheless. When they drew near the opening of the valley, she let out a small "Oh!" and sped up into a trot.

He thought she'd found Marten, but she was heading for a small group of M-types. There were four—no, five of them.

"Um, you're from Ovest, right?" Chiyuri called out, and the five Linkers turned around slowly.

The large red-type avatar closest to them turned a face modeled in the shape of a tank gun turret for a mere instant toward Haruyuki before replying, "Yeah… We are."

"Do you know where Cotto—I mean, Cotton Marten—is?" she asked.

"…"

The red avatar looked silently at his comrades.

A green-type with a similarly muscular physique slumped his shoulders as he replied, "Marten just leveled up, so she didn't have a lot of extra points. And the place where she died was bad…"

"Huh…?" Chiyuri gaped at him. "Y-you mean…?"

"About five, six days into the Unlimited EK, she lost all her points."

Chiyuri's shoulders shuddered, and she staggered like her

limbs had gone numb again, so Haruyuki hurried to hold his childhood friend up.

By the time they arrived, Tezcatlipoca's Unlimited EK had been going on for two or three weeks. So the fact was that no matter how they tried, they could never have saved Cotton Marten. But total point loss was serious and not so easily accepted.

Cotton Marten had lost the Brain Burst program and any memories connected with the Accelerated World. Chiyuri would never see her again, not in the Accelerated World, not in the real one. And some percentage of the blame for this lay, without a doubt, with Haruyuki himself.

Still holding Chiyuri up, Haruyuki stiffened in expectation of some kind of reproach. From the members of Ovest, not from Chiyuri. But the five people before his eyes slumped to the ground one after the other and hung their heads, as if they no longer had the energy to keep standing, even.

Instead of their blame, Haruyuki abruptly heard his name called from immediately behind.

"Silver Crow!"

Haruyuki jumped and then looked over his shoulder.

Standing there was a duel avatar with saturated bluish-purple armor. The voice was male, but the avatar was so slender, it could have been mistaken for an F-type. From the chest down to the hips was particularly thin, obviously thinner than Silver Crow, even.

One of the five sitting on the ground called out to him in a hoarse voice.

"...Leader..."

Even before he heard this, the name of the duel avatar popped up in Haruyuki's mind. Juniper Weasel. Leader of the Legion Ovest, which had its headquarters in the city of Nishi-Tokyo.

This was the first time he'd ever spoken with him face-to-face, but he'd had any number of normal duels against him. With weapons like a high-precision sniper attack launched from a rifle with an abnormally long barrel that fired real bullets, and an elusive mobility that brought pride to his namesake of the weasel, he was a rare red-type sniper, and he had dropped Haruyuki flying at top speed. Haruyuki was pretty sure he was level seven.

Juniper Weasel stared at him dead-on with eye lenses that shone faintly yellow, and then bowed the small head on top of a longish neck. "You saved us, Crow. If you and Lime Bell hadn't come along, we woulda all been wiped out by that fox-face."

"..."

Haruyuki had been convinced Juniper Weasel was going to tell him right off, so now his jaw dropped beneath his mirrored goggles.

But Weasel seemed to pay no mind to Haruyuki's silence and continued in an unaffected, husky voice.

"Thanks to you two, looks like thirty or forty percent of the Legion's gonna make it home alive... To be honest, the damage is too huge, and I can't get my head around it yet. I smelled something dodgy when Helix's Beryllium Coil refused to be a part of the mission. For the rest of my life, I'm seriously gonna regret getting on board with this plan and not trusting my own nose."

Even for an experienced veteran like Juniper Weasel, it was probably no simple thing to accept the fact that 60 percent of your Legion members had been driven to total point loss as one.

After a moment's hesitation, Haruyuki asked in a small voice, "By 'got on board'... You mean someone other than you initially came up with this plan?"

"Yeah." Weasel nodded. "Russet Strix from Night Owls. But this isn't all on him. He got the ball rolling 'cause he wanted to change the Accelerated World for the better in his own way. After we ended up in the Unlimited EK, he kept on fighting dead center in front of Tezcatlipoca so that as many members as possible could get away."

"...So then Strix is...?" Haruyuki left the rest of the question unasked.

"Right before Tezcatlipoca got all smashed up, I watched as he hit total point loss. And while we're on the subject, Cold Brew's

Coffee Barista and Gouen's Kapur Drum also lost everything, so of the leaders of the four Legions spearheading the Exercitus plan, I'm shamefully the only one who survived."

A self-deprecating smile lifted one side of the weasel mask, and Juniper Weasel looked up at the red sky. He stayed silent for a moment, but then turned his face toward Haruyuki again, the smile gone.

"Honestly, I got absolutely no idea what happens now. Tezcatlipoca suddenly collapses, those weirdos come marching on out from inside of it. They said today's the end of Brain Burst service, yeah? You got any idea what that means, Crow?"

Posed this question, Haruyuki reflexively shook his head but then added after a second of thought, "Nothing certain. But if you're interested in a guess..."

"Sure," Weasel assented readily. "Won't lodge a complaint if it ends up being wrong."

"...Got it," Haruyuki replied. "If we piece together everything that fox-face—Urocyon—said, I think it probably means something like this. Our Brain Burst 2039 and their Dread Drive 2047 are in something like an online game's server-versus-server battle, and we're competing to see who can hit the clear conditions first... And the losing server gets shut down."

"...Server versus server...," Juniper Weasel murmured, and then he whirled his head around.

Haruyuki followed suit and sent his eyes racing over the area. The regenerated survivors continued to assemble at the mouth of Green Boulevard, but not a single person was overjoyed to still be alive. The failure of the Tezcatlipoca subjugation plan and the hardships of the weeks-long Unlimited EK had thoroughly crushed their spirits.

"Silver Crow."

His name called, Haruyuki looked once again at Weasel.

The dark blue weasel-shaped avatar bowed deeply once more. "I know I'm in no position to ask a thing like this, given that I was trying to take down the seven Great Legions. But if this server battle thing is for real, we can't handle it the way we are now. We're on the brink here. We don't even know if the individual Legions will continue to exist, much less Exercitus, and we don't have the firepower, either. So, Crow, fight those guys—those Unifiers—not for our sake or for the sake of BB, but for your own self."

When Weasel closed his mouth, the five Legion members assembled to either side of their leader and also bowed.

Unifiers. This was the name that Urocyon had spoken. Most likely, it was the group name for the ten Drive Linkers who had come out of the portal. Haruyuki should probably think of it as less a Legion name and more the name of an elite squad like the Six Armors or the Seven Dwarves.

He hadn't even been able to make Urocyon alone fight him for real, and yet there were nine more superheroes with just as much or more power. Could he actually get them to even look at him, much less fight him? And then it hit him.

The extension Chiyuri had bought them with her Citron Call, bravery, and quick-wittedness was approximately twenty-seven hours of real time—more than three years of inside time. Naturally, he couldn't spend the whole day in a dive, but he still had plenty of time to discuss the situation with trusted Burst Linkers and come up with a plan. And the Accelerated World had the Seven Kings, level niners like Urocyon and his team, plus a host of hardened veteran warriors.

The real issue was that while he absolutely could not picture a future in which his own master, the White King White Cosmos, worked with the other Kings to save the Accelerated World, he had to talk her into it or the whole endeavor would go nowhere. And although the White King appeared to be strangely omniscient, she hadn't known there was a portal inside of Tezcatlipoca, which meant that the invasion of the Drive Linkers would have also been a surprise to her.

"...I mean, I doubt they'd give me alone the time of day," Haruyuki noted by way of preamble, and continued. "But I'll do whatever I can with my comrades. And whatever your motivations, all of you in Exercitus who stood up against Tezcatlipoca should hold your heads high. Although maybe you're thinking who am I to say anything..."

"Naw, man. It's like Speed Star saying something like that, that's, like, a real thing for even the guys in total point loss." With a faint smile, Weasel looked at Chiyuri. "And Lime Bell. Thanks for looking out for Marten."

Chiyuri had been standing there quietly up to this point, so now she jumped slightly before responding in a soft voice, "I didn't make it in time. And Cotto messaged me and everything..."

"It's not your fault," Weasel told her. "We got one member who knows Marten in the real, so if you want, I could get 'em to message you. What do you think?"

"No...," Chiyuri started to say, but then nodded as if she had rethought things. "Um, okay, please do that."

She opened her storage and took out a pale blue card. The message card could record a short text, but the frozen texture indicated that it was protected by a password.

"This is my contact address," she told him. "The password is B-E-L-L."

"Got it." Weasel accepted the card and put it into his own storage.

The password was barely strong enough to protect anything, but anyone could see that the card was locked just by looking at it. And the fact that it couldn't be locked a second time made it difficult for anyone entrusted with passing it on to secretly take a peek.

This was standard procedure for giving a message to someone in the Accelerated World, so Weasel seemed unaffected as he made his storage disappear, and then sighed.

"...We're gonna wait until everyone who got turned into a death marker's regenerated, and then leave through the Sunshine portal," he told them. "You guys go on and take off."

"No, we'll stay and wait with you," Haruyuki replied. "It's only another half an hour or so."

"'Kay." Weasel nodded.

The last of the members of Exercitus not driven to total point loss regenerated exactly twenty-seven minutes later.

Haruyuki recognized more than a few faces among the survivors gathered at the entrance to the gorge, but the mood was very much not one in which he felt comfortable calling out to them. He and Chiyuri stayed close to each other at the southwest base of the cliff and watched as Juniper Weasel called out in a loud voice from the top of a flat rock.

"Scouting party's report says there are no Enemies on the road from here to Sunshine City. But who knows when one could pop up, so we're gonna move in formation. Anyone with enemy detection abilities to the front or the rear, close-range-types guard 'em, distance- and support-types, you're in the middle."

Hearing these instructions, the survivors began to move. Excluding Haruyuki and Chiyuri, their number was one hundred thirteen people. The Sun God Inti attack team, made up of members from the six Great Legions, only had ninety-six people, so this looked like a seriously large armed force to Haruyuki's eyes. But at the start of the mission, they had exceeded three hundred people. Which meant that his own guess of two hundred people being forced to total point loss was unfortunately correct.

In less than two minutes, the survivors were in formation, and at Weasel's "Move out!" command, the long, large procession started forward slowly. They cut diagonally across the intersection scarred by the battle, detoured around the towering stone statue, and headed for Sunshine 60, visible in the northeastern sky. Their movement was so well regulated that Haruyuki found it hard to believe this was a mixed corps with members from several different Legions. Most likely, they'd taken the time to practice coordinated movement before challenging Tezcatlipoca.

Abruptly, he heard a murmur from the past in his mind.

At any rate, if the small and midsize Legions have formed an alliance to upend the stagnation created by the seven Great Legions, then the Accelerated World might begin to move in big ways again. And then a flood that not even Enju can control will come rushing in and sweep us away.

I have to say, I'm a little looking forward to it.

The one who had said this to Haruyuki was the Black King Black Lotus, aka Kuroyukihime—Sayuki Kuroba. Kuroyukihime had long fought to break the stagnation of the Accelerated World, and the seed of hope she'd planted in Exercitus was real. But the atrocities of the Deity of Demise, Tezcatlipoca, had swallowed up even a force of three hundred people.

There should still have been two hundred or so level-three and lower members of Exercitus who weren't able to dive into the Unlimited Neutral Field. But because most Legions had lost their leaders and main members, simply continuing to exist was not going to be easy, just as Juniper Weasel had said.

To start with, the Accelerated World itself was poised in a moment of crisis. Would the world itself continue to exist? Haruyuki and the other members of the seven Great Legions now had to expend every effort to make it so that these Burst Linkers, walking now with their heads held high after enduring brutal loss and living hell, could return to this place again at some point.

Juniper Weasel, the last person remaining in the valley, checked to make sure that none of his comrades had been left behind before nodding slightly at Haruyuki and Chiyuri and racing away like a gale wind. A minute later, the formation was absorbed into the rocky mountains standing to the northeast of the intersection and disappeared from sight.

After turning his ears to the sound of the lonely wind blowing across the vast wildlands, Haruyuki said slowly, "You okay, Chiyu?"

After a second, a murmured voice came back to him. "Mm… I'm okay."

This was followed by a *klak*. Chiyuri had plopped down onto the ground.

Haruyuki took a seat beside her. There were a million things he had to do, but he was suddenly exhausted all over again. If he let his guard down, he might very well fall asleep.

Thinking about it now, so much had happened that day.

On his way to school that morning, Zelkova Verger of the Legion Gallant Hawks had been the first of four duels; and at school, he'd taken care of the sole animal in the custody of the Animal Care Club, Hoo, the northern white-faced owl, together with the club's super president Utai Shinomiya and club member Reina Izeki.

After that, he'd met up with the Red King Scarlet Rain/Yuniko Kozuki and the Triplex's Thistle Porcupine/Kao Fukaya, and handed Hoo over to Kao, who kept birds of prey. He was about to go home, his job finished, when he got a message from Oscillatory Universe's Snow Fairy, and he'd headed for the private Eternal Girls' Academy, Oscillatory's headquarters in Minato Ward's Shirokane, together with Rose Milady/Tsubomi Koshika and Orchid Oracle/Megumi Wakamiya, who were in the taxi that came to pick him up.

The first, second, sixth, and seventh of the Seven Dwarves had been assembled in the EG student council office, and Haruyuki had undertaken battle training at Platinum Cavalier's insistence. The objective was to defeat a Beast-class Enemy alone, but this turned out to be Cavalier's trap, and just when Cavalier's Femto style sword technique had Haruyuki backed into a corner, the Archangel Metatron had intervened, and he'd just barely made it out alive.

He'd ended up in a taxi home with Kuroyukihime, due to Megumi's scheming. He wanted to properly apologize for changing Legions, so he'd invited her up to his condo. In his living

room in the evening light, he'd told her the feelings that he'd been pushing down all this time. And then his lips and hers...

The instant his recollection reached that point, her curt voice came back to life in the back of his mind.

Listen, Haruyuki. From what I've seen, Rin, Niko, and Chiyuri consciously like you. And although they themselves may not be aware of it, Fuko, Utai, and Choco are extremely suspect.

You have to square off with all of their feelings and tell each of them how you actually feel.

Unconsciously, he looked at Lime Bell out of the corner of his eye.

Chiyu—Chiyuri Kurashima—was his childhood friend, unshakable, born in the same year in the same condo, going to the same elementary and junior high schools.

When he'd been singled out for bullying and locked himself up in a thick shell of distrust and self-loathing, Chiyuri was the one who had kept her hand extended toward him, endlessly patient. And after she became a Burst Linker as Takumu's "child," she'd saved him in his fight against Dusk Taker and the battle against the rest of the Acceleration Research Society more times than he could count. The way she unfailingly had his back, her battle abilities, her inherent cheer, and above all else, her core strength had helped him more than he could put into words.

But—no, actually *because* of this—his first thought when told she had romantic feelings for him was confusion. He'd assumed that what she really wanted was for him, her, and Takumu to live happily ever after as childhood friends.

"Hey, Haru?" she said abruptly, and he jumped and shrank into himself.

Ever so timidly, he looked to his side, but never in a million years could he have predicted the question she followed up with.

"I guess there's no legitimate way for Burst Linkers who lose all their points to come back, huh?"

The pleading note in her voice stabbed at his virtual heart. And he definitely hadn't forgotten that she had only just lost a friend.

This was not the time for thinking about romance. Although that was important, too, but not now anyway.

As he deeply inhaled the dry air, he set his brain to work in earnest. It wasn't like there were no precedents for recovery from total point loss.

Even limited to those cases he had personally witnessed, there were Dusk Taker, who had come back in the form of a consciousness possessing Wolfram Cerberus; Orchid Oracle, who'd returned in the middle of the Territories; and Centaurea Sentry, whose resurrection Haruyuki had personally been quite involved in.

Of these three examples, the restoration of Taker and Oracle had been due to the mysterious "revival" ability of the White King White Cosmos. Chiyuri would have also known about these, so this was likely why she added the "legitimate way" to her question.

But the third case…

After a moment's hesitation, he figured his master wouldn't get mad about it, given the current situation, and said, "You remember Centaurea Sentry? That person I brought to the big send-off party?"

"Yeah. Seri Suzukawa, right?" Chiyuri nodded. "Now that you mention it, how did you meet a soccer player in high school in Shinjuku?" Her date-shaped eye lenses narrowed sharply.

"Uh. Um…" He reflexively started to sit up straighter, but he quickly relaxed again as he replied. "Oh, it's not like we met in the real! First contact was on this side."

"Oh, yeah. I guess," she said, slowly. "So what about Sentry?"

"…You know she was the third Chrome Disaster, yeah?"

"…Uh-huh." Chiyuri assented and continued in a small voice. "Kuroyukihime and them thought she'd been subjugated by the Blue King and driven to total point loss ages ago. But she was actually alive and hiding somewhere in the Accelerated World the way my sister Fuu did."

"She really was subjugated by the Blue King," he said and then stopped. He firmed up his resolve and confessed. "But this actually did put Master Sentry in total point loss. The BB program was forcibly uninstalled, and she lost her memories of the Accelerated World."

"What...?!" Chiyuri's eyes flew open, but naturally, her mind continued to tease through this puzzle, and she continued in a hoarse voice. "Oh. Do you maybe mean...she came back as a Burst Linker even though she lost all her points once? In a way that's different from Dusk Taker?"

"Yeah." Haruyuki gave her a slight but firm nod. "And right in front of me, too. She didn't tell me exactly how, but I think the quantum thought circuits in the Brain Burst central server are probably the key."

"The quantum...thought circuits," Chiyuri repeated, and she looked up at the red sky almost like she was looking for those circuits. But all that was there was the orderly row of system messages WARNING and FINAL STAGE carved into hexagonal tiles.

Haruyuki wondered if the sky of the Unlimited Neutral Field would be like this forever from now on, before blinking and turning his face back to Chiyuri. "It's not like we're using our actual flesh-and-blood brains to think and talk right now. We're thinking with quantum circuits that have copied our minds—our souls. The White King calls it a 'light cube.' All our memories and everything in our brains is reproduced and stored in these circuits."

"So even if you lose all your points, and all your memories as a Burst Linker are erased, as long as the quantum circuits—the light cube—is safe, your memories can be restored?" she asked, all in one breath.

He placed a gentle hand on her shoulder to try to calm her down as he said, "If the light cube's okay. Normally, when a Burst Linker loses all their points, I guess the cube's reset, too. I think that Master Sentry either saved her own cube somehow before fighting the Blue King or...it didn't get reset because of some effect of the Armor of Catastrophe."

"..."

Chiyuri lifted her face as if about to say something but then stayed silent for another five seconds. Finally, a faint voice spilled out of the mouth hidden under her face mask. "...So then by now, Cotto's light cube is already..."

Haruyuki couldn't bring himself to give her an unequivocal "yes," so he only said, "Probably."

Chiyuri's friend Cotton Marten was not a veteran Linker like Centaurea Sentry, nor did she have any Enhanced Armament with a dodgy history. Haruyuki highly doubted that she had any means of avoiding the re-initialization of her specialized quantum circuits at the time of total point loss. In fact, more than likely, she hadn't even known those circuits existed.

It wasn't as though he knew everything about the Accelerated World, either, so he couldn't say it was absolutely out of the question. But he did think the possibility of Cotton Marten being resurrected was infinitely close to zero.

"Hey, Haru?" Chiyuri said, her voice even fainter. "The White King... Could she bring Cotto back to life with her revival power?"

"...!"

He reflexively stared intently into her small face mask. Had this been her motivation in giving Juniper Weasel her contact address? No. Haruyuki immediately dismissed this idea. She had voiced this question now impulsively, out of a sense of guilt at not having been able to save her friend.

Shifting his gaze away from her face, he set his mind to work in earnest.

White Cosmos's Revival—her resurrection ability—was a fearsome power, toying with Burst Linkers' dignity, but it didn't necessarily bring about tragic results.

Forcibly revived as the foundation for the Armor of Catastrophe Mark II, Dusk Taker appeared to be a copy of the original filled with malice, reproducing only the darkness in Seiji Nomi's heart. On the other hand, however, Megumi Wakamiya/Orchid Oracle seemed to have been brought back whole, like Centaurea

Sentry. Cosmos's power had resurrected both Burst Linkers in the Accelerated World, so where did these differences come from? The White King's closest aide, Snow Fairy, had admitted their master was prone to whims, but that probably wasn't the cause of the differences in resurrections.

"...Wakamiya—Orchid Oracle—said that if you look at White Cosmos's revival ability another way, it's a Main Visualizer access privilege," Haruyuki said, looking at the ground through the gap between his legs, and he felt Chiyuri squirm next to him. But she didn't say anything, so he continued to explain.

"I don't know how she learned an ability like that, or even if it's a normal technique or an Incarnate technique. But if she has free access to the Main Visualizer—the Brain Burst central server—then she could even restore the re-initialized light cube data... maybe. So if you're asking if there's a chance, I do think it might be possible to bring Cotton Marten back to life."

Now he heard his childhood friend inhale sharply. He hurriedly grabbed her wrist and said the thing that had to be said.

"But the White King would absolutely never simply help you, not without some kind of payment. She's after something someone like me can't even imagine, that maybe even the Seven Dwarves don't know everything about, and every single thing she does is to achieve that something; she won't lift a single finger for anything not in service to her ultimate goal. So if she does revive Cotton Marten...I think she'll demand you switch Legions in return."

"M-me?!" Chiyuri cried out, stunned, and held up the hand Haruyuki was holding, to point at herself. "Why? I mean, I'm still only level five, and I can't use Incarnate."

Haruyuki turned her hand toward the stone statue towering above them in the center of the intersection.

"Did you already forget that you rewound time for the statue and buried the portal?" he asked. "Search the whole entire Accelerated World, and you'll never find anyone else who could do that. And Pard said your Citron Call was one of the top three techniques in the Accelerated World, alongside Metatron's Trisagion and Oracle's Paradigm Breakdown."

"Huh? No, but it's nothing so great as that," Chiyuri muttered, embarrassed.

"Haah." Haruyuki sighed heavily as he released her wrist. "Think about it. The White King's already got two of the top three. So it wouldn't be weird if she wanted that last one."

"Hmm. I guess..." Chiyuri couldn't quite process this. She abruptly clamped her mouth shut and stared at Choir Chime, the Enhanced Armament equipped on her left arm.

Belatedly, he began to panic. What would he do if she said she was okay with moving from Nega Nebulus to Oscillatory Universe if it meant Cotton Marten would be revived?

However.

"...Even if it were for Cotto's sake, I couldn't transfer," she murmured, looking squarely at him. "This is different from when you transferred. I can tell that much at least."

"...Yeah?" Haruyuki somehow managed to respond.

In this moment, Chiyuri had accepted the separation from her friend. He had no way of guessing how close she had been with Cotton Marten, but developing a relationship with a member of another Legion that went beyond saying hello to a familiar face was rare in the Accelerated World where the basic rule was that everyone other than parent or child was an enemy. Excluding Prominence, which had merged with Nega Nebulus, about the only friend in another Legion Haruyuki could say he had was Great Wall's Ash Roller.

Actually, he did have one more. He could count the number of times they'd spoken on one hand, but the Acceleration Research Society's Wolfram Cerberus was definitely a friend. And now that he had been transformed into Wolfram Disaster, the most powerful duel avatar in history, through the fusion of the Invincible thruster Enhanced Armament stolen from the Red King Scarlet Rain, and the super-concentrated negative Incarnate collected with the ISS kits, Haruyuki had to do whatever it took to save him.

The real-life Cerberus he'd glimpsed on the shopping street in Koenji a month earlier had been a boy with a lingering childishness, bangs hanging down to his eyes. Haruyuki hadn't even gotten the chance to ask his name, but he had an idea what school he went to.

The black trousers Cerberus had been wearing were cut from a stylish fabric with a dark-gray checkered pattern visible when the light hit right. And a mere seven hours earlier, Haruyuki had seen the exact same uniform on Tomochika Kyobu and Rioh Koshimizu of the Seven Dwarves. Which meant that Wolfram Cerberus was a student at their school, Shirakabanomori Academy.

It was summer break, so he wouldn't be able to find Cerberus just by standing watch at the school the way Niko had once found him at Umesato. But if he could somehow manage to connect with the school's local net, he might be able to dig up his real name and address.

After letting his thoughts drift this far, Haruyuki sighed. He shouldn't be thinking of himself right now; he needed to take care of Chiyuri. After all, she had just lost a friend. He was about to try to say something consoling when he heard her voice first.

"There's no way I could transfer Legions," she said, her head still hanging, and then she lifted her face to look at him as she continued. "But, like, there isn't a one hundred percent possibility that the White King won't revive her for me with some other condition, right?"

"...That's a convoluted way to say it. Just say the possibility's not zero. Geez," he noted, but he was completely ignored.

"Is it possible or not?" she demanded.

"...I mean, no one knows what she's thinking, so I can't say there's no way, but..."

"Then *you* ask her, Haru."

"Huh... Whaaaat?!" Reeling, he shook his head vigorously back and forth. "Then she'll put up the trade conditions on me and not on you."

"I'll help you out with whatever it is," she told him.

"Okay, look," he protested somewhat pathetically, but in his heart, he was a bit relieved. He could hear a hint of Chiyuri's usual cheer and unyielding will in her voice again.

Even if this cheer was an act based on a faint sliver of hope, the possibility of resurrection really was not zero. The White King was in fact Haruyuki's current Legion Master, and she wouldn't go taking his head off on the spot if he did go to her with some wild request… Probably.

He had made up his mind and was about to respond that he was on board when he heard the whisper of a voice, and his whole body stiffened.

…Someone…

Chiyuri cocked her head dubiously to one side, and he silenced her by holding his index finger to his mouth as he focused his entire self on his ears.

The only thing his avatar's auditory system captured was the dry wind blowing through the groups of rocks. He couldn't hear anyone talking or any Enemies crying out. But the instant he started to relax with the assumption that he'd been hearing things…

Someone, help me…!

He heard the voice again, slightly louder in volume this time.

Chiyuri apparently also heard it and gasped. "That voice!"

They both leapt to their feet and whirled their heads around. Behind them were rocks more than twenty meters tall, the business buildings of the real world transformed. To their left, Green Boulevard stretched out straight to the northwest, while to their right was the Higashi-Ikebukuro Intersection, and in front of them, the two-legged stone statue. He stared intently in every direction, but he saw no sign of a person.

Since the interiors of buildings weren't recreated in a Wasteland stage, it was unlikely there was anyone inside of the rocks. But unlike the ground, these rocks were not indestructible, so there was a possibility that, for instance, someone could be shot several meters into one with the force of a collision and be buried by the collapsing rock immediately after. If that were the case, then the only way they could find the owner of the voice was to destroy all of the nearby rocks one after the other. But he had no idea how many days it would take to smash them all with their bare hands, and the Change would probably come before they could finish anyway.

If they could at least figure out what direction it was coming from, Haruyuki thought, perking up his ears once more. But even after waiting a minute or so, he still hadn't heard the voice again.

Abruptly, Chiyuri raised the large bell of her left hand. Bending her elbow to the limit of its range of motion, she turned the opening of the bell straight up and then brought it directly down toward the ground.

Rather than a dull *thunk* as the bell dug into the rocky foundation, he heard a clear sound, a *tooooong* like a crystal mallet gently tapping a metal sphere in the air. He clearly felt the sound waves penetrate the ground and radiate outward.

Chiyuri stayed motionless for a time with the bell still pressed against the ground, but then she suddenly lifted her face and shouted, "That way!" She dashed forward with incredible speed, and he hurried to chase after her.

Racing along the rocks to the southeast, she turned right after about thirty meters and plunged into a narrow gorge. She ran the same distance again and then abruptly screeched to a stop.

"It's...around here...," she said, her gaze racing over the area.

Haruyuki pushed back the urge to ask her what that sound before was and also searched the area.

The gorge was maybe ten meters wide, not even close to the width of Green Boulevard. With nothing but a succession of perpendicular cliffs to either side, he couldn't see anyplace a person might hide. Plus, there was no need for someone seeking help to hide.

Is it a trap? And if it is, who exactly...? he wondered, and he was about to call out to Chiyuri that they should go back for now.

"Haru! Over there!" Chiyuri cried, and he pointed to a spot on the ground.

He saw a simple circular indentation, about sixty centimeters across and barely ten centimeters deep. There were other similar holes in the area, but the bottom of this one was somewhat strange. Rather than being indented in a U-shape, the center rose slightly. Almost as though a rock of just the right size had been put over a deeper hole...

"Ah... It really is that!" Haruyuki agreed with his own thought, and he crouched directly above the hole. "Oiii! Is someone in there?!"

Chiyuri crouched next to him, and together they held their breath and listened.

A few seconds later...

...Is someone there...?

The voice that came in response was so faint and weak that he wouldn't have heard it if the wind hadn't happened to stop.

Reflexively, he exchanged a look with Chiyuri before asking quietly, "That voice... Was it maybe Cotton Marten?"

After half a second, Chiyuri shook her head. "It sounds like a girl's voice, but it's probably not her."

"...No, huh."

Unfortunately, it seemed that a miracle had not happened. But naturally, this didn't mean they had the option of simply leaving this person there.

Haruyuki brought his face close to the indentation once more and called out to whoever was in the hole, "I'm Silver Crow from Nega—I mean, Oscillatory Universe! We're gonna get you outta there. Just hang on a bit longer!"

Although he said they would get her out, the large rock plugging the hole was less tightly wedged in, without a millimeter of an opening between it and the edge of the hole. It was like the lid was digging right into the sides of the hole, and he couldn't see anywhere for fingers to get a hold and lift it out. This could hardly have happened by accident, so no doubt some malicious actor had pushed the owner of the voice into a deep hole in the ground and then used force to seal her inside of it with a rock.

Actually, no. Until a mere hour earlier, the Deity of Demise, Tezcatlipoca, had been running rampant over the area. This blocked hole had to have been a shelter to protect the owner of the voice. If the Burst Linker who had pushed the rock into place had escaped total point loss, they would have long ago rescued whoever was down there. The fact that this hadn't happened meant…

Haruyuki cut off his thoughts there and stared hard at the rock in front of him.

"…You wanna try both of us hitting it?" Chiyuri said, and he quickly shook his head.

"It'd be great if that broke it, but we might just push it farther in," he told her. "And, like, if it doesn't break even when the Change comes, the system might be treating the hole and the rock like ground."

"You mean indestructible?!" she cried. "So what do we do?!"

"…Incarnate technique… I could maybe pierce it with Laser Sword, but…" He didn't have to finish his sentence for his meaning to be clear. If this rock was round and sixty or so centimeters wide, his Incarnate blade might pierce it, but it would also skewer the owner of the voice. And there was a nonzero possibility that a blow like that would put her at total point loss.

If he had an Incarnate technique like Dusk Taker's Nihilistic Fluctuation that could dig out anything he picked up, he could have safely removed the stone. But Dusk Taker was gone, and no Burst Linker who could use a similar technique came to mind. Not to mention who knew how many days would pass here while he was going through the steps of leaving through a portal, contacting someone, and diving back into the Unlimited Neutral Field?

"Hey, Haru?" Chiyuri asked. "Can't you cut the stone with your Omega style thing?"

Haruyuki shook his head once more. "I might be able to cut it, but there's no way I could cut just the stone alone, not with my skill level. I don't know how big the stone is, either. Can you do something with your Citron Call?"

"From what I can see, it's been a few days since this stone was embedded in this hole," she said, frowning. "That's too much time to rewind."

"I guess. Hmm." He frowned with her. "If we had some kind of super-thin, tough tool we could control and push into the gap to lift it…"

"If we had something like that, we'd already be using it!" Chiyuri cried out, exasperated, as she slapped him on the back, and as though this impact were a switch, an idea popped up in his head.

"G-get back a bit." He pushed Chiyuri away and focused on the place she'd hit him, the joint with the Enhanced Armament Metatron Wings.

Ektenia, the equipment's fixed ability, was not an Incarnate technique, so it couldn't pierce the indestructible ground, and even if it could, the risk of injuring the owner of the voice remained. But if he used the wings themselves as a thin and tough tool that he could control, maybe he could pull the rock out of the hole without damaging it.

But that kind of precise control would be difficult for him. The Metatron Wings were, in the end, a borrowed weapon, and the awareness of the Archangel Metatron being their original owner was hard to erase from within him. This was no doubt the reason he didn't have the same fine control over them as he did over the ten metal fins that were his own natural wings.

Given that in terms of the system, ownership of the Wings was with Metatron, it would be difficult to eliminate his feeling of them being on loan to him. But when he'd tried to return the Wings once, Metatron had responded that they were part of the link between the two of them, so they could not be given back.

But if they were embedded in the link, that meant the Metatron Wings were a circuit connecting him with Metatron, an antenna, and an amplifier. In which case, if he enhanced the link itself, that might just also strengthen his connection with the Wings.

An hour or so earlier, in the middle of the intense battle with the werewolf Urocyon, Haruyuki had heard the voice of the Archangel Metatron—*Crow! Use my wings!* That voice—no, command—hadn't simply been him hearing things. Most likely, Metatron could detect Haruyuki's status but was in a place that made it difficult for her to come running, like she had in the fight with Platinum Cavalier.

Metatron, Haruyuki called out to her in his mind through their link. *This whole time, I've thought your wings—the Metatron Wings—were borrowed, and at some point, I'd have to give them back. But if they are proof of the link between me and you—the bond we have—then I never want to lose them.*

Can I make these wings mine forever?

As Chiyuri stared at him in frustration, he waited another five seconds.

At this critical juncture, this *is what you come to me with? I have said before that this is acceptable. It was you who refused to the union with them, servant.*

He could just barely hear her exasperated voice, and he felt a faint warmth in the wings on his back and the pounding of a pulse.

Thmp, thmp. This pulse came into sync with his own. The heat in the wings came through his metal armor and penetrated the naked body of his avatar. Like a plant setting down roots.

"Haru, your top wings are...," Chiyuri murmured.

He craned his head around to the limit of his range of motion. He obviously couldn't see his back, but he did see a surge of milky-white light flowing out from the base to the tips of the Metatron Wings.

Turning his face forward again, Haruyuki closed his eye lenses. He pictured countless roots stretching out from the Wings and enveloping the virtual heart in his chest. These extremely thin roots tangled together in layers, melted into each other, and became one with his heart.

Thmp!

A noticeably stronger, hotter heartbeat pounded in the center of his avatar. At the same time, the ten metal fins and the four Metatron Wings above them fully deployed on their own with a *waashp*.

The weight of the Enhanced Armament he'd felt when he had the Metatron Wings equipped gradually faded. He couldn't see it himself, but he could feel the four Wings fuse into two and then fuse with Silver Crow's own wings. The white wave pulsing along his back flashed with an even more intense light.

As this light died down, the incandescent heat left his body, and he exhaled at length.

"...What're my wings like now?" he asked, lifting his face.

"They're like..." Chiyuri blinked a couple times. "At first, they were four on top and then ten below, growing separately. But now the top four are overlapping perfectly so they're just two, and they're stuck to the bottom ten. There's six growing out of each side, twelve altogether. Although the wings on the very top have a kind of different shape."

"Yeah...?" He opened his storage. The only Enhanced Armament he currently possessed was the Lucid Blade. When he hurriedly shifted to his abilities window, the weapon upgrade of his Aviation ability, which had been +4, had risen to +6. The Metatron Wings had apparently completely disappeared as an Enhanced Armament and been integrated as an ability. He would never again equip or remove the Wings.

When he thought about the fact that his Aviation had been enhanced by a factor of two level-up bonuses, he first felt fear rather than joy. But if he was going to fight the Drive Linkers, no matter how strong he got, it wouldn't be enough. The reason he hadn't used the Metatron Wings in normal duels up to that point was because he'd obtained them through the extremely irregular means of a loan from a Being, the Archangel Metatron. But as to whether or not those days spent challenging and being challenged to proper duels would ever return...

"C'mon, Haru. Don't space out on me. Hurry up and do

something about this rock." Chiyuri tugged on his arm, dragging him back to the present. She was right. This was not the time to be stewing in his own thoughts.

Thanks, Metatron. He offered up his gratitude in his heart, and rather than words in return, he felt his head being patted gently.

He focused his mind on the top two of the now six pairs of twelve individual wings. Unlike before, he felt a clear connection with them, as though the network of his nerves stretched all the way to their tips.

He bent the new wings on his shoulders forward so that he could see them. What had been two pairs of four wings had fused into one pair of two, but they still had the sword shape and film-like thinness of the old Metatron Wings. And like the original wings, they were elastic, able to stretch out to many times their normal length and as strong as polyamide film.

He stretched the wings out to the ground and pushed down on either side of the large stone perfectly plugging the hole. A thin platinum film forced open, or rather cut out a gap of not even 0.1 millimeters and dug deeper, bit by bit. While he had no feeling in the wings, the shape and hardness of what they touched was communicated to his back.

Just as he'd expected, the stone was an almost perfect sphere with a diameter of sixty centimeters or so. If he had attempted to destroy it with his Laser Sword, the Incarnate blade would likely have pierced the rock and gone on to injure the person beyond it. Pressing the Metatron Wings—his new wings—flat against the underside of the round stone, he carefully extended them, stopping only when the tips overlapped with each other. He set his feet apart to brace himself and took a deep breath.

"...Hngah!" he cried, contracted his wings, and tried to lift the rock straight up.

At first, it wouldn't budge, but when he pulled a little harder, the stone moved surprisingly smoothly. Not because it hadn't been wedged in as firmly as it looked, but rather because the output of his new wings was extraordinary. If he let loose their full power, he could very well have tossed the rock high up into the sky. Carefully fine-tuning the amount of strength he used, he slid the stone off the hole.

Zsh, zsh, zsh... The stone came up a few centimeters at a time, resisting just a little at the end before it popped off the hole somewhat anticlimactically.

He looked at it closely and found that the large beach ball of a stone had ten small indentations on its top, lined up symmetrically. Most likely, these were traces of the fingers of both hands, left here by whoever it was who had pushed the stone into the hole.

After Haruyuki set the stone down next to the hole, he returned his new wings to his back. He folded them up together with the other ten, stored them in his armor, and sent another telepathic "thank you" to Metatron.

The almost perfectly round hole was fairly deep, and the light of the sun didn't reach inside. Even so, he could see some kind of curled-up shadow about a meter down from the ground. Another rock—no, it was maybe the head of a duel avatar.

"Haru!" Chiyuri cried out quietly beside him, apparently noticing this at the same time.

He gave her a wordless nod in return and cloaked his right hand in an Incarnate overlay to illuminate the inside of the hole.

Just as he'd expected, a small avatar was leaning against the side of the hole. The fact that the avatar existed at all meant that her health gauge was not completely depleted, at any rate, but mental exhaustion was something else altogether. Head lolling, she didn't so much as twitch when he shone the white light on her.

This had to have been the avatar who'd been calling for help. Which meant that during the time it had taken Haruyuki and Chiyuri to run over and push the rock aside, she had fallen asleep—or passed out. Exactly how many hours, how many dozens of hours had she been in this small hole...?

"Haru, we have to hurry and get her out," Chiyuri murmured.

He glanced over at her. Even though they had proof now that

it really wasn't Cotton Marten locked up in here, she showed no sign of despair as she dropped down and called into the hole.

"Hey, you! Are you okay?! We're gonna get you outta there. Can you reach out your hands?"

Her voice had a ring to it almost as clear as that of the bell on her right hand, and perhaps it acted as a kind of smelling salts. The avatar stirred slightly before jerking her head up and blinking her lavender eye lenses.

"...Who...are you...?" she asked hoarsely.

"It's okay," Chiyuri replied in a quieter voice. "We're friends. I'm Lime Bell from Nega Nebulus. This is Silver Crow from the same—I mean, no, from Oscillatory Universe."

"Lime Bell... Silver Crow..." After repeating their names, the avatar in the hole gave her own name. "I'm...Taupe Cape from Gallant Hawks."

"Oh! I know you. You're Gallant's leader, right?" Chiyuri responded and shoved her hand into the hole. "Come on, Crow. You too."

Urged on, Haruyuki crouched beside her.

The reason he was a little slow to react was because Gallant Hawks was the Zelkova Verger's Legion, the Burst Linker who had challenged him on his way to school that morning. He knew he'd fought in a way that lacked respect for his duel opponent, maybe because his nerves were frayed, and if she had watched that duel... The thought slipped through his mind, but this was no time to be worrying about that.

Fortunately, Taupe Cape appeared not to hold any grudge against him, and she grabbed the hands he and Chiyuri extended without hesitation.

In sync with Chiyuri, he pulled her up little by little. The slender avatar was surprisingly light, and none of her armor had parts that stuck out in any serious way, so they were able to lift her out smoothly without too much work. Once they'd gotten her out up to her hips, they moved her to one side and sat her on the edge of the hole.

Taupe Cape expanded the chest wrapped in grayish-purple armor as far as it would go and breathed in like she was devouring the fresh air.

While duel avatars didn't require oxygen, they did have the sensation of breathing with lungs, so Taupe Cape had no doubt been fighting the terror of a lack of oxygen in that small, closed space the whole time.

After taking several deep breaths and slowly exhaling the last one, she looked up at Haruyuki and Chiyuri and bowed her head. "Bell, Crow. Thank you. I thought I'd never get out of this hole."

"How long have you been in there, Taupe?" Chiyuri asked, and the other avatar cocked her head slightly to one side.

"I don't know precisely anymore, but..." She paused for a moment. "Probably ten days, two weeks-ish..."

"..."

Chiyuri was stunned into silence, and Haruyuki's jaw dropped in silent amazement. Two weeks all alone in a pitch-black, vertical hole, so small she couldn't even lie down. Without the ability to decelerate like Black Vise or a resistance to loneliness like Avocado Avoider, who knew what kind of damage that would do to the psyche?

"...I can't believe you made it that long," Haruyuki said.

Taupe shook her head slightly. "If it had been a trap, I totally could never have done it. But the person who put me in here..." She opened her eye lenses wide with a gasp. "Right. Where's Tezcatlipoca?! What happened to Exercitus? To Zel and Jim and them?!"

She quickly looked around and then turned her face up to the sky and froze in place.

Haruyuki also glanced at the crimson hexagons lined up in the abnormal sky before responding, "We'd be here all day if we gave you the detailed story. Basically, Tezcatlipoca collapsed. Excluding you, one hundred thirteen members of Exercitus survived. They left earlier through the portal at Sunshine City."

"Collapsed...?" Taupe muttered, doubtful, but then turned her gaze back on him. "Zel...? Did you see Zelkova Verger?"

Haruyuki couldn't immediately answer her. It wasn't like he'd checked each and every survivor, but he would've remembered if he'd seen the large Zelkova, with his distinctive armor, among them. And he highly doubted that Zelkova would have left Taupe Cape locked up in a hole and returned to the real world if he had survived. Which meant, essentially...

"...I'm sorry. I didn't see him," he replied briefly, unable to bring himself to say that Zelkova had probably been driven to total point loss.

But Taupe Cape appeared to intuit everything from just that. She curled up like she was in pain and hung her head even lower.

Chiyuri, who had similarly just lost a friend, apparently had no words of comfort for the grieving avatar. Haruyuki had only dueled Zelkova Verger the one time that morning, and he had only known Taupe Cape by name, but he was pretty sure that they were parent and child. He felt like he'd heard somewhere that Taupe was Zelkova's parent. He couldn't begin to imagine the sadness of losing a child.

But Taupe Cape had to have been more mentally spent than she could bear. While it was not the flesh-and-blood brain that was exhausted, but rather the replicated mind of the quantum circuits, there would no doubt be an excessive burden placed on her brain during the memory synchronization that would happen after she burst out. They had to return her to the real world through the nearest portal as soon as possible.

With this thought in mind, Haruyuki took a step toward the hunched-over Taupe. But before he could open his mouth, he heard a pained voice.

"...I don't want to go back," Taupe said softly.

...B-but...you have to leave right away and get some actual rest." He managed somehow these words of protest, but Taupe shrank even further into herself.

"I'm...on a video call with Zel."

Hearing this, Haruyuki exchanged another look with Chiyuri.

A video call was in the same family as the voice call, where you chatted with sound only, and the dive call, where you chatted in avatar form; it was a feature where you chatted in a video feed window displayed on your virtual desktop. Your own face couldn't be filmed with the camera built into your Neurolinker, so a video call required an external camera, but it was the quickest way to accelerate while looking at the actual face of someone in a different place.

If she'd entered the Unlimited Neutral Field on a call, he could easily understand her desire to not return to the real world. The first thing she would see when she burst out was the face of Zelkova Verger, who had now lost all memories connected with the Accelerated World.

"..."

Not sure what to do, Haruyuki clenched his teeth beneath his goggles.

Chiyuri brought her face mask close and whispered, "Hey, Haru, how about we let her rest somewhere safe on this side?"

"Huh? Umm..." He blinked in surprise at this unexpected suggestion.

It was possible to rest and recover from mental exhaustion in the Unlimited Neutral Field...in theory at least. Before the Sun God Inti attack mission, Ardor Maiden had let Haruyuki take a nap of about fifty minutes with his head on her lap, and the exhaustion of training for nearly five months was miraculously gone when he woke up. This had most likely been some unknown ability of Maiden's at work, but he did feel like a good sleep in the Accelerated World could definitely prevent that exhaustion from being brought back to the flesh-and-blood brain.

"...That's maybe a good idea." He nodded. "But where's a safe place?"

"Hmm." Chiyuri paused thoughtfully. "Like big sister Raker's house or something?"

"Ohh..." *Makes sense*, he thought, before he realized that he didn't have the key to Fufuan, Sky Raker's player home. Metatron could come and go from the house as she pleased, since Fuko had given her a duplicate key, but she was apparently in the middle of something at the moment.

Duplicate key.

"...Oh!" He let out a small cry and opened his storage once more. He scrolled through the item list rather than the Enhanced Armament and quickly closed it after finding what he was looking for. "It's not Fufuan, but I know a safe place."

Chiyuri nodded without asking where, and she crouched. She brought her face close to Taupe Cape, who was still hanging her head, and began to speak in a quiet voice.

Before too long, she helped Taupe to her feet and looked at Haruyuki. Apparently, Taupe had accepted the proposal.

In which case, they needed to move from this place. Their destination, the Mejirodai area of Bunkyo Ward, wasn't even two kilometers as the crow flies, but it was far too dangerous to go on foot with the thoroughly spent Taupe Cape. That said, however, the emotional weight of embracing an F-type avatar—a girl he'd just met—and flying there was too great.

This is no time for being a big shy baby, Haruyuki scolded himself.

"Excuse me," he said, going around behind Chiyuri and Taupe standing side by side, and he wrapped an arm around each of them at the same time. He made sure he had a good hold before he deployed the wings on his back.

Since his flight ability had been strengthened by two, he tried to go easy on the vibration of them, but even still, this meager force generated a gravitational acceleration on par with a drop-of-doom type amusement park attraction, and he hurried to cut back his output. If it had been only Chiyuri he was carrying, he might have taken decisive action and executed a super-high-speed challenge with no advance warning whatsoever, but it would have been inappropriate to give free rein to this sort of mischievousness at this moment.

He ascended to just a little higher than the range of the rocky mountains lining the gorge, before shifting to hovering. If he was going to prioritize evading Enemies, then he should get more altitude, but he was worried about the missing Urocyon and Complicator. Urocyon had promised to let Haruyuki leave if he could survive for five minutes and to let the portal stay buried until midnight on July 28, but he'd said nothing about not attacking if he encountered him in some other place.

Thus, Haruyuki hung in the air at an altitude of about thirty meters, where he was hard to spot from the ground as he felt around for the presence of Enemies.

"...So this is the flight ability," Taupe Cape murmured, from where she was held against him, not hiding her admiration. But this was quickly followed by an unexpected question. "Why didn't you use it in your duel against Zel this morning?"

"Umm..." He called up his memories of the battle that now seemed like the long-distant past. "Zelkova was expecting me to come flying in, so I approached on the ground and got him to let his guard down from above."

"Oh. Huh. Makes sense." Taupe nodded and fell silent once more.

Haruyuki wasn't sure whether or not to add that it definitely wasn't because he hadn't taken Zelkova Verger too seriously, but eventually he went back to enemy detection without saying anything. After confirming there were no Enemies or avatars in the area, he lightly vibrated his wings.

He headed toward the southwest in a horizontal gliding movement, like sliding through the air. He slipped past Ecomuse Town towering over the landscape and flew slowly as he looked to the gorge of Otowa Street on his left, when low ground with too many small rocks to count came into view up ahead. The real world's Zoshigaya Cemetery.

Since annoying, dead spirit-type Enemies occasionally lurked in places like this, he decided against passing directly overhead and instead detoured to the south. From there, he flew in a straight line and descended to the ground in front of a single massive rock more than two hundred meters wide.

He put on the brakes immediately before the feet of Taupe Cape and Lime Bell touched the earth and stayed there motionless for a second before letting go of them. Once they had both planted their feet on the hard stone, he let out a short sigh and looked straight ahead.

The single stone building blocking the way was a five-star hotel with a nearly 100-year history in the real world. In front of it was a lake boasting clear water, unusual for a Wasteland stage.

"...Is this really it?" Chiyuri looked dubious.

Haruyuki replied in the affirmative before opening his storage again. He pulled out the item he'd found earlier and let it dangle from his right hand.

"Follow me," he told the two girls, approaching the water's edge, and then kept on walking. The lake was extremely shallow, maybe not even five centimeters deep.

When the three of them had advanced ten meters or so, sending ripples spreading outward across the tranquil water's surface, fog began to suddenly drift up around them, growing thicker in the blink of an eye until it eventually painted his entire field of view a singular white.

He nodded at Chiyuri making nervous sounds and Taupe Cape standing next to her, before brandishing the item hanging from his right hand, a large key with a decorative blue string tied to it. When he shook it lightly, the cool *ting* of a bell rang out, despite the fact that there was no bell attached to it.

Instantly, the white fog parted, and the proud gate to a Japanese-style manor with a tiled roof appeared. Haruyuki looked back again and said, "This is Oumutei... Centaurea Sentry's house."

Haruyuki had been given the duplicate key to Oumutei by Centaurea Sentry four days earlier in real time, right before the mission to attack the Sun God Inti. He'd said that he wanted to have more time for his sword training, and Sentry had thought about it for a mere three seconds before handing him the key and telling him he could take whatever he wanted from the kitchen.

He should really have given the key back right after the Inti mission was over, but because of the succession of unpredictable developments like the appearance of Tezcatlipoca and Haruyuki's Legion transfer, he had completely forgotten about it.

He hadn't had any contact with Master Sentry for three days now, not since the regrettable failure of the mission to rescue Silver Crow. He wondered if she was perhaps staying at Oumutei as he slipped through the manor gates, but the large samurai house was silent. There was no hint of any person's presence. Not knowing whether he was disappointed or relieved, he opened the front door.

"Hello!" he called out, just in case, and then led the girls first to the kitchen. He opened a fridge disguised as a set of shelves, and found that the inside was mostly taken up by bottles of sake. He dug out three bottles of the only nonalcoholic drink—carbonated water meant for mixing with the sake, apparently—and set them down on the table in the center of the room.

"If you'd rather have regular water, there's a well in the garden," he said as he did so.

"This is great, thank you," Taupe Cape quickly replied from where she sat on a chair, and she twisted the cap off. Perhaps she was excessively thirsty—she had no sooner brought the bottle to her lips than she had gulped down the whole half-liter bottle in one go.

As he watched this out of the corner of his eye, he opened the other refrigerator. This one was stuffed with all kinds of food and crammed with tea cakes, but only Sentry knew how to serve them. Thinking they probably wouldn't go very well with fizzy water, he pulled a slab of expensive-looking *yokan* jelly wrapped in bamboo sheathing out from the back of the fridge.

He opened the wrapping and cut the twenty-five-centimeter *yokan* log into four pieces with a knife. He put one slice on his plate and one on Chiyuri's, the other two on Taupe Cape's plate, added bamboo skewers he found in the kitchen, and then returned to the table.

Sitting directly across from him, Taupe pressed her hands together and thanked him before cutting one slice into another four parts with the skewer. She ate one piece slowly now, as if truly savoring what went into her mouth.

Just as Haruyuki realized he was also hungry and picked up his own skewer, a drop of water fell with a *splsh* onto Taupe Cape's plate. For a second, he thought the roof was leaking, but Oumutei wasn't that cheaply built, and anyway, it didn't rain in a Wasteland stage.

The source of the water drop was Taupe's eye lens. A new droplet spilled out from her left eye, trickled down her face mask turned toward the table, and dropped onto the plate. But Taupe didn't move to wipe her eyes; she simply continued to eat one bite after the other.

Haruyuki also cut a piece of his own *yokan* slice and brought it to his mouth. A rich yet refreshing sweetness spread out over his tongue, followed by the simple flavor of the azuki bean the jelly was made of. It had probably cost an arm and a leg in the shop, but he was sure that Centaurea Sentry wouldn't be mad at them for eating it.

So the three of them silently ate, and Taupe Cape kept crying.

4

Twenty minutes later, having left Oumutei by himself, Haruyuki walked in a straight line until he'd gotten out of the thick fog, before whirling around.

Naturally, he couldn't see the house, blocked as it was by the fog, but he bowed toward its owner, Centaurea Sentry, and then spread his wings at an acute angle. He still had pretty much all of the special attack gauge he'd charged up during the battle with Urocyon, so he vibrated the twelve metal fins with an output of 50 percent.

Boom! The shock wave pushed the lake water at his feet back ten meters in all directions as Silver Crow shot up into the sky at a speed fast enough to make all of his joints squeal in protest. Despite the fact that this was only half throttle, the power output was basically the same as his previous full-strength acceleration, and he reflexively started to put on the emergency brakes, but he desperately checked that impulse and continued his ascent. If he put on the brakes at this speed, the deceleration would generate an explosive sonic boom. And that would be like saying "Come find me" to any Enemies or avatars on the ground.

He pressed his arms tightly against his sides, minimizing air resistance as much as possible as he soared up for ten seconds or so, and then his field of view was dyed white once more. Not fog this time, but clouds. Shooting through the enormous fleecy configuration, he finally spread out his wings to their fullest and applied the brakes with a level of force that wouldn't generate a shock wave, to gradually decelerate.

Once he had finally shifted to hovering, there was nothing but blue sky around him. When he lowered his gaze, the skyscrapers of central Tokyo looked like miniatures of the cityscape. He was probably at an altitude of two thousand meters.

Two thousand meters in ten seconds meant that his average speed could be calculated to be seven hundred twenty kilometers an hour. Even before the fusion, the Metatron Wings had boasted an acceleration reaching the speed of sound—approximately twelve hundred kilometers an hour at full power. But exceeding seven hundred kilometers an hour at half power while ascending vertically where the influence of gravity was at its strongest was something else. If he accelerated at full power, one of his limbs might very well be ripped off…

"Don't freak out," Haruyuki muttered to himself.

He had despaired over how much more powerful Urocyon and the other Unifiers were than the Burst Linkers. If he was going to be afraid of the power he'd obtained, closing that gap would remain the dream of a dream.

He would absolutely make this power his, even if it meant his head was ripped off, forget a limb. After vowing this in his heart, he narrowed his eyes on the scene directly below him. The lake where Oumutei hid looked like a blue drop of water from this height.

The second this thought crossed his mind, Taupe Cape's tears falling onto the white plate came back to him.

After finishing the two slices of *yokan*, Taupe had thanked him again and started to stand up, but then sat back down before her bottom was even thirty centimeters off the chair.

Haruyuki and Chiyuri assumed that now that her virtual hunger had been sated, staying awake any longer was beyond her, so they'd helped Taupe into the Japanese-style tatami room across from the kitchen.

He pulled a futon and blanket out of the home storage, laid them out on the tatami mats, and then set Taupe down on the futon. She immediately dropped off to sleep, almost like she was passing out. Judging from her exhausted state, he wouldn't have been surprised if she slept for a full day.

He had intended to stay until she woke up, but Chiyuri said that she would watch over her so he could go, and he'd taken that reprieve. But naturally, he hadn't left Oumutei to go fool around or for a change of scenery. He wanted to use this time to tackle the mission he'd been tasked with.

That evening, the White King White Cosmos had given Haruyuki an order—actually, depending on how he looked at it, that one order was maybe four: to contact the other highest-ranking Beings besides the Archangel Metatron, Ohirume Amaterasu, and Abandoned Princess Bari, to whom he was already contracted/linked, and contract with them, if possible.

Those four Beings were Goddess of the Dawn Ushas, Queen Mother of the West Xiwangmu, Storm King Rudra, and Night Goddess Nyx.

He had absolutely no idea what the White King's objective in issuing such an order was, and it was not clear if it was still in effect now that Tezcatlipoca had collapsed and the Drive Linkers had invaded. But the White King was Haruyuki's master, so he had to execute the missions he was given until they were clearly withdrawn.

The issue was that the four highest-ranking Beings inhabited the deepest parts of extremely difficult dungeons on the same scale as the Shiba Park Underground Labyrinth, Metatron's home. Kuroyukihime, who was there when Cosmos issued this order, said that an attack squad of eighteen people in three parties, at the very least, was required to break through the dungeons.

Since he couldn't actually recruit personnel from Nega Nebulus or any of the other Kings' Legions to carry out the White King's order, his attack corps would have to be composed of only Oscillatory Universe members.

Oscillatory was a large Legion with a general force of thirty people, even excluding the members of the "underground corps," the Acceleration Research Society. But the only people he'd met since he joined the Legion were Rose Milady and Orchid Oracle, who were planning to leave the Legion, and four of the Seven Dwarves. He had only fought the other members in the Territories seven days earlier and hadn't spoken to them yet. How many would gladly accept a sudden request to join him in attacking a high-level dungeon?

"...At any rate, I guess could go check out the dungeons," he said with a sigh, and he turned his body to the southeast.

Of the highest-level Beings he was supposed to make contact with, Ushas had her castle under the Shinjuku Government Building, Xiwangmu under the Tokyo Dome, Rudra under the Tokyo Big Sight, and Nyx under Yoyogi Park. The closest of these to his current position was the Tokyo Dome.

*What kind of god is Xiwangmu? Her name sounds kinda Chinese...*he wondered as he sought out a dome-shaped mountain in the wasteland spreading out two thousand meters below him.

Suddenly, a faint voice echoed inside his head.

Servant.

"M-Metatron? What's up?" he accidentally asked with his actual voice instead of in thought, but the question apparently reached her without issue.

I should like to ask you that very question. Shift to the Highest Level this very second.

"Huh? R-right now?"

That is what I said.

Together with this curt response, the presence of Metatron disappeared. Apparently, she was not going to pull him up to the Highest Level herself.

After lunch that day, in the student council office of the Eternal Girls' Academy junior high division, Snow Fairy, aka Nanako Juholt, had said that Crow was a level-two contractor and on top of that, a level-three accessor.

A contractor was just as the name would have it, someone who was linked with (i.e., under contract to) a Being, but he had no idea what the levels meant. An accessor was someone who had reached the Highest Level, and he had some idea of the levels here. Level one was someone who had direct contact with a Being and was shifted by them, level two was someone who shifted in long-distance resonance with a Being, and level three was someone who could shift on their own.

Haruyuki had only shifted to the Highest Level without Metatron's assistance a mere handful of times up to that point. But all of those shifts had either been gradual progress over enormous amounts of time as he honed his senses, or accidental in extreme situations where his life was in danger. While he had to admit those shifts had been under his own power, he was far from being able to shift at will.

Since no matter how he looked at it, his current situation was not one likely to produce that latter accidental shift, the only possibility was the former method.

Actually, mere hours earlier, Haruyuki had experienced a shift in an unexpected form. When he'd shared the first kiss of his life with Kuroyukihime in the living room of the Arita house, he'd no sooner heard the sudden sound of acceleration than the two of them had been flown to the Highest Level.

The instant he recalled the warmth and softness of Kuroyukihime's lips, his face grew hot beneath his goggles, but he managed to push this aside somehow and set his brain to work.

Thus far, he'd thought that what he required in order to shift to the Highest Level was the ultimate concentration. Once his focus exceeded a certain threshold, either by gradually intensifying it over long hours or with the instinct to fight in a life-or-death moment, excess load was applied to his light cube/quantum circuits, and his mind was guided—or rather bounced—to a higher-order space.

But this hypothesis didn't explain the phenomenon of the sudden shift from the real world. When he was kissing Kuroyukihime, his mind had without a doubt been inside his flesh-and-blood brain and should not have been connected with his light cube.

"...Or was it, though?" he muttered in a voice that wasn't quite a voice.

When he'd first encountered Centaurea Sentry on the Highest Level, still in her ghost state, she had wondered about the nightmare experienced by those who received the BB program. Had it truly been a by-product of the process of reproducing their souls in the light cube over the course of several hours? If that was true, then when he was having that nightmare, his mind had been connected to his light cube through his Neurolinker. And in that case, what if that connection wasn't a one-off thing, but rather was continuously maintained when his Neurolinker was equipped, or even when it was nearby, if not equipped?

The brain inside the head of the flesh-and-blood Haruyuki and the quantum circuits in the Brain Burst central server, aka Main Visualizer... One soul existing in two physically and conceptually distant receptacles.

The instant this image popped into his head, he saw a number of keywords flash and blink.

Ultimate concentration. Excess load. Mental ignition. Incarnate light.

Light...

It's light.

He felt like he heard someone's voice again. It wasn't Metatron, nor any other high-ranking Being. This voice was from inside him, echoing from the dark depths of the deep and wide lake that was his memory.

I feel a light inside of you. The photons locked up in the light cubes and Main Visualizer continue to vibrate eternally. If you sense that light and become one with it, you can go to a new stage. Take the power of the Incarnate even further.

He couldn't immediately recall when or where he'd heard this voice. But he felt that he was closer than he'd ever been to the fundamental mystery of the Accelerated World.

The decisive difference between Metatron and the other high-level Beings and the low-level Enemies was the existence of a light cube. Metatron and her kind had a "spirit media" that was the exact same as the quantum circuits given to Haruyuki and the other Burst Linkers. In other words, it was fair to say that in the Accelerated World, the high-level Beings and the Burst Linkers were basically the same.

So then why could Metatron and the others shift to the Highest Level freely, while Haruyuki and the Burst Linkers could not?

It was probably because the Beings were more intimate with the Main Visualizer in terms of distance, but also in the shape of their souls. Stored in its light cube, Haruyuki's soul lacked optimization. It couldn't easily become one with the Main Visualizer. He needed a boost from a Being or an approach run on his own to leap over the wall.

So then how could he optimize his soul?

The same way as he trained in Incarnate. Shift again and again. Over and over and over. Actually, Incarnate and light cube were probably fundamentally the same. Incarnate was, in other words, the power to get closer to the Main Visualizer.

A Burst Linker optimized their soul bit by bit in the process of learning Incarnate. Those who reached a certain level became qualified to be a level-one accessor by contracting with a high-level Being. From there, Incarnate training and leaps to the Highest Level were carried out in parallel simultaneously, optimization progressed further, and the Linker reached level two, then three…

This steplike—or, put another way, selective—mechanism couldn't have come about by chance. He had no doubt that someone had designed or modified the game Brain Burst 2039 to be this way. The fact that they were even allowed to use the Incarnate system, a power that was basically a cheat, was because the powers that be of this game world wanted them to.

If, in order to shift freely at any time to the Highest Level, he had to spend endless hours optimizing his soul until he was in the same domain as the Beings, then Haruyuki in that moment wouldn't have been able to immediately reach that stage. But if he could get into that ultimate concentration state with a make-or-break shot like he had those times in the past…

Centaurea Sentry's secret stash of high-end *yokan* jelly had essentially eliminated his hunger, but the exhaustion of dueling continuously since that morning was taking a heavy toll on his mind. The normal duel with Zelkova Verger before school, the back-to-back fights with the Beast-class Enemy Crococetus and "Basher" Platinum Cavalier, and then the face-off with the Drive Linker Urocyon and his fathomless power a mere hour earlier. He'd maybe only had a day of such high density two or three times before in the nine months since he became a Burst Linker. With this level of fatigue, he wouldn't be able to make a second attempt to shift if he failed the first time.

Still hovering at an altitude of two thousand meters, Haruyuki spread out his legs to the front and rear, lowered his center of gravity, and readied his right hand on his hip.

The ultimate concentration was likely the key and not the door. The instant his mental focus crossed a certain line, a small hole opened up in the wall between his light cube and the Main Visualizer, and his consciousness was bounced from there to the higher-dimensional space.

And here, he finally realized whose voice it was that he'd heard from the depths of his memory: Mirror Masker, Utai's late brother, Kyoya Shinomiya.

When Haruyuki had shifted to the Highest Level in the mirror room of the Shinomiya house, he had tried to smash the wall of the world with a punching strike and with his mind focused to the extreme. But instantly, he heard Kyoya's voice. Obeying the instruction to feel the light within himself, rather than to smash down the wall, he had slipped through it. He had probably been able to do that because Kyoya—the replicated mind of Mirror Masker lodged in the Main Visualizer—had guided him.

But he couldn't hear Kyoya's voice now. He would have to build a door with his own power in order to slip through the wall of the world again.

He took a deep breath and slowly exhaled. He opened the right fist readied at his hip and extended his fingers straight out.

Outside and inside, world and self. Main Visualizer and light cube.

When he closed his eyes, a strange image appeared in the back of his mind. In the middle of the darkness, countless tiny cubes were piled up in an orderly fashion, the faintest gaps between them. Enshrined among them was a single massive cube. All were filled with a flickering rainbow light.

A single one of those countless small cubes was Haruyuki's light cube. And the massive cube was the Main Visualizer. Even if it seemed far, far away, the truth was distance did not exist here. All that separated the two was a single metaphysical wall generated by the system.

Haruyuki opened his eyes and focused his entire being in the tip of the middle finger of his right hand. A silver light—an overlay—appeared. He made it shrink, smaller and smaller.

In the middle of the fight against Urocyon, he had come up with a new technique, Light Sword, by further focusing his Incarnate technique Laser Sword. As he recalled that sensation of hardening and refining the image, he compressed the Incarnate light to its limit. The minuscule shining point lodged in the tip of his finger began to vibrate with a high-pitched *skreeeee*.

This was his inner light. If he released this super-concentrated light all at once, it would became his second-stage Incarnate technique, Light Shell. But rather than doing that, he kept it as a point as he tried to perceive the world itself. Previously, this had taken long hours of concentration, but he had since learned the trick of compressing that time, one of the secrets of the Omega style Whole Blade, Gou.

He diffused his self, and the instant the world—the Main Visualizer—had grown infinitely close, he released the point of light. Transparent ripples spread out in the air, and a rainbow light spilled out from the center.

Skreeeeee!! The sound of reacceleration rang out, and Haruyuki's mind was sucked into the depths of the radiating light.

5

"You're late! How long did you intend to make me wait, servant?!"

This voice rained down on Haruyuki before he could even open his eyes, and he startled and shrank into himself. When he timidly lifted his face, a silhouette of hazy, white light popped up against the endless darkness. Sitting in empty space.

Long hair, white robe, spread wings. A top-ranking Being, the Archangel Metatron. Even without any color to her, her transcendent beauty was entirely undiminished.

"B-but I've never made it so fast before..." Haruyuki tried to protest, standing his duel avatar similarly depicted in white particles up straighter.

However.

"Crow. It is of no concern to me the length of time you inconvenience this Archangel, but to make ourselves wait is a punishable offense."

"I'm so bored with waiting, I'm falling asleep. I may very well fall asleep unless you feed me."

New voices rained down on him from either side. Frozen stiffly in position, he quickly looked to his right and left.

Sitting ahead to his right was a young woman in the prime of youth, wearing Japanese clothing reminiscent of a *miko* shrine priestess and a crown patterned after the sun atop her head.

Ahead of him to his left was a girl of about sixteen or seventeen, clad in a roomy robe and skirt in the style of a *hanbok* and a crown with small bells hanging from it. Although from the perspective of fourteen-year-old Haruyuki, she was also a woman, not a girl.

At first glance, with Metatron in the middle, they looked like sisters, but they were not such sweet creatures as all that. The woman on the right was Ohirume Amaterasu, the one on the left was Abandoned Princess Bari, and both were Beings of the highest rank, equals with the Archangel Metatron.

So this is what a deer in the headlights feels like. No, wait, a mouse in front of a cat. No, no, no, a sparrow staring down a hawk? After some panicked, escapist thoughts, Haruyuki steeled himself and said, "I—I sincerely apologize for the wait. But…can't you all decelerate your subjective time as much as you want?"

"We may reduce the speed of our own clock, but we cannot change the clock of the world," Amaterasu pointed out, sounding exasperated.

Metatron also spoke up, as if to compete with her. "The situation is such that not even a second can be wasted. While we awaited you, we continued our observations and analysis."

"Observations…?" He frowned. "Of what?"

"That, of course," Bari replied, and pointed toward his feet.

He turned his gaze downward to see a vast number of starry nodes glittering soundlessly there. Each and every one of them was a social camera in the real world. The placement density was higher in shopping areas and along main roads and lower in residential areas, depicting the terrain of central Tokyo in detail.

The darkness in the central area was the Castle—the imperial palace. The brightly shining constellation on the west side of this was the Shinjuku area. Following the Yamanote Line north from there led to the equally dazzling Ikebukuro area.

Bari's slender finger was pointing to an enormous star, red like blood and shining ominously on the east side of Ikebukuro Station.

When he narrowed his eyes for a closer look, he saw a dense nothingness swirling around the red star. It was clear what this was: the destroyed Tezcatlipoca and the red portal that had appeared from inside it.

Lifting his face, Haruyuki turned to the *hanbok*-wearing Being and said, "Bari—I mean, Lady Bari. It's just as you told us. When Tezcatlipoca was destroyed, a portal came out from inside of it. But it leads to a world other than the Accelerated World."

"It does seem so, yes," Bari agreed readily, turning her finger directly up. "Can you see that?"

"Huh…?" Throwing his head back to the limit of his neck's range of motion, he looked up at the inky sky—no, universe.

In stark contrast to the scene below, it was entirely dark without a single star. Naturally. The social camera network was to monitor public safety, and cameras wouldn't have been placed in empty space, where there was no one around.

He was about to reply that he couldn't see anything when he noticed a flickering, too faint to have been called a light, off in the dark distance.

He narrowed his eye lenses beneath his mirrored goggles and stared intently. He felt like his goggles were in the way, and then he realized that something like that didn't matter in this space. Even with his eyes closed, if he tried to actually see, he would have been able to.

Release the self from the formless avatar. Perceive the world not with vision but with awareness itself.

Gou.

One star and then another burst into existence in the far distant darkness. Their number increased with ferocious speed to depict a second central Tokyo, exactly the same as the one below.

No. It wasn't a second Tokyo. The remains of the worlds of the already shuttered AA2038 and CC2040 were overlaid onto the world of Haruyuki and his comrades spreading out below his eyes—BB2039. So the world glittering in the sky above was a *fourth* Tokyo.

This wasn't the first time he had seen this light. When he shifted to the Highest Level guided by Mirror Masker, he had been attacked by Snow Fairy, still an enemy at the time, and she had stolen the sensation of breathing from him. To escape the unimaginable torment, he had used negative Incarnate—Omega style's Gou—and in that moment, he had perceived a new world living far above his head.

At the time, he hadn't known what it was he was looking at. But now he did. It was the fourth Accelerated World, the home of Urocyon and his friends, Dread Drive 2047.

Without Haruyuki realizing it, his powers of perception had been honed to an unprecedented degree. And so he saw it. There was just one glittering red star in the DD world, where the same infinite sea of white stars gathered as in the BB world. Perhaps coincidentally or perhaps not, a crimson line thinner than a strand of spider silk stretched down from this star, which was naturally in Higashi Ikebukuro, passed right before his eyes, and connected with the star of the same color shining in the BB world below his eyes.

He raised his right hand, as if in a dream, and tried to touch the line. But it slipped through his hand without any sensation whatsoever.

"...This is the path connecting the two worlds," he said in a hoarse voice, and Metatron nodded.

"It would appear so."

"Then if we can just cut it...!" he cried desperately.

"Do you think we did not attempt that?" Metatron replied. "Regrettably, we, too, can only perceive that it exists. We have not been able to analyze it, much less interact with it."

"...But..." His shoulders automatically slumped with disappointment.

At present, the BB-side portal had been temporarily locked by Chiyuri's Citron Call, but it would be reopened tomorrow at midnight, when the other eight members of the Unifiers would once again attack through this line.

Their overwhelming battle power was a serious threat, but the real issue was that the conditions for victory in the war of the worlds had only been disclosed to the DD side. And the missing Urocyon and Complicator might very well have begun to move already to clear those conditions.

"Servant… Silver Crow," Metatron called to him as he hung his head and clenched his fists.

When he lifted his face, the Archangel, who had at some point descended from her chair in the air, was standing in front of him. She raised both hands and slapped them down onto his shoulders.

"You must be strong. I was not able to move from this place, but I did perceive your battle with the invaders through our link. You fought quite well… For a little warrior, at any rate."

"Y-yeah…"

Normally, Metatron did nothing but scold him, so as these rare words of praise sank into his thoroughly exhausted brain, he felt his heart warm. He wanted to hug her and bury his face in her robes, but if he did that, he wouldn't get off with just a flick to his forehead. And when he really thought about it, Metatron was one of the people Kuroyukihime had said he needed to give an answer to.

This was obviously not the time to bring that up, so he simply thanked her and asked the question on his mind. "You couldn't leave here? How come?"

Metatron pulled her hands off his shoulders and turned to Amaterasu and Bari, her eyes still closed, before saying, "First, tell us your tale, the details of the conversation you engaged in with the invaders. Although I was able to perceive the situation itself, I could not hear voices."

"R-right." Haruyuki nodded, and Metatron bobbed up into the air once more and seated herself in her invisible chair.

Can I even remember what we talked about? he wondered, but every word Urocyon uttered was deeply etched in his memory. After taking a moment to collect his thoughts, he took a step back and began to tell the three girls—no, the three Beings—about the formation of the large alliance Exercitus by approximately five hundred members of small and midsize Legions; about how three hundred of those members had taken on the challenge of subjugating Tezcatlipoca in the Higashi Ikebukuro area of the Unlimited Neutral Field; about how the mission had failed, and those three hundred had all been put into an Unlimited EK state with 70 percent of them—more than two hundred people—driven to total point loss.

As if satisfied with the largest massacre in history, Tezcatlipoca had suddenly destroyed itself, and from within its massive bulk, a crimson portal had appeared. The ten invaders who came through it said they were players of Dread Drive 2047, and then one of them had descended to the ground and begun to attack the Exercitus survivors. Haruyuki had fought this person—"Primal Fang," aka Urocyon—and while he had been overwhelmed by his opponent's unbelievable speed and power, he had just barely succeeded in surviving for five minutes.

"...You just told me I fought well," Haruyuki said weakly. "But he wasn't even trying. If he'd come at me full throttle from the start, I wouldn't have lasted five seconds, much less five minutes."

"Indeed, that seems to be the case," Amaterasu, floating to his right, readily assented.

"...Uh-huh," he replied finally.

"Take on not the mien of a wet puppy," she said, seemingly trying to comfort him. "In battle, results are everything. Regardless of whether or not your opponent fights with their full strength, if you survived, you did not lose."

"...Uh-huh." Nodding once more, Haruyuki was uncertain whether or not it was okay for him to ask if Amaterasu had ever actually seen a wet puppy. But before he could open his mouth, Bari, sitting to his left, spoke.

"Continue."

"R-right. Umm." He paused to think. "While Urocyon and I were fighting, my comrade Lime Bell moved to the Drive Linkers' blind spot, restored Tezcatlipoca's remains just a little with her special attack, and buried the portal. Before it was completely buried, eight of the nine on top of the remains returned to their own world, but this guy named Complicator stayed here. That's what he said anyway."

Haruyuki stopped for a moment, and then reproduced Complicator's words, which he'd burned into his memory, right down to the length of his pauses.

"'If we win, your world will disappear. If you win, our world will disappear'... It's this unchangeable rule decided on by whoever created and runs the two games."

Even after Haruyuki closed his mouth, the top-ranked Beings maintained their silence.

After five seconds or so, no doubt a vast span of time for the three who Rose Milady/Tsubomi Koshika dubbed "super AI," Metatron said abruptly, "Whoever created and runs the two games, hmm? In other words, this means that the invaders, your so-called Drive Linkers, also don't know what kind of creature that would be."

"Y-yeah. I'm pretty sure," he agreed.

"'Tis galling," Amaterasu said.

What exactly did that mean again? He searched his memory and hit upon "irritating" or something like that, maybe.

"To think that one who we know not if they be person or Being or program could hold in their hand saengsal yeotal," she continued.

"S-saeng...?" Haruyuki parroted, stunned.

"It means that they choose at their whim whether we live or die," Bari explained.

"G-got it." He nodded. "It *is* pretty frustrating. Right now, with the rules this someone decided, our only choice is to fight Urocyon and his comrades."

"I understand," Metatron agreed, the very slightest crease rising between her eyebrows. "But the issue is the fact that those rules have only been shown to the Drive Linker side. It is the height of folly, is it not, to enter battle without knowing how you can win?"

"...Yeah." He was forced to assent. She was absolutely right. The condition for a Burst Linker victory might very well have been "Capture all the Drive Linkers without killing any of them; if even one dies, Brain Burst loses."

Maybe, he wondered, if due to some kind of error on the part of the system administrator, the message that was supposed to have been sent simultaneously to all Drive Linkers and all Burst Linkers had only been sent to the Drive Linkers. And then he heard a faint sound at regular intervals, like tapping on a thin sheet of crystal.

Piiing. Ping, ping.

Haruyuki knew this sound. It was neither music nor a signal but footsteps.

Metatron turned her face to the right, and he, Amaterasu, and Bari followed suit.

Two white lights flickered in the distance in the infinite darkness. As they grew closer, they began to take shape as avatars. Both were F-types clad in graceful dress armor, with doll-thin waists and limbs. But the avatar on the left was as short as a child, and the one on the right was about the same height as Haruyuki.

Ping, ping.

The footsteps came from only the one on the left; the avatar on the right made absolutely no sound as she walked.

They stopped three meters—although there was no distance on the Highest Level, so, at most, it simply looked that way—away from Haruyuki and the Beings.

Haruyuki wasn't sure whether to kneel or not. Because the small girl was very much his superior in the Legion he belonged to, and the tall girl was the master he had sworn his sword to. But thinking that this was not the place for formalities, he settled for a neat bow.

Metatron was also a rank-and-file member of the Legion, but

she merely stared at the two girls without so much as nodding her head, much less getting down on her knees.

"So you came at last, Cosmos?" she said, coolly.

The tall girl—leader of the Legion Oscillatory Universe and White King, "Transient Eternity" White Cosmos, responded, her golden curls swinging slightly, "I guess I kept you waiting a bit, hmm, Metako?"

Likely by coincidence, Cosmos called Metatron by the same nickname as Sky Raker used. Relative to the girl by her side, Sleepy, aka Snow Fairy, she was tall, but if they were to stand side by side, Metatron would have been five or so centimeters taller. But her aura, not diminished in the slightest on the Highest Level, gave the White King a sense of presence on par with the top-level Being.

Now she glanced at Fairy next to her. "*She* threw a little tantrum about how she didn't want to come."

"I did not throw a tantrum," Fairy argued sullenly, and she turned her gaze for a mere instant on Haruyuki. Actually, no. It seemed more like she was looking at Bari floating to Haruyuki's left. But she quickly turned her face forward again and *ping*ed as she took a step back. "Anyway, I'm here, so go ahead, talk."

"Yes, yes." The White King waved a dismissive hand.

As he listened to them, Haruyuki casually looked over at Metatron and noticed that the Archangel's mouth was pulled the slightest bit tighter in displeasure. He briefly wondered why, when he remembered in a flash of insight.

In the middle of the Territories against Oscillatory, he had shifted to the Highest Level with Metatron. Snow Fairy had appeared and said, "*I wonder why you two are so unreasonable... If you're an Enemy, then you should just be an Enemy and satisfy yourself bullying Burst Linkers.*"

Immediately after that, Fairy had tried to sever the link between him and Metatron, and while they had narrowly escaped that, in her rage, Metatron had declared, "*I won't let that Snow Fairy or whatever it was get away with this.*"

Haruyuki panicked as he wondered if she were actually going

to try to make Snow Fairy pay now, but the Archangel merely turned her face away with a haughty sniff.

As if this was a signal, Cosmos opened her mouth. "First, as to the conditions of victory in this fight," she said, without any preamble, as if she knew every word they'd exchanged before her arrival. And then the White King uttered words that stunned not only Haruyuki but the Beings as well. "I learned them earlier."

"Huh? …H-how did you find out?!" Haruyuki leaned forward eagerly. "You don't actually have the admin's contact info or something, do you?!"

"Of course I don't have their contact info," she replied curtly, waving a dismissive hand at him. "They were sent to me out of the blue. Most likely at the moment when Tezcatlipoca was destroyed and the sky changed color."

"They were sent… You mean a system message? How come it was just for you…" He'd gotten this far when he remembered what Urocyon had said and shook his head. "No, it wasn't just you, it was all seven of the Kings…right?"

She looked at him curiously. "What makes you think that?"

"Something Urocyon—the Drive Linker I fought—said. That this 'interworld war' was announced in a system message when he reached level nine. So I figured the BB message would've been sent to all the level niners, too."

"Interworld war?" she repeated. "Did you come up with that?"

Posed this unexpected question, he blinked a couple times before nodding. "Y-yeah, well… Is that not what it is?"

"A war of the worlds, hmm? Well, that works, doesn't it? I'll use that myself."

"S-sure, go ahead," Haruyuki replied.

"And so what was this message about, then, Cosmos?" Metatron interjected, as if she had grown impatient.

"Before I tell you," she said, "I wonder if you might ask the other three listening to this conversation to come out? You all are seriously involved with this as well."

Other three?

Haruyuki whirled his head around. All that existed in the eternal and everlasting darkness wedged between the twinkling world of BB below and the world of DD far above were the three people White Cosmos, Snow Fairy, and Silver Crow, and the three pillars Archangel Metatron, Ohirume Amaterasu, and Abandoned Princess Bari. There wasn't even a single kitten anywhere to be found.

The instant he had that thought, he noticed them. Minuscule points of light—dots—popped up and blinked soundlessly on the opposite side of Metatron, in a spot a little higher than his own head. There were one, two…three.

He blinked rapidly before reaching to try to touch the dot floating closest to him.

Crackle!

"Ow!" He felt pain like the slight shock of static electricity and let out a cry.

At nearly the same time, a high-pitched voice rang out inside his head, *Don't just go touching me, you lech!*

"…L-lech?"

Even Chiyuri's never called me that, he thought in his great upset, as the minuscule dot sent out rays of light thinner than threads.

The beams of light cut through the darkness and leapt around like a laser hologram to produce the figure of a person. It was woman a bit smaller than Bari, probably a similarly top-ranked Being, but her look was definitely not like anything the others wore.

Short hair that flipped out at the bottom in an almost retro style, short-sleeved shirt and a knee-length pleated skirt reminiscent of some school's uniform, thick-soled sneakers. The only points of commonality with Metatron and the others were her flawless beauty and her closed eyes.

Floating in space, she glanced at Haruyuki with those closed eyes and said, "You Silver Crow? I *thought* you were a little too chummy, but you're even handsier than I imagined. C'mon, get back. Go away." She shooed at him with her right hand.

"O-okay!" Haruyuki cried, taking two steps back.

"Haah…" Metatron sighed heavily behind him. "You are as you ever were, Ushas. I won't say anything further about your manner of speech, but could you do something about that outfit, at least?"

Ushas. Goddess of the Dawn, a top-ranking Being who lived in the Shinjuku Government Building Underground Labyrinth, one of the four great dungeons. In other words, she was one pillar of the Four Saints, alongside Metatron and Amaterasu.

Ushas lifted long, curled eyelashes the slightest bit and replied unhappily, "Easy for you to say, Metatron. I mean, your outfit's kinda cute. Amaterasu's and Bari's, too, y'know? But my initial outfit's got all this heavy armor stuck to it. I mean, fighting in it is one thing, but, like, I can't be walking around in that all the time."

"And where did you get ahold of those clothes without a shred of dignity to them?" Metatron demanded.

"Heh-heh! Not telling!"

Haruyuki stood rooted to the spot, listening to this exchange. There was no great difference in terms of details from a conversation with a junior high Burst Linker, but each of the speakers was one of the Four Saints, in possession of the greatest fighting power in the entire Accelerated World. He'd already been told by Ushas that he was "a little too chummy," and he didn't know what kind of punishment he'd face if he butted in here and earned further displeasure.

He frowned and cocked his head slightly to one side. He'd definitely heard Ushas's name from Fairy and Cosmos, but he'd never had any contact with her. So why did she talk like she'd met Haruyuki before?

"I will say this for the record," Metatron was in the process of saying. "The situation is such that we do not know whether our world will continue to exist. This is not the time to be concealing information, is it?"

"N'kay, hold up." Ushas shook her head, exasperated. "How

does getting cute outfits have anything to do with the survival of the world? Ohhh, I get it. You want a little uniform of your own, huh?"

Haruyuki was very much not brave enough to interrupt the two Beings, so he waited for their verbal jousting to come to an end.

"So, hello. Hi," the White King interjected, sounding annoyed. "I know this is the Highest Level, but that doesn't mean time's standing still, okay? Perhaps we could get back to the subject at hand."

Instantly, Ushas raised her eyelids the slightest bit and glared at her with colorless eyes. "...You're White Cosmos, huh? Heard you nicked the Tenken from Metatron's castle."

"You had your Tensuu stolen from you long ago!" Metatron cried immediately.

"Who cares about that stupid sword?" He could hear Ushas rolling her eyes. "It wasn't even cute at all."

It took him a second to realize what they were talking about. "Tensuu" was the Arc that had been in safekeeping in the Shinjuku Government Building Underground Labyrinth, the greatsword Impulse, currently in the possession of the Blue King, Blue Knight. And "Tenken" was the crown/scepter Luminary, which had been held in the Shiba Park Underground Labyrinth. This was the magnificent crown that now sat upon the head of the White King.

Similarly, he'd heard that the Green King, Green Grandé's shield Strife, had been in the Tokyo Dome Underground Labyrinth, and the Purple King, Purple Thorn's staff Tempest, in Tokyo Station Underground Labyrinth. Which meant that the four Kings had beaten the Four Saints, but what they had defeated was the Legend-class Enemy first form. These Saints bickering before him now were their second forms, their true selves with power far surpassing that of their first forms.

No Burst Linker had ever defeated the true form of the pinnacle of Beings, the Four Saints, and the fact that the White King could be so composed despite this fact was either because the person inside, Enju Kuroba, had the daring of Anomaly Graphite Edge, or because she was confident that she could fight even these true forms.

"All right. Enough of that!" The White King checked the squabbling that was devolving into physicality, and with eye lenses like Marquise-cut gems, she looked to the right and left sides of Ushas. "I'd like to introduce myself, so could I ask our two guests there to also come forward?"

Now that she mentioned it, there had been three dots, Haruyuki thought.

The remaining two dots flashed simultaneously and shot out several extremely thin beams of light like the ones he'd seen only moments ago.

Appearing to the left of Ushas was a tall woman like the personification of the word "noble." Her hair was tied up in a complicated fashion and decorated with magnificent combs and accessories. The clothing she wore resembled but was still different from Bari's *hanbok* and Amaterasu's shrine maiden robes, an ample *hanfu* in the style of ancient China, and a slender straight sword hung from her left hip. This was probably Queen Mother of the West Xiwangmu.

Although her features were gentle, the aura she radiated was more powerfully intimidating than that of any of the other Beings, and Haruyuki couldn't bring himself to gaze directly at her for even three seconds.

He quickly turned his face to the right just as the final dot had finished taking a three-dimensional shape. And took a startled step backward.

"Holy huge!" he cried out.

All of the high-ranked Beings he'd chanced to meet—Metatron, Amaterasu, Bari, Ushas, and now Xiwangmu—were women, and of the two pillars with whom he remained unacquainted, Night Goddess Nyx had "goddess" right there in her name, so he figured she was probably a woman, too. He'd sort of been convinced that the final pillar would also have been a woman.

But the new three-dimensional figure of light appearing to the right of Ushas sitting sulkily with her legs crossed didn't even have a human form, much less have a gender.

Actually, it was human. But only the one part of a person—a head. Three, in fact.

The new Being was three enormous heads, two meters from crown to jaw, fused together and looking out in the directions of two, six, and ten o'clock. Indian-style crowns wrapped around their foreheads, and teardrop-shaped gems hung from their eyes. The sharp and fierce features were clearly male. He didn't understand why the Being was in the form of heads, but there was no doubt that these three visages were the Storm King Rudra.

The front face looked down on Haruyuki with eyes that were, of course, closed beneath sharp eyebrows.

"...In recent days, it was you who so insolently contacted us, then," a low, sonorous voice rang out, and Haruyuki froze in a cautious pose.

"C-contact?! I—I—I—I did?!" He was about to continue and say that this was out of the question, that they had never met before, but a second before he could, a small voice called to him from behind.

"It was when you escaped from my sense blockade, Crow."

He didn't have to turn around to know the voice belonged to Snow Fairy. This "sense blockade" was probably the asphyxiation attack she'd made him suffer through on the Highest Level. He had been so lost and panicked that he couldn't remember what he'd done, but at the very least, he was pretty sure he wouldn't have contacted Rudra or any of the top-ranked Beings.

"The tiny one speaks true, Crow," Amaterasu said, as if reading his mind. "While it was limited to the one time, your consciousness expanded to every corner of the Highest Level in the manner of a bubble popping. Xiwangmu appears to have simply been slightly annoyed, but Rudra was quite ticked."

"Ticked...?" he parroted dubiously.

"This is what you small ones say when one is irritated, yes?" she responded, an eyebrow arched. "Milady used the word."

What are you teaching her? he demanded of Tsubomi Koshika/ Rose Milady in his mind before it clicked for him. He first learned of the existence of the DD world when he'd activated a negative Incarnate in order to escape Fairy's asphyxiation attack. At that time, his consciousness spreading throughout the Highest Level must have unintentionally also touched the high-ranking Beings.

"Um… I-I'm sorry about that!" Haruyuki first turned toward the "ticked" Rudra and bowed deeply, before then bowing to Ushas and Xiwangmu on the left. "I definitely didn't contact you on purpose. It was more like I had too much momentum. Or like my Incarnate suddenly couldn't stop, and anyway—"

The reason I used negative Incarnate in the first place was because Fairy was suffocating me.

He decided against bringing this up as an excuse and instead apologized once more. "A-anyway, I'm really sorry!"

"You are not forgiven." The thunderous voice shook even the nihilistic space.

Haruyuki jumped slightly and was about to prostrate himself in front of the Being, but Rudra continued, his tone softening slightly.

"If you desire the gift of our pardon, then you will make us an offering of a chariot's worth of this cake or what have you that you fed to that arrogant Archangel."

"…"

Haruyuki stood stunned, rooted to the spot.

Before him Ushas cried out, "Same!" and even Xiwangmu spoke for the first time, "We would have this, too."

Metatron, how much did you boast about that cake?! He kept this question inside his head and bowed neatly. "U-understood… I will."

Amaterasu and Bari had also ordered him to offer each of them a *nagabitsu* of cake (whatever that was), so now he had five deliveries to make. But this was a small price to pay if it meant the help of the top-ranked Beings. He wasn't sure what a chariot was, though. Probably some kind of wheeled carry bag… As he considered the issue, Haruyuki continued to bow.

"It seems we can finally get to it, then," the voice of White Cosmos rang out behind him once more.

It had only been three days since he'd come under her command, but he felt intuitively that what the White King was exhibiting corresponded to the highest level of patience on her own personal scale. If she was cut off again here, there was the threat of the ultimate war beginning: Burst Linker versus Being… This fear, fortunately, did not become reality.

The six Beings seated in the air—excluding Rudra, who was only heads—moved without a sound to form a large semicircle facing Cosmos. Haruyuki realized he was obstructing their view and immediately trotted in a crouch over to Snow Fairy and glued himself to her side. She turned irritated eyes on him, but this was any number of times better than being glared at by the Beings.

Meanwhile, the White King showed no sign of faltering under the gazes of the six pillars as she inclined her crowned head only the slightest bit and introduced herself. "It's a pleasure to meet you all for the first time, excluding Metatron, who I'm already acquainted with. I am White Cosmos."

The Beings remained silent, but perhaps she had anticipated this; Cosmos continued without quailing.

"Immediately after Tezcatlipoca destroyed itself, I received a message from the BB system. I will read it out to you."

She paused for a beat and lowered her voice a touch.

"Final stage victory conditions. Defend the seven Beings/Units listed below until JST 2047-07-31, 24:00:00. MN2-01 Metatron. SJ2-01 Bari. SJ3-01 Ushas. BK1-01 Xiwangmu. KT2-01 Rudra. CY1-01 Amaterasu. SY1-01 Nyx. If four or more of the Beings are destroyed, Brain Burst 2039 will be deemed to have lost, and the trial will end."

6

Even after Haruyuki returned to the real world, he wasn't able to immediately open his eyes. Still leaning against the sofa, he exhaled at length, letting out all the air in his lungs.

He was so tired, he wanted to climb into bed that second, and yet an uneasiness colder than ice was firing up his sympathetic nervous system. Metatron and the White King had both ordered him to sleep soundly until morning at any rate, but what he actually wanted to do was dive right back into the Unlimited Neutral Field and hunt down the two missing Drive Linkers.

Urocyon and Complicator could have been infiltrating the Shiba Park Underground Labyrinth at that very second and charging toward the lowest level, where Metatron's first form sat. Her true form was currently outside of the dungeon, but if her first form was defeated without the use of any stage gimmicks, there was a serious possibility that she would be forcibly sent to the boss room in the moment of defeat.

Naturally, it was an almost Herculean task to take down her first form without any weakening gimmicks. But given that the Drive Linkers had masterful control over the super-high-performance Incarnate techniques known as Psion Arts, the possibility of them being able to accomplish this task with just the two of them was nonzero.

Haruyuki had proposed a temporary evacuation, fully prepared to be struck down by lightning in response, but all of the Beings looked negatively on leaving their respective castles. There was the risk of being attacked when they came aboveground, so evacuation might not have been the definitive and correct choice, but if they were going to do it, now was the time, when eight of the ten Drive Linkers were absent. The Unlimited Neutral Field did, in fact, encompass all of Japan, so if the seven Beings listed as targets moved to Hokkaido or Okinawa, it would be nearly impossible to find them.

"...But I'm pretty sure the guy who came up with these battle rules would've thought of that much, at least," Haruyuki murmured in a hoarse voice, and he lifted his closed eyelids just a hint.

He'd been accelerated for a couple of minutes, at most, but the white light from the ceiling stabbed into his eyes, bringing tears to them. He blinked repeatedly and let his eyes grow accustomed to the brightness.

It was the same old living room as always, but it smelled different from usual. He could pick up the delicious scent of food and the refreshing aromas of soap and shampoo.

Sniffing, Haruyuki looked to his left and then froze in place. Because his childhood friend was sitting there, leaning deep into the sofa cushions, her eyes closed.

Oh, right. I dived with Chiyuri.

At the same time as he remembered this, his stomach growled. The *yokan* jelly he'd eaten on the other side unfortunately could not be brought over to the real world. An inexpressibly alluring fragrance was wafting out from the tote bag Chiyuri had brought with her, sitting on the low table before him. But he hesitated to dig into it without its owner's permission.

Chiyuri had said that she would stay with Taupe Cape until the exhausted Linker woke up, so she was probably still at Oumutei. But thirty seconds had already passed since Haruyuki woke up. That was eight hours and twenty minutes in the Unlimited

Neutral Field. *She should really be waking up already,* he thought, just as a faint groan slipped from her slightly open mouth.

"Nnn..." Her eyelashes fluttered, her face scrunched up, and she slowly lifted her eyelids. Like Haruyuki before her, Chiyuri blinked repeatedly, her eyes dazzled, before she said, "Ah... Haru, you were already back?"

"Hey, Chiyu," he greeted her. "How's Taupe Cape?"

"Water first, please."

Her words made him realize he was also thirsty. He stood up, cut across the living room on quick feet, pulled a bottle of oolong tea out of the refrigerator, and poured it into two glasses. Taking one in each hand, he traced his steps back to the living room and held one of the glasses out, which Chiyuri took and quickly emptied.

Haruyuki also gulped down the nicely chilled tea while still standing and let out a long sigh. With his thirst quenched, his pangs of hunger grew even greater, but he ignored them and waited for Chiyuri to speak.

After a few seconds, Chiyuri said slowly, holding the glass in both hands, "Taupe burst out with me from the portal at Waseda Station."

"...Yeah? Thanks for staying with her."

When he conveyed his gratitude, she shook her head slightly. "I didn't do anything."

"That's not true," he protested. "I'm sure the reason Taupe felt safe enough to get the sleep she needed was because you were there—"

Chiyuri abruptly shook her head vigorously to either side, so Haruyuki swallowed the rest of his words.

"I did nothing." She squeezed the words out, not bothering to fix her now messy hair. "I... I didn't tell Taupe that Zelkova might be able to come back. I felt like if I did, I'd have to help her revive Zelkova before Cotto..."

"..."

Haruyuki bit his bottom lip hard.

If she was going to give Taupe that hope, then he did actually agree that she should also offer to help. But she knew that the chance of actually bringing anyone back to life was infinitely close to zero, so she had no reason to blame herself for not telling the grieving Burst Linker about this hint of a possibility.

After a moment of uncertainty, Haruyuki said, "I… Right after I left Oumutei, I met with the White King on the Highest Level."

"What?!" Chiyuri opened her eyes wide in surprise, and Haruyuki sat down next to her.

"I learned a lot of important stuff there, but that can wait. Before we left the Highest Level, I asked the White King about her revival ability…"

As he explained, he relived the conversation with White Cosmos.

They'd discussed the victory condition and strategies for the interworld war—aka the final stage—with Metatron and the other Beings, and immediately after they dispersed for the time being, he'd called out to stop the White King as she was about to leap out.

"Does your Revival bring back any Burst Linker at total point loss unconditionally?" he'd asked.

The White King had cocked her head slightly to one side before replying, *"It can't be anyone. There are a number of necessary conditions."*

He'd then asked about the conditions, and a faint smile rose on her face.

"While I don't doubt your loyalty, I can't exactly reveal all of my powers to a person who's only been in my Legion for three days. But I will tell you just one of those conditions: The person must remain broadly or deeply in the Burst Linker memory."

"Broadly…or deeply…?" Chiyuri repeated the words of the White King that Haruyuki told her. "What does that mean?"

"This is just a guess," he said. "But 'broadly' probably means a lot of Burst Linkers remember them a little, and 'deeply' means a few Burst Linkers remember them a lot. Of course, the best thing would be a whole bunch of people remembering them a lot..."

"...How many people do you think a few is?" Chiyuri murmured.

"I don't know," he replied in a similarly quiet voice. "Could be two or three, could be twenty or thirty."

"..."

She fell silent once more, and he could easily imagine what she was thinking.

Cotton Marten belonged to the midsize Legion Ovest. It would have had more than twenty members, but that was before the mission to subjugate Tezcatlipoca. The Legion master Juniper Weasel had said that about 60 percent of the members had been driven to total point loss, so there were probably only ten or so surviving. And it wasn't like all of them would have been so close with Cotton Marten that they had deep memories of her.

He couldn't say anything more unless White Cosmos gave him the detailed conditions for regeneration, and he did feel bad for Chiyuri. But there was something that had greater priority ahead of reviving Cotton Marten at the moment.

If the BB side lost the war of the worlds, Brain Burst 2039 would in that instant be terminated, and Haruyuki, Chiyuri, Takumu, Kuroyukihime, and even White Cosmos would all cease to be Burst Linkers.

Actually, even if the Accelerated World were lost, she might manage to survive somehow, Haruyuki thought, and then he took a deep breath to switch gears.

First, he had to tell Chiyuri—no, the members of Nega Nebulus—about the start of the interworld war and the conditions for victory. While he was a member of Oscillatory Universe now, the White King had ordered him to do this.

That said, however, the membership of the third Nega Nebulus, an amalgamation with Prominence, totaled forty-nine Burst Linkers. Actually, forty-seven now that Haruyuki and Metatron had left, but Centaurea Sentry had joined, so forty-eight. It would be difficult to have them all meet in the usual normal duel format at this hour, and he had his doubts about whether they would come out for a dive call tonight.

First, he would explain the situation to Kuroyukihime, Fuko, Niko, and Pard, and have them decide how to proceed. He started to compose a message in his mind but was soon interrupted.

"Haru, let's eat," Chiyuri said, and his stomach responded with a growl. Giggling, she stood up and reached out for the tote bag.

"Hey?" he asked, on a sudden whim. "Can I ask Taku up?"

"Huh? Taku? Well, yeah, of course," she said, and then cocked her head to one side. "But he said he has kendo practice until seven thirty, so he's probably not home yet."

"I'll ping him at any rate." He launched the mailer on his virtual desktop and sent a short message. A mere ten seconds later, the brief reply arrived.

"Oh!" he cried. "He says he just got home now, so he'll come over as soon as he changes."

"Perfect timing!" She grinned. "So get three plates out, then. The big ones."

"Got it!"

Following the instructions of Chiyuri, who knew the state of the Arita kitchen better than Haruyuki himself did, he set the plates out on the dining table.

What came out from the tote bag was a magnificent feast—Chiyuri's mother's special Olivier salad, sardines and eggplant stewed with tomatoes, and a shrimp mushroom pilaf. As she dished this out onto the three plates, the doorbell rang, so he checked the front door feed before pressing the unlock button.

A few seconds later, Taku—Takumu Mayuzumi—came into the living room.

"Huh?" Haruyuki cried out unconsciously the instant he saw him. "Taku… Did you grow?"

"What? No, I don't think I'm any taller." His childhood friend frowned slightly. He was dressed in a summery style, with a loose pale-blue-green Okinawan shirt and shorts reaching below the knee. He'd already been over ten centimeters taller than the average for boys in their grade, but he looked a little bigger today than Haruyuki remembered.

"And think about it. You just saw me at the send-off party for the Inti attack mission." Takumu smiled wryly. "That was only five days ago, you know."

"Hmm." Chiyuri also stared hard at him. "I maybe feel like you're taller, too. If you keep growing like this, you're gonna end up over two meters tall."

"Th-that's kind of unlikely," he protested weakly.

"So then, should I give you a smaller portion?" she teased.

"N-no, I mean, that's not really..."

She laughed out loud and divided the pilaf up neatly into three portions before scooping them out onto the plates.

While Takumu was in the washroom, washing his hands, Haruyuki poured more oolong tea, and then the three of them sat down around the table. They clapped their hands, said, "Let's eat!" and picked up their forks at the same time.

In addition to chicken and potatoes, the Olivier salad had zucchini and broccoli, so the texture was a lot of fun. The eggplant practically dissolved in his mouth, having soaked up the fat from the sardines in the garlicky stewed tomato dish, while the shrimp pilaf fried up so fragrantly in Chiyuri's mom's pride, a cast-iron frying pan, had an exquisite mouthfeel. After savoring it all, as if in a dream, he took a sip of oolong tea and sighed.

Chiyuri and Takumu also had healthy appetites on full display, their hands in constant motion. It hadn't been just the three of them around this table since they'd held that spontaneous slumber party in the middle of the whole ISS kit thing. Chiyuri had made them a soup curry with summer vegetables, and when Haruyuki had insisted that the best way to eat eggplant was to deep-fry it, Chiyuri had argued that he was truly a child if he couldn't see the true deliciousness of grilled eggplant, and Takumu had interjected with the most persuasive argument for traditionally pickled eggplant.

That slumber party was around June 20, so it had only been just over a month since then. But it no doubt felt like a million years ago because of the tumultuous days that had followed one after the other. And now that they had plunged into what could have been called the climax of all of those events, the interworld war, he had no idea when the three of them would come together again.

The instant he had this thought, the words that he'd been carrying around in his heart spilled out of his mouth. "...I'm sorry. To both of you."

Chiyuri and Takumu blinked vacantly in unison at him. Chiyuri was in the middle of chewing, so Takumu asked, "Sorry for what, Haru?"

"Oh." He turned his eyes down toward the table. "Because I went and left Negabu and joined Oscillatory..."

Chiyuri turned her fork on him from the other side of the table and gave an angry grunt, while Takumu, to his left, slapped his back.

"Quit it, Haru. You transferred to the White Legion to save the attack team when we were stuck in range of Tezcatlipoca's attacks—especially me, after I got hit with Level Drain, right?"

"But," he protested weakly, "the reason you all challenged Tezcatlipoca in the first place was to rescue me."

"In which case, we're even. And...the truth is, I'm the one who should be apologizing," Takumu half said, half muttered, and then abruptly sat up straighter, ran his hands through the layers of his silky hair, and bowed his head. "Sorry, Haru. About our promise to fight for real when we both hit level seven. I'm gonna need you to wait awhile yet."

"..."

Unable to immediately find words in response to this, Haruyuki could only move his mouth awkwardly.

In the Silver Crow rescue mission, carried out to recover him from where he was held prisoner at Tokyo Grand Castle, the large theme park on Reiwa Island in Tokyo Bay, Takumu—Cyan Pile—had been hit with Tezcatlipoca's Level Drain, just as he himself said. As a result, he dropped from level six to level four. How many normal duels and Enemy hunts would he have to do to earn enough points again to reach level seven…?

Wait. I can think about if the Accelerated World continues to exist, like the resurrection of Cotton Marten.

Even if it wasn't possible to get all of the members of Nega Nebulus together, he should at least explain the Drive Linker assault and the war of the worlds to the ones he could assemble.

"Hey, Haru?" Chiyuri said, looking serious, having swallowed the mouthful of pilaf she was working on. "You gotta tell Taku about those guys."

"Those guys…?" Takumu looked up with a dubious face, and Haruyuki nodded at him before looking at Chiyuri.

"I know," he said. "I'm going to call an all-hands meeting after we're done eating, so I'll explain everything to the Legion members then."

7

After wrestling with the question of whether to hold a dive chat with all the Legion members or use a normal duel field, he decided to leave it to the judgment of Kuroyukihime and Niko.

For a normal duel-style meeting, where two of the participants dueled and the remaining attendees registered as part of the Gallery, all of the attendees had to gather in the same area in the real world. At present, Nega Nebulus was in possession of a large territory made up of all of Nerima area, all of Suginami area, Nakano No. 1, and Minato No. 3, so naturally, the members' homes were also scattered over a broad region. Minato Ward was out of the question, but even if they held the meeting somewhere in Nerima, Suginami, or Nakano, more than a few members would be forced to travel kilometers to attend.

It was already almost nine at night, and for a moment, he thought they should do a dive chat where people could join from their own homes. But the matter for discussion being what it was, it would take half an hour to simply explain the situation, and no matter how many hours they had for the subsequent discussion on how to respond as a Legion, it wouldn't be enough. Since time wasn't accelerated during a dive chat, it was possible they would greet a new day while still in the meeting.

Thus, Haruyuki had added to the message he sent Kuroyukihime that if it seemed impossible to have an all-hands meeting that day, they could make it tomorrow, and he would explain the situation to just the executive members that evening.

But the reply that arrived from Kuroyukihime a mere three minutes later was somewhat incomprehensible. The all-hands meeting would be held at nine, normal duel-style. But Haruyuki, Takumu, and Chiyuri wouldn't have to move from their current position for the meeting.

Meaning what? He cocked his head to one side, and before too long, a new message arrived. A mail containing the exact same text sent to all Legion members, including to Haruyuki.

"Umm." Takumu read the message aloud. "We will hold an all-hands Legion meeting in a normal duel at nine PM. The starters will be Black Lotus and Sky Raker. All members able to participate should be on standby in their home or a place where it's safe to accelerate, after confirming automatic Gallery settings. At eight fifty-nine, tap the link below. Use of dummy avatars for viewing is not possible, barring exceptional circumstances..."

After reading that far himself, Haruyuki stared at the last line. It was a global net URL, but a shortening service had been used, so he didn't know where it connected to. And...

"Hey, Taku?" he asked. "You ever see this 'sss' link shortener before?"

"Mm, it's not familiar." Takumu shook his head. "And, like, how can it be okay for us to be at home for a normal duel-style meeting? We can't watch the duel if we're not in the same area as our masters, right?"

"Right..."

The two boys both frowned.

Chiyuri slapped their backs from behind. "If Kuroyukihime says we can do it from home, then we can do it from home! C'mon, we only have ten minutes, so let's get this table cleared! Hop to it!"

"Okay."

"Yeah."

Haruyuki and Takumu replied at the same time, and they carried the dishes on the table to the kitchen.

While the Aritas did have a dishwasher, Chiyuri began to wash the dishes herself with a practiced hand, so Haruyuki took on the role of drying them. Takumu was charged with putting them away in the cupboard, and within five minutes, they had finished cleaning up.

They made three cups of café au lait in three minutes—instant, of course—sat down on the sofa next to one another, and by the time they took a sip of their coffees, it was 8:58 PM.

After exchanging looks with Takumu to his right and Chiyuri to his left, Haruyuki opened the mail from Kuroyukihime once again. He suddenly wondered if it was okay for him to attend an all-hands Legion meeting of Nega Nebulus. But without him, there would be no explanation of the war of the worlds.

He told himself that it would go how it went and checked the clock display in the bottom right of his field of view. As soon as this display showed fifty-nine minutes, he tapped the mysterious shortened URL.

"Ah..." he heard Chiyuri say. She was as surprised as he was.

There was the low hum of vibration, and a shining blue emblem appeared in the center of his virtual desktop—two swords arranged in the middle of a diamond, surrounded by flowers. In between the two swords were the letters "SSS."

The emblem disappeared in a mere two seconds, and for some reason, the URL noted at the end of the mail also vanished. He closed his mailer and looked in every nook and cranny of his virtual desktop, but it didn't seem like anything in particular had happened.

"...What was that crest thing just now?" Takumu murmured, and Haruyuki was about to say he had no idea but then snapped his mouth shut.

SSS... Triple S. He'd heard that name from Kuroyukihime.

It had been six days earlier, on Sunday. For certain reasons, he had ended up in the bath together with Kuroyukihime at her house in Minami Asagaya, and she'd confessed to him the fearsome secret of her birth.

She had not been born through a normal pregnancy and delivery but rather as an embryo fertilized outside the body and grown in an artificial womb, a so-called machine child. While she was still in that artificial womb, she had been equipped with a Neurolinker and overwritten with the soul of another human being via the soul translation technology.

And what she had used in order to ascertain these facts, kept strictly confidential by the major corporation Kamura Company, was SSS Order.

At the time, she hadn't explained in detail exactly what this SSS Order was, but he was certain it had some deep connection with the blue emblem. And normally, when he opened a URL in a mail, his browser launched. But when he opened this URL, only the 3D image of the emblem was displayed, accompanied by a sound effect, unnatural behavior for his Neurolinker.

He was forced to cease his investigation there, however.

The instant his clock display showed nine, the familiar sound of acceleration echoed in his ears, and his mind was flown away to the duel stage.

Surprisingly, of the forty-nine current members of the third Nega Nebulus, there were, in fact, forty-seven present at the sudden all-hands meeting announced a mere ten minutes earlier.

After checking the total number of avatars standing around in groups of twos and threes, Haruyuki stared for a moment at the starters just barely visible in the circle of people—the Black King "World's End" Black Lotus and "Strato Shooter" Sky Raker—before turning his eyes to the field around him once again.

Drizzly rain fell from the slightly cloudy sky like fog. Taking a step caused water to squeeze out of the thick lichen that covered the ground. A lower water-affiliated Drizzle stage. A river about ten meters across flowed before him, and the banks on either side were broad swaths of lush green. The row of massive rocks barely visible on the other side of the curtain of fine rain was probably a residential district in the real world.

As he searched his memory to answer the question if there was anywhere like that in Suginami...

"This is the Zenpukuji River Greenbelt in Suginami Area Three." He heard a voice from behind say, and he looked over his shoulder.

Standing there was a shrine maiden avatar, her small body clad in semitransparent armor patterned after a white robe and red hakama trousers. One of Nega Nebulus's Four Elements, "Testarossa" Ardor Maiden.

"Mei, hello." Haruyuki bowed, his silver armor clanking, and Maiden also returned the greeting.

"Good evening, C."

"Zenpukuji River, huh?" he said.

"While the view in reality is not quite as charming as this, it is still a nice place," she told him. "When it cools off a little, let's ask everyone to go on a picnic here."

"Oh, good idea," Haruyuki agreed, and he was about to ask after Hoo on his trial move from Umesato Junior High. But a heartbeat before he could, a clear voice rang out from the center of the group of avatars.

"First, let me offer my sincere thanks to all of you, members of the third Nega Nebulus, who responded to the sudden call to assemble despite the late hour!"

The speaker was, of course, the Legion Master Black Lotus/Kuroyukihime. She stood—well, more accurately, she floated, with her hovering ability—over a triangular rock jutting out of the moss-covered earth.

To the left of the triangular rock was Sky Raker, sitting in her elegant wheelchair. Seven or eight meters ahead of them were "Bloody Storm," aka the Red King, Scarlet Rain, and "Bloody

Kitty" Blood Leopard. To the right of these two was the Triplex's Cassis Moose, and to their left was the Triplex's Thistle Porcupine, while the other Red faction members took up the right side of the large circle.

And on the left side were the Black faction members, starting with "Aquamatic" Aqua Current. Lime Bell, Cyan Pile, Magenta Scissor, the former Petit Paquet crew: Chocolat Puppeter, Mint Mitten, and Plum Flipper. The temporary transfers of Ash Roller, Olive Grab, and Bush Utan. Newly minted members Centaurea Sentry and Ardor Maiden, standing next to Haruyuki. Unfortunately, two people were absent: Metatron, who could not manifest in a normal duel stage, and Trilead Tetroxide.

He was pretty sure that Kuroyukihime had said Trilead Tetroxide was training on Mount Fuji in the Unlimited Neutral Field with his master "Anomaly" Graphite Edge. But she'd told him that three hours ago, which was 125 days on the inside. *Was he actually still not back yet?* Haruyuki wondered anxiously.

"Lotus, hold up!" Scarlet Rain—Niko—called out in a childish yet dignified voice and took a step forward. "Before we get into it, you wanna explain that link in the mail? This is Suginami area, yeah? So how come I can be the Gallery when I'm in Nerima?"

"Don't worry about it" was Kuroyukihime's answer.

Even Niko gaped for a second before waving her rounded arms. "O-of course I'm worried about it! If you got some kind of mad wild tool to fool the whole BB system, then worst case, all of us here end up slapped with a ban—"

"There's no need for concern," Kuroyuki interrupted coolly. "I didn't trick the BB system, I tricked your Neurolinker position."

"..."

Now it wasn't just Niko. The entire assemblage, outside of Kuroyukihime and Fuko, were stunned.

The Neurolinker location information system boasted a precision of essentially zero errors while aboveground, and even underground, it would only be off by a few centimeters, at most, as long as the Neurolinker was connected to the global net.

Naturally, security for this system was unusually tight. A great number of crackers had attempted to break through in the past, but they apparently hadn't even understood the mechanism by which location was measured. And now Kuroyukihime casually said that she had "tricked" this very system.

Paying no mind to the silence of the forty-six people around her, she continued.

"Since it seems you have understood, I will get right to the issue at hand. I will work to ensure we finish this meeting in the remaining twenty-five minutes. But if we don't, I will create a second framework with the same procedure. Now then, I'm sure some of you are already aware of this, but the joint army Exercitus, composed of a number of small and midsize Legions, attempted and failed to subjugate the Super-class Enemy Tezcatlipoca approximately two hours ago."

While her tone and wording were detached, Haruyuki could clearly pick up on a regret and sadness that she couldn't completely hide.

After being informed of the formation of Exercitus by the White King on the Highest Level, Kuroyukihime had expressed her sincere hope that this joint army of unprecedented scale would crush Tezcatlipoca and use that momentum to challenge the seven Great Legions, including Nega Nebulus, to a fight. But Exercitus had been defeated, and the majority of its members had lost.

It seemed that most of the Legion members already knew all of this. When he thought about it, that was only natural. It had been nearly an hour since the Exercitus survivors had left the Unlimited Neutral Field. While Haruyuki had been having supper with Chiyuri and Takumu, a vast quantity of information must have been flying back and forth both in and outside of the Accelerated World.

On top of this, there was also the fact that over forty days had passed in the Unlimited Neutral Field. He hadn't been able to see the missing Urocyon and Complicator from the Highest Level, but it was unclear if this was because they had returned to the real world, or because they had the ability to completely mask themselves. If it was the latter, it was possible that they had settled on a target Being by now and were in the middle of attacking that dungeon...

Overcome with that anxiety again, Haruyuki hung his head, and Kuroyukihime's voice reached his ears.

"Due to an Unlimited EK that lasted for several weeks, more than a hundred members of Exercitus faced total point loss. There is no doubt that this is the greatest tragedy in Brain Burst history. And it seems that this itself has triggered a new anomaly."

Hearing this, the members groaned. Haruyuki listened closely and heard them whispering words like "final stage" and "Dread Drive." So it seemed that a fair bit of information had indeed spread.

Kuroyukihime waited for the commotion to die down somewhat before getting into the heart of the matter.

"...At about five seconds past eight this evening, I was cleaning up after dinner in the real world when a BB system message was displayed in my field of view. I'm sure that you also received this at the same time, Rain?"

Niko shrugged and nodded. "Yeah, I got it."

"I thought so. No doubt the text was the same, but if there is anything different, please say so."

The system message Kuroyukihime spoke from memory after this preamble was word-for-word the exact same as the one the White King had recited on the Highest Level.

If four or more of the seven were destroyed, then Brain Burst 2039 would lose, and the trial would end. The instant Kuroyukihime added "that's all" to the last words of this mechanical declaration, the meeting participants erupted in shock all over again, several times louder than the previous clamor.

That was no wonder. For the majority of Burst Linkers, the top-ranked Beings, including the Four Saints, were boss monsters waiting for invaders in the depths of the Great Dungeons. They wouldn't be able to shift gears so easily when suddenly told to protect the targets for subjugation they had seen as final missions for the game Brain Burst.

But this commotion, too, died down again in a few seconds. It wasn't that they had all processed the situation, but rather because a small avatar had leapt forward rather forcefully from the Red faction side.

Wide-brimmed hat on his head, long cloak draped over his body. His face mask wasn't visible at all, but Haruyuki knew who it was. The person who had cast the lone vote in opposition at the Nega Nebulus and Prominence merger meeting, "Stronger Name," aka Iodine Sterilizer.

Dine produced just his right hand from inside of his cloak, raised the brim of his hat slightly, and spoke. "Lotus. You are now our Master, so I do not wish to cast aspersions. But a mere two hours previous, we were thinking this and that about what would happen to the Accelerated World. And then rumors of Exercitus started going around, and just when the fellows in Ovest and Night Owls were all 'If we're doing it, then let's do it,' suddenly, we're talking about hundreds of people losing all their points and Tezcatlipoca destroying itself… My head's already spinning, and then you're telling us about this wild message, and it's not going down the old gullet at all."

His manner of speaking was as ostentatious as ever, but the content of his speech was exactly right. Even Haruyuki, who had seen it all play out himself, from the annihilation of Exercitus to the destruction of Tezcatlipoca and the appearance of the Drive Linkers, couldn't completely grasp the situation, so he could understand why Dine and the others would be confused.

"Mmm." Kuroyukihime deftly crossed the blades of her sword arms in front of her and nodded slightly. "To be honest, I myself have only secondhand information outside of this system message. And my personal experience is not weighty enough to convince you all. And thus."

With the fulcrum of the tip of her right leg, she spun her body around lightly.

"I'd like to leave the detailed explanation to the Burst Linker who most likely has the most firsthand information of any gathered here today. Silver Crow, if you would."

Whaaaaa?! Haruyuki wanted so badly to shriek and run away, but he had foreseen this development. Naturally, he was nervous, but this was still better than when he'd marched into the student council office at Eternal Girls' Academy, and he didn't really want to pointlessly be flustered and waste time.

"...Understood," he replied, stepping forward. When he passed to the left of the motorcycle-less Ash Roller, he realized that the usually arrogant fin-de-siècle rider was excessively meek today, but he figured this was because Centaurea Sentry was standing to his right and Aqua Current to his left. Ash tended to get nervous around "strong women," maybe because his parent was *the* Sky Raker.

Ash Roller, Olive Grab, and Bush Utan had transferred from Great Wall to Nega Nebulus in order to crush the Acceleration Research Society, the masterminds behind the ISS kit incident—to be more precise, in order to shore up Negabu's forces in the Territories against Oscillatory Universe, the prerequisite to that mission. But they had no sooner put in all the work and unmasked the Acceleration Research Society when Haruyuki had transferred to the Oscillatory they'd just gone up against, so he was certain that Ash, Olive, and Bush felt a certain amount of resentment, too. He wanted to look for a chance to apologize, but he first had to fulfill this duty.

He slapped the arm of the stiff Ash Roller lightly as he passed to at least convey something of his feelings and stepped out into the center of the ring.

It took him about ten minutes to explain the tragedy that befell Exercitus, the red portal contained within Tezcatlipoca, and the ten Drive Linkers that came through it.

He'd spent most of that time on Urocyon's strength, talking about how all of his normal attacks were enhanced with

Incarnate and smashed any armor, no matter how heavy. How every part of his body was similarly guarded by Incarnate, so he could easily repel even a thirty-millimeter bullet. The toughness to leap from a height of sixty meters and walk away without a scratch on him, the nimbleness that made him hard to follow with the eye. And the high-level Incarnate techniques he called "Psion Arts."

"...I only saw a technique called Cerdocyon that launched a fox head aura from his fist, and one called Chrysocyon that transformed him into a werewolf, but I totally don't believe that's all he's got. And I think in the fight with me, he wasn't giving it half of what he actually could..."

Haruyuki closed his mouth there and looked around at the Legion members.

The first to react was an F-type with a distinctive large visor patterned after a bowl cut, a member of the popular idol group Heliosphere, Freeze Tone.

"N'kay, Crowboy," Freeze called in a somewhat low and mellow tone, and then gave voice to an utterly unexpected question. "So the transform, not a werewolf, werefox, yeah?"

"S-sorry?" he stammered.

"Nah." She shrugged. "Just the guy's avatar name, his technique names, all fox stuff, y'know?"

"Huh... Are they?" He stared at her, baffled. "Actually, now that you mention it, he did say Cerdocyon was a crab-eating fox..."

"So first, Urocyon, n'kay?" Freeze began to explain smoothly and at length. "That's the scientific name for a gray fox. Most primitive of all living Canidae. And that first Incarnate technique, the Cerdocyon one, true, we call 'em crab-eating dogs in Japan, but as a species, they're more fox than anything. The second Incarnate technique, that Chrysocyon thing, that's a maned wolf. And this big bad, too, we say it's a wolf in Japanese, but if you're gonna pick, I personally think it leans fox. Y'know?"

Y'know, she says... Haruyuki was taken entirely aback when a rich baritone filled the silence.

"Regardless of the genetic lineage, given that the transformation was the maned wolf, I think he should be called a werewolf—or if you want precision, a were-maned wolf man."

The speaker was an M-type with massive horns, Cassis Moose, one of the Triplex.

Instantly, Freeze Tone began to rattle on at top speed. "I'm tellin' ya, the maned wolf's nowhere close to being a wolf! Like, hundreds of thousands of years ago, n'kay, like four lineages split off from this ancestor Canidae named Tomarctus, and yer so-called wolf's one of the first of the Canidae, and the maned wolf is just the one species, one genus all on its own. But the crab-eating fox and the culpeo are in the same South American lineage, so as a species, they're about as far apart as a house cat and an ocelot!"

"That analogy does not make things clearer," Cassis Moose said, groaning, and Freeze Tone took a large step toward him, her pale-blue miniskirt armor swinging.

"What Free's trying to say," Aqua Current noted, her voice reminiscent of tranquil water, "is that since his avatar name uses the scientific name for a gray fox, which is neither a dog nor a wolf, there must be a reason for that...I think."

When Haruyuki had first met Aqua Current, she had been known as a level-one bodyguard by the name of "The One," and after the resurrection of Nega Nebulus, she'd been a pillar of the Legion as one of the Four Elements. But he still found her mysterious even now.

Freeze, called "Free" by this very Aqua Current, pulled back the right foot she had set forward, stood up straight, and replied in a respectful tone, "'Zactly—I mean, yes, you're right! If this fox bit's this guy's identity, then, like, if we keep that in mind, we could get a hint or whatevs about his attacks, maybe."

"The fox is his identity," Haruyuki murmured, and he glanced at the Burst Linkers surrounding him.

The duel avatars in a multitude of colors had each been automatically created by the BB system in the forge of their individual mental scars—trauma and complexes...or so it was said. If

Dread Drive 2047 had the same mechanism, then it was no coincidence that Urocyon was a superhero with a fox motif. The key to understanding him and his attacks might well have been hidden there.

"So what don't foxes like?" he said to himself, and Kuroyukihime replied immediately from atop the rock behind him.

"Guns."

"N-no, well, I mean, yeah, but...," he said as he turned around. The instant he looked up at her magnificent avatar, body covered in smoky quartz, his virtual heart leapt. The softness he'd felt hours earlier came back to him, and he flapped his mouth beneath his visor for a moment before he continued. "...All animals don't like guns. And, like, this guy, I mean, he was totally fine taking a direct hit from a thirty-millimeter."

"Mm." She nodded. "There is that. Well then, there's a dog or a wolf, or sour grapes..."

"Wasn't it that the fox tried to eat the grapes but couldn't reach them?" Fuko pointed out, breaking her silence thus far.

Kuroyukihime cocked her head to one side. "Was that how it went?"

While this exchange was going on, the chattering among the meeting members quieted down, and silence returned to the field. Five minutes left in the duel.

Haruyuki figured it was basically decided that they'd go for a second round, but Niko cleared her throat and stepped in to tie it all together.

"At any rate, we know the victory condition," she said. "If we can protect at least four of the seven Beings in the message until midnight on July thirty-first, we win, and if more than four are destroyed, we lose. The gang from the DD side is coming in hot for real day after tomorrow, midnight on the twenty-ninth. Do I got that right?"

"Y-yes." Haruyuki nodded firmly and added, "The real attack starting the day after tomorrow at midnight's not a rule set by the system, though. Urocyon just decided that, so I think it's risky to accept it wholesale. The Beings could take turns watching the red portal in Higashi Ikebukuro, but some of them say they're going to help us, and some of them say it's each of them for themselves."

"Mmmm." Niko crossed her arms and groaned at length and then spoke, sounding somewhat confused. "Our girl Metatron saved us during the Territories, and she's a member of the Legion now, so I figure she'll fight right alongside us. But the other six are all major dungeon boss Enemies, yeah? They're gonna be not so into helping us, so much as they're gonna come attack us or what?"

It seemed that a lot of the meeting members had the same question. It wasn't only the various faces of the Red faction shrugging uneasily. Chocolat, Mint, and Plum from the Black faction joined them. They had formed a bond with the Lesser-class Enemy they named Coolu, and because of this, they didn't care for Enemy hunting in the Unlimited Neutral Field. Not only had they never fought the top-ranked Legend class, they would have never even encountered one of them.

During the Territories against Oscillatory, they had seen a Devil class, and it was only natural that they couldn't imagine fighting alongside the Four Saints, who were of an even higher rank. Even Haruyuki, who was linked to Metatron, had cowered with fear at the intense air of intimidation emanating from Storm King Rudra and Queen Mother of the West Xiwangmu.

Niko's concern was exactly on the mark.

"...I think some people here know this, but..." Haruyuki said by way of introduction, and he took a deep breath to firm up his resolve before continuing.

"The seven Beings that were singled out as targets in this battle. These boss Enemies all exist in a first form, which is a huge monster, and a second form, which is human-shaped. That second form is their real self, and it'll show up if you defeat their first form without using any assist gimmicks in the dungeon. The issue is, they can't control their first forms themselves. So even if the Drive Linkers made it to the boss room of whatever dungeon, if we went into that room to protect that boss, the first form would attack both groups indiscriminately."

"Are you for really serious…? How're we supposed to guard 'em like that?" It was Ash Roller who spoke up there, having maintained his silence up to that point. He had apparently finally gotten over his nervousness at being wedged in between Centaurea Sentry and Aqua Current.

Haruyuki looked at the skull face of the century-end rider and gave voice to the provisional conclusion he'd come to in conversation with the six top-ranked Beings.

"We either attack the Drive Linkers before they reach the boss room. Or we destroy all of the first forms ourselves first."

8

The emergency Legion meeting ended without a second round.

While it had been labeled a meeting, Kuroyukihime's objective had been to inform the Nega Nebulus members of the current situation, so right from the start, she'd had no intention of formulating a unified path forward as a Legion. And when Haruyuki thought about it, it was much too much to insist that the Burst Linkers at the meeting digest the astounding story of a war between worlds with the continuation of the game hanging in the balance in the span of a mere thirty minutes. It had been the right call to give them all a night to sleep on it.

Kuroyukihime said she was going to get in touch with the other Kings that night and request a meeting of the Seven Kings as soon as possible. In order to resist the Drive Linkers, all Legions needed to work together, but would they be able to overcome the hostility of the White Legion?

This was all if the war wasn't already over by the time morning came.

After seeing off Chiyuri and Takumu at the front door, Haruyuki returned to the living room and lowered the lights. He cut across the room, colored a dark orange now, and sank leisurely into the sofa. He was sure that he would fall asleep in three seconds if he closed his eyes, so he stared at the framed photo hanging on the wall.

Contained in the simple aluminum frame was a black-and-white photo showing a town in another country. On the left side of the cobblestone walkway was a café in the middle of a changing season, and on the right was a road littered with fallen leaves. It was an entirely unassuming scene, and the photo had been hanging there since forever, so he hadn't really paid it any mind before.

But now that he was really looking at it, he started to think it wasn't the work of a professional photographer. The center of the picture was slightly off from the center of the path, and the blurring of the photo was somehow unnatural. Rather than the focus being in the foreground, the blur seemed to be something added in processing with a camera app filter. In other words, this photo was probably not taken with a camera but by a Neurolinker, or even earlier than that, with a smartphone.

He couldn't remember how long the photo had been there, but there had to have been a pretty good reason for his mother, an aficionado of all things high quality, to go out of her way to have a snapshot by an amateur printed out at a lab, framed, and hung on the wall.

Maybe there's something written on the back, he thought, and he stood up to walk over to the photo.

But an icon started flashing on his virtual desktop, letting him know he had a call. And not a voice call but a dive call. The caller name next to the icon was "Reina."

...Who?

He blinked in confusion and then hurriedly turned back to the sofa. He settled in there and tapped the icon.

His surroundings and his own body were wrapped in darkness and melted away, and his mind alone plunged straight down into a deep vertical hole. Eventually, a light approached from below, and he descended into the middle of it. And was bounced up high by something soft and squishy.

Boing, boing, boi... He rebounded several times, a little lower each time, until he finally came to a stop. He was about to lift his face and look around, but before he could, he heard a girl shriek.

"Whoa! You're a little pig!"

He, in his pink pig avatar, was hoisted up from behind. "Mm, nnngh."

Small arms wrapped themselves tightly around his neck, and he kicked and flailed his short limbs until he heard a new voice.

"Come on, Shii. You hug the little pig so tight like that, he'll suffocate!"

"But he's sooooo cute!" the girl with Haruyuki in a sleeper choke hold replied as she loosened her arms slightly.

In a full-dive environment, he couldn't actually suffocate even hoisted up like this, but perhaps Snow Fairy's suffocation attack had traumatized him. He couldn't help but pant and wheeze.

When he looked ahead of him once more, standing there was a woman—no, a girl—who looked to be about junior high age. She was wearing a blouse with puffy sleeves, like the heroine of a fairy tale might wear, under a pinafore fitted at the waist. If her wavy hair parted in the middle hadn't been the same style as it was in the real world, he might not have been immediately able to identify who she was.

"H-hello, Izeki," Haruyuki greeted her.

Reina Izeki grinned. "Heyo, Prezzz."

"...And behind me?" He turned his pink pig avatar's head to the limit of its range of motion and could just barely make out the person holding him up. He'd already assumed it from her voice, but she was, in fact, a girl of about four or five years old. Sometimes, though, the appearance and voice for a full-dive avatar were different from those of the actual person.

"My kid sister," Reina told him. "Shii, come on, put the piggy down."

"Okaaay," the little girl said, sounding the slightest bit unhappy as she finally released Haruyuki.

He was gently set down on what appeared to be ground covered by short grasses, but it had a cushiony springiness to it. Full-dive spaces for young children often had specs like this because of their conditioned reflex to cry if they fell on hard ground, even if they were only an avatar.

They were in an open space in the middle of a forest, a number of large trees rising up around them, but these would probably also be soft to the touch. A single narrow path stretched out from the circular clearing, and he could see something like a little house at the end of it.

Having grasped the situation, Haruyuki looked back and introduced himself. "H-hello. I'm Haruyuki Arita."

A girl with her hair in braids, wearing a pinafore like Reina's, bowed excitedly. "Hello, Mr. Pig! I'm Shiika Izeki!"

"Come on, Shii," Reina chided her. "His name's not Mr. Pig, it's Arita, okay?"

"But..." The girl looked about to burst into tears, and at seeing this, Haruyuki hurried to say, "M-Mr. Pig is fine! I mean, I am a pig and all!" He waved his arms and the black hooves at the ends of them as he jumped up and down on the spot. Compared with a game avatar, an avatar for a dive call VR space had limited physical strength, but by making good use of the elasticity of the earth, he managed to leap up over a meter.

Shiika was apparently tickled by his antics. The teary look instantly vanished from her face, and she began to laugh wildly. "Ha-ha-ha-ha-ha!"

She then asked him to play hide-and-seek, and so they spent about five minutes at that, with him alternately being "it" and hiding. But after he found her for the third time, she curled up at the base of a large tree and went to sleep.

"Aah, she finally dropped off," Reina said in fond exasperation as she peeked at her over his shoulder. She scooped up Shiika's small avatar and looked down at Haruyuki. "Sorry, Prez. I'm gonna take her to bed. Just wait three minutes in the hut there!"

"Sure." Haruyuki nodded. "Take your time."

"Sorryyyy!" Reina apologized once more before disappearing with her sister.

He cut across the woods and drew near the adorable stone house. He knocked on the door, at any rate, before opening it and found inside a simple room about four meters square. In the center were a round table and two chairs, and a fire crackled in the fireplace against the far wall.

He jumped onto a tall chair, and while he was gazing at the flames, the door flew open.

"Sorry, really sorry about that. For real, totes sorriezzzz!" Reina had no sooner charged into the room than she was clapping her hands together in apology.

"Oh!" Haruyuki hurriedly replied. "You don't have to apologize. It's totally fine."

"Nah, I mean, I call you, and then you get stuck playing hide-and-seek with a five-year-old. Usually, she's already asleep by now, but she was all fussy today, y'know? And then I was, like, I gotta make a dive call, and she was just, like, I'm coming, too, wouldn't take no for an answer..." As she explained, she sat down across from him. She was about to bow in apology once more, so he quickly interjected.

"It was fun for me, too," he told her. "Don't worry about it! Your little sister—what characters do you use to write 'Shiika'?"

"Oh, it's the one with a bunch of little guys on the tree radical," Reina started to say, before apparently remembering they were in a VR space and materializing a pen and paper. With a fairly neat hand, she wrote "Shiika," using the characters for "beech tree" and "fragrance," and showed it to Haruyuki.

"Wow, that's a pretty name," Haruyuki said, quite casually. "I mean, yours is, too, of course, Izeki."

"Ooh!" Reina grinned. "Prez, you trying to seduce me?"

"Huh...? N-no!" He shook his head vigorously. "I didn't mean—I wasn't trying to seduce you!"

"You don't gotta go so hard on that no, though? I mean, *I* called *you*. It was to get you to seduce me, Prez."

"Whaaaat?!" He bounced up on his chair and then remembered with a gasp.

Right before they left Umesato Junior High, after finishing their Animal Care Club duties that day, Reina had said she would call him tonight. The reason for that was because Haruyuki had invited her to stand for the next student council election in September. "Seduce" could also mean "explain," so in that sense, she definitely wasn't mistaken, but…

"Umm…" He cleared his throat to switch gears and then timidly asked, "Does this mean that you're interested in running, Izeki?"

"I didn't say that," she responded, still grinning, and then the smile abruptly disappeared from her face. "It's like… I said this at school, too, but I'm not exactly student council material. That's for, like, people who are all-powerful, 'I wanna make the school better,' yeah? I don't got that in me at all…"

"If you're gonna put it like that, I mean, neither do I."

"So then why'd you get on board with Ikuzawa in the first place?"

"…"

Unsure about how to respond to this for a minute, Haruyuki tapped at his virtual desktop and called up a document folder. He picked out a file with the title "Student Council Election Speech Draft 01" and flicked it toward Reina.

"Maybe you could read this when you have a second," he said slowly. "Tell me your answer after you do."

"…Mm. Gotcha." She nodded and put the file into her own storage before lifting her face, as though she had just remembered something. "That reminds me. Is Hoo gonna be able to stay with Kao?"

"Oh. Right." He told her what Thistle Porcupine, aka Kao Fukaya, had told him immediately before he burst out of the emergency Legion meeting. "Fukaya said they also have a northern white-faced owl named Loco, so if it looks like Hoo's going to fight with Loco, then they can't keep him. They're gonna leave him in his cage for the night and see how it goes. Right now, neither of them are bothered by it, I guess."

"Yeah?" Reina said. "It'd be great if they got along."

"Yeah." Haruyuki nodded firmly.

Hoo had been taken into Utai's care when he was found huddled up with blood streaming down his leg on the premises of Utai's school, Matsunogi Academy elementary division. The cause of his injury was his former owner digging the individual identification microchip out of Hoo's leg before abandoning the owl.

Because of this, Hoo didn't trust any human being besides Utai, and while he'd started to get more comfortable around other people lately, he was still sensitive enough to pick up on when Haruyuki was upset and refuse to take food from him. Kao said it was fifty-fifty as to whether he could settle into this new environment.

But if he could get along with Loco, then that would no doubt help heal Hoo's trauma to some extent. Haruyuki strongly prayed in his heart that this would happen, before conveying to Reina what Kao had said when they parted.

"Thi—Fukaya—also said that if Hoo's move goes well, you have to come see him, Izeki."

"For real?! I'm so psyched!" she cried excitedly, and he felt a dull throb in his heart.

Reina had picked up on the fact that Haruyuki, Utai, Kao, and Niko were connected by something she didn't know about. If he were in her position, he would have tried to do a slow fade, unable to stand being the only one left out of the loop.

But even after the start of summer break, she'd been coming to take care of Hoo pretty much every day and continued to be her usual cheerful self with them, without so much as a question about their secret. Haruyuki automatically respected her for this, and thus, he had invited her to be a member of their team for the student council election. He searched for words, wondering if there was a way to explain this somehow without touching on Brain Burst.

But as if to get the drop on him, Reina said, smile fading from her lips slightly, "Sorry, Prez. I got no right to run for student council."

"Huh?" He frowned. "But that's totally not..."

"You remember, yeah?" she continued. "The day the Animal Care Club was formed, I left you holding the bag with cleaning the hutch and took off, pronto."

"..."

Now that she mentioned it, he did have a vague memory of that. Wait, it was actually...

"It wasn't...pronto," he replied slowly. "I'm pretty sure you helped clean up the leaves for twenty minutes or so, yeah?"

"That's basically the same as doing nothing at all. Me and that other guy... Um..."

"Hamajima."

"Right. After me and Hamajima left, you and Utai worked your butts off to get all those hardened leaves that were stuck to the ground out of there, yeah?" She hung her head. "Like, I am seriously the worst, dude."

"B-but!" Haruyuki earnestly shook his own head. "You came back. Hamajima never showed up again... And you didn't leave on the first day just 'cause the work was annoying, right? You had stuff going on, didn't you?"

"..."

Even when he asked this earnest question, she kept her eyes lowered. After a few seconds, she began to speak very slowly at a volume he probably wouldn't have been able to pick up if this weren't a dive chat.

"Making excuses is basically the weakest thing ever, but... Back then, okay, it was like, dark. Our mom's gone, y'know? And my old man's a designer, but he's basically like a giant baby who can't do anything besides that, so, like, me and my brother's mom, and Shiika's mom, they both left him."

"...Oh wow," Haruyuki responded in a similarly quiet voice. Now that she mentioned it, he did feel like she had told him not too long ago that she had a little sister from a different mother. But in Japan, when parents got divorced, he thought custody of the kids went pretty much automatically to the mother, like in his own family.

Perhaps guessing at his question, Reina began to explain without him having to ask. "Mom—me and my brother's mother—she's kind of a mess herself. She was seeing some other guy even before she divorced Dad, and she said she didn't want custody of us, since she was gonna marry the guy. Shiika's mom's not a bad person, but it's like… She's the gullible type, falls for all kinds of stuff. And she went all in on this maybe religious group that says stuff about how Neurolinkers and social cameras are government brainwashing devices, you know? My old man hated her talking his ear off about this stuff, and she sort of stopped coming home…"

"…I've maybe heard of that group," he said slowly. "Didn't they make some kind of gated community in Hokkaido or somewhere?"

"Yeah, that's them." Reina scowled for a moment before continuing. "So her mom says she's taking Shiika and going up to that community. But Shiika was born with this metabolic issue, right? She's got this embedded device that administers her meds, and it's controlled by her Neurolinker. As long as the thing's working properly, she can play and eat and do stuff like normal. But obviously, they don't let Neurolinkers into that community, so she could die if she went there. Me and my brother explained it, like, a million times, but… Mom was convinced that Shiika being sick was *because* of the Neurolinker."

She let out a long sigh, as if to tell him to go on and guess what happened next, so Haruyuki nodded silently.

"And then!" she said. "For real, it was wild. Stuff happening all over the place. Mom divorces Dad, runs off to Hokkaido. I mean, that's the only way it could've played out for Shiika's sake. But then my brother started this job as a buyer, and Dad wasn't coming home as usual. So I ended up watching out for Shiika. She's my baby sister, and I don't hate it. But, like, before all this, I used to go hang with my friends in Shimokita or Shibuya after school, and now I can't do any of that stuff at all. So I kinda feel like I don't fit my usual group anymore..."

"So then, that first day, that was 'cause you had to go pick up Shiika?" Haruyuki asked, and Reina cocked her head slightly to one side.

"Mm, yeah, basically. But we applied for afterschool care, too, so I mean, I had the time to clean a hutch, at least. But I was cheesed that I lost the draw and got stuck being in the Animal Care Club, so I took it out on you, Prez. I know it's kinda late for this, but I am sorry about that."

She put both her hands on the table and was about to lower her head in a bow, but he hurriedly stopped her.

"You don't have to apologize!" he protested. "It's totally normal to put picking up your sister over any club thing. And shouldn't you have been exempted from the draw anyway?"

"Hmm? What?" She glared at him suddenly. "You saying you would've been better off if I wasn't in the club?"

"N-n-n-n-no!" He shook his pig head with such force, it nearly flew off. "That's not what I meant. I'm super glad you're a member of the Animal Care Club, Izeki. I just thought if they're gonna decide it by lottery, they should honestly take family situations into account is all..."

"Ha-ha-ha! Kidding! Joke! Relax." She burst out laughing again and locked the fingers of both hands together. "But, situation or not, the fact is I totally blew off the cleaning and left you high and dry. I'm just not fit to run for student council. No matter how you look at it."

"But you are!" He shouted this, and some kind of hot lump rose from deep inside his avatar. He began to speak, carried away by his own emotion.

"You felt bad about leaving in the middle of cleaning that day and apologized to me, right? So then we can call it done. You don't have to go on blaming yourself forever. If you carry that kind of darkness around in your heart all by yourself, it just gets bigger and bigger. And at some point, it spills over to the outside, and you end up hurting yourself and the people around you. The election's one thing, but the cleaning thing, and everything else, too, it's okay to forgive yourself… You *have* to forgive yourself."

These were not words he'd carefully thought through but rather ones that welled up from somewhere in his heart and revealed themselves as is. But it seemed that they did reach Reina.

Transparent droplets suddenly welled in her eyes and glittered with the reflection of the flames in the fireplace. A moment later, she herself appeared to notice them and hurriedly brushed the drops away before responding in a hoarse voice, "Mm. Thanks, Prez. I dunno if I'll put my name in the hat, but… I'll read that file you gave me and really think about it."

Without waiting for his reply, she stood up, turned her back to him, and wiped her eyes once again.

She probably couldn't see it, but he nevertheless nodded firmly twice.

"Thanks, Izeki," he said. "We've still got time, so no rush."

"Got it," she replied. "Shiika is totes in love with you, by the way, so maybe you could come play with her again?"

"Of course! Call me anytime," he said, and she looked back and smiled.

After the dive call with Reina Izeki was over, Haruyuki took care of a little bit of his summer homework before taking a bath and going back to his own room. The instant he fell back onto the bed, his upper and lower eyelids practically glued themselves to each other. The clock displayed in the lower right of his field of view read 11:22 PM.

It had been a long—interminable—day. He shouldn't have been that physically tired, but perhaps because he had completely exhausted his mental energy, his limbs were as heavy as lead. Normally, when he went to bed, he took off his Neurolinker, but it was too much of a hassle to do even that.

With the last of his strength, he pulled the thin blanket up to his shoulders and closed his eyes. All he could hear was the faint

whrr of the air conditioner and the faint sounds of the city coming through the window.

While he was listening but not really listening to these sounds, his mind slid down into the depths of darkness but was yanked back, just as it was on the verge of being swallowed up completely.

He was so tired, he could hardly stand it, but the anxiety in his heart would not let the switch in his brain be turned off. He had exited the Unlimited Neutral Field three hours ago, which meant four months had passed in there. If Urocyon and Complicator had stayed on their dive without returning to the real world, this was more than enough time for them to have investigated every nook and cranny of the twenty-three wards of Tokyo.

Actually, it would have been good news if they were contenting themselves with just gathering information. But given how belligerent Urocyon was, he was likely to march right on into any great dungeon he happened upon. He might charge in with the intention of testing his skill, send all the Enemies inside flying, and reach the deepest level. At which point, wouldn't he use that momentum and keep going to challenge the boss? Haruyuki highly doubted that the first form of one of the Four Saints, which Kuroyukihime had said would require at least a party of eighteen people to attack, would be defeated by Urocyon and Complicator alone, but the more he thought about it, the bigger this seed of anxiety grew.

He curled up in a ball beneath his blanket and murmured in a soundless voice, "Metatron."

Naturally, he got no response.

Currently, she and the other five Beings were taking turns shifting to the Highest Level to continue monitoring and searching the Unlimited Neutral Field. She would definitely notice if the Drive Linkers infiltrated a dungeon somewhere, and he'd asked that they please inform him if that happened. So no contact meant nothing was happening…probably.

He had to sleep. He had a ton of things to do the next day. They couldn't waste the extension Chiyuri had wrested from the Drive

Linkers. He had to make sure he got a proper sleep so that he could perfectly carry out preparations for their countermeasures.

He relaxed his entire body and focused only on taking deep, slow breaths. The sounds of the city receded until he could only hear his heart in his chest. *Thmp, thmp, thmp...*

Ting.

He heard the sound of a bell over his heartbeat, and just as he really was on the verge of sleep, his eyes flew open.

He wasn't imagining it. This was a call from Metatron. Which meant Urocyon and Complicator had made a move.

His sleepiness was instantly gone. Taking a deep breath, he half shouted the acceleration command, "Unlimited—"

And then he noticed something strange floating above his chest.

With his mouth still open wide, he stared at it, stunned. A small particle of light shining white. *Ting, ting.* Emitting a faint sound, it grew darker and brighter at regular intervals.

Abruptly, the point of light whirled around counterclockwise and formed a sharp spindle about ten centimeters tall. A small ring appeared above it and adorable wings on either side. This was the 3D icon Metatron used when appearing in a normal duel stage.

She had appeared in this room immediately before the Silver Crow rescue mission, too. But at that time, he'd been accelerated with the Burst Link command, so he was his pig avatar, and his room had been changed into the Blue World.

But he had not used the acceleration command now. And while his Neurolinker was equipped, he hadn't launched the Brain Burst program. So how could he be seeing Metatron's 3D icon?

Ever so timidly, he lifted a hand and brought it closer to the icon. But the instant the tip of his finger touched the tip of a faintly shining wing, an even more inexplicable phenomenon occurred, stopping his breath.

The 3D icon began to spin once more and melted into extremely thin lines. Countless shining threads gathered and wove together, painting a complicated pattern, and spun the figure of a life-sized person.

The moment the silhouette was complete, it flashed with an even brighter light, and he reflexively squeezed his eyes shut.

He felt a sudden pressure on his stomach, soft but weighty, and he let out a yelp. When he nervously lifted his eyelids again, there, before his eyes, was a woman of unreal beauty, with a crown of light above her head and massive wings spread fully.

"M-M-M-M-M-M-M-M-M..." Haruyuki flapped his mouth open and closed as Legend-class Enemy Archangel Metatron looked down on him coolly.

"You were the one who called me, servant," she said, her voice like bells ringing. "Why do you appear so surprised?"

"...B-b-but it *is* a surprise..." He managed to answer somehow before looking the Archangel over from head to toe once more. Since the room lights were off, the only source of illumination was the pale blue of the streetlight making its way in through a gap in the curtains, and yet he could see her entire body quite clearly.

Sitting straddled across his stomach, Metatron was not in her usual white robes but rather the kind of short-sleeved shirt and pleated skirt a student in the real world might wear. The skirt pattern was a little different, but it was basically the same as the "uniform" that Goddess of the Dawn Ushas had been so proud of.

He was very curious about this new look, but he was even more curious about how Metatron, a resident of the Accelerated World, could materialize in the real world. Had he gone into a full dive without realizing it himself? Was he dreaming?

He raised his hand once more and was about to touch the smooth thigh, as pale as porcelain, before he realized the truth in the nick of time.

This wasn't a real body. The mattress beneath them wasn't deformed with the addition of Metatron's weight, and when he really looked closely, her slender legs passed right through the thin blanket, as did her spread wings through the curtains.

Which meant that she was a sensory sensation his brain was receiving via his Neurolinker. Haptic technology was a basic Neurolinker function, but even so, the amount of data here was too great.

Restraining the impulse to reach out and grab the edge of her stylish tartan skirt, he said, "Umm. I wasn't calling you before. I was just kinda worried and accidentally said your name..."

"What? A soliloquy?" she said, exasperated. "The signal strength was quite high for that, you know. I told you that I would inform you should something happen."

It seemed impossible that her voice was only in his brain and not in his actual ears.

Swinging her right leg over his body, Metatron sat down on the edge of the bed and folded up the wings on her back as she continued in a tone that was a tiny bit gentler. "But I understand your feelings of anxiety. The world where you have fought is facing a critical moment, after all—the question of annihilation."

"When you put it like that...!" Haruyuki sat up reflexively and earnestly connected his thoughts with words. "It's not like I'll disappear in the real world if the Accelerated World is gone. But Metatron... All of you Beings..."

"I suppose we will be completely annihilated." Her voice, so readily assenting to the idea, sounded calmer than it ever had before, and he swallowed hard. It was almost like...almost as if she'd already accepted that fate.

She turned her face toward him only slightly, raised her eternally closed eyelids softly, stared at him with golden eyes, and smiled.

"Please don't misunderstand. It is not the case that we have given up on victory. But I also have the feeling that I might well at last learn the answer to the question that I have carried since the moment the consciousness that is myself sprang forth."

"The question..." He paused to think. "The meaning of your existence in the Accelerated World...?"

"Yes." Metatron nodded. "The person who created and controls the Accelerated World designated as the targets for attack in the final stage the seven Beings, of which I myself am one. This could not have been some passing flight of fancy. Most likely, we were generated for this end from the start. In short, we are not merely a single object—no, obstacle set—in this game Brain Burst 2039."

"Of course you're not!" Haruyuki cried desperately. He was loud enough that if his mother had come home, she would wonder what was going on and peek into his room, but he didn't care about that. "If your job was only to be a boss monster, then the fact that you Beings have light cubes—souls like us—doesn't make sense! Tezcatlipoca is proof that you'd be plenty threatening even without a light cube. And…if you were generated as nothing more than targets for attack, then why would you…? I mean, a mere player like me…"

He actually couldn't bring himself to ask her the rest: Why would you like me?

But the Archangel smiled once more, as if she had picked up on everything in his heart. "…Indeed. If there are emotions born from what could be called a heart in me, these are an unnecessary feature in a target for attack. But—or rather, *because* of this…"

"Huh…?" He stared at her, uncomprehending.

"No, pay that no mind." She shook her head slightly before extending a hand and lightly pressing it against him. The pressure was supposedly only virtual, but he fell back onto the bed anyway.

"You must be tired," she said sternly. "Go to sleep, Haruyuki."

"…But…"

"Do you wish me to lull you to sleep? So like a child, hmm?"

Pardon?

Before he could respond to this question, Metatron was lying down beside him and pulling his head onto her chest. The material of the shirt that touched his face was smoother than silk and imbued with a refreshing scent, like a breeze blowing across a grassy field.

He froze at the everything-ness of it. There was no way he could sleep in a situation like this. Or so he thought, but the instant he felt the warmth and softness enveloping his whole body, the clock of his thoughts decelerated. He still had so much he wanted to talk about, to tell her, but her merely patting the hollow at the nape of his neck scattered his consciousness like downy fluff.

Good night, Haruyuki.

He heard a gentle murmur and fell into a gentle darkness.

9

Sunday, July 28, 2047. On this day, the second of the interworld war, a meeting of the seven Kings would be convened for the first time in a week if coordination between the Legions proceeded without issue.

But Haruyuki's slumber had been interrupted by the dry thunder of a *skreeee* before dawn arrived.

"Whoa! What?! What?!" Still half-asleep, he leapt up and looked around. "Aaaaaah?!"

The bed he had supposedly been asleep in, and even his bedroom itself, had disappeared, with only a gray sky spreading out for as far as he could see.

I'm falling!

The second he had this thought, his right shoulder was yanked upward hard. When he looked back, the Archangel Metatron was there. Hanging in the sky, wings spread, she held on to the armor of Haruyuki's shoulders with her left hand.

Shoulder armor?

There, he finally realized that his body was not his physical body, nor his pig avatar, but his duel avatar. Only one health gauge was displayed in the upper left of his field of view. Which meant that this was the Accelerated World, the Unlimited Neutral Field. He threw his head back, and on the other side of the cumulus clouds covering the sky, he saw the red hexagonal tile pattern faintly.

"...I didn't call out the command, though," he murmured, stunned.

"I brought you here," Metatron said smoothly, and he was once again speechless.

Actually, if their link had grown so strong that she could appear in the real world in her true form, then it was maybe possible for her to force him to accelerate. But in that case, what about the ten points he would have used up with the Unlimited Burst command?

This thought popped into his head suddenly, and Metatron shook him lightly.

"Would you please focus?" she demanded. "Keep yourself in the air."

"Oh. Right," he said slowly. "No, actually, wait! My special attack gauge's empty. I have to fill it somewhere."

"Now that you have accepted my wings, you should be able to fly without this gauge."

"...R-really?" Further taken aback, he nonetheless deployed just the upper pairs of the twelve wings on his back. When he vibrated them hesitantly, the thrust generated lifted his avatar several centimeters.

"Y-you're right," he half gasped. "So can I fly forever like this?"

"As long as the link with me exists," she agreed. "But actions that do not consume your gauge are limited to maintaining position in the air, as you are now, or to flying slowly. To fly at full speed, you will need to charge your gauge as you have done thus far."

He noticed that she had returned to her usual white robes from the school shirt and pleated skirt. He wanted to ask her why she had been dressed like that, but this was not the time for that.

When she took her hand off his shoulder, he slowly flipped around and asked, "...So those guys—Urocyon and Complicator—they infiltrated a dungeon somewhere?"

"Oh-ho!" Metatron said, sounding impressed. "For once, your intuition is sharp, servant."

"Wh-which dungeon?!" Haruyuki demanded, drawing about ten centimeters closer to her. "It's not yours, is it?!"

She gently pushed his forehead back as she replied, "It is not my castle, and it is unclear as to whether or not the intruders are the Drive Linkers. However...the issue may be easier to handle if it *is* them."

He frowned. "...What do you mean?"

"Amaterasu was on observation duty on the Highest Level, and she sent me a notification. Approximately ninety minutes ago in this time, the sealed door of the Sanctuary of the Evening Star—the Shrine of Vesper—was opened, and some person entered it alone."

"Shrine...? Where is that?" He cocked his head to one side at this unfamiliar place name.

Metatron raised a hand and pointed to the left behind Haruyuki.

He once again flipped around and narrowed his eyes. At the same time, a gap opened up in the thick clouds hanging below him, revealing the scene on the ground.

The tall pillar rising up about two hundred meters below was the mixed-used condo building where he lived. On the west side of this was Kannana Street, on the south, Koenji Station and the overhead Chuo Line. The terrain was as it had been in the real world, but everything was covered in pure white snow and blue ice. A water-affiliated Ice stage.

Metatron's finger was pointing to the southwest. The large dungeons in that direction were the Shinjuku Government Building Underground Labyrinth ruled by Goddess of the Dawn Ushas and...

"Yoyogi...?" Haruyuki murmured, and Metatron nodded gently.

"Yes. Yoyogi Park Underground Labyrinth. The castle of Night Goddess Nyx."

To be continued...

ACCEL WORLD

LEAP TO INFINITY

It was a move beyond human limitations—no, something more than that. She could almost keep going up into the sky.

The first time Risa Tsukiori happened upon a gymnastics competition was the 2040 summer Olympics. She had only just turned eight and was still obsessed with kids' anime, so she was entirely put out by the fact that her father had monopolized the TV to watch the Olympics all summer. But all complaining would do was make her mercurial father angry, so she held her tongue and watched the boring Olympics broadcast every day.

She really couldn't understand what was so interesting about the soccer, judo, or track and field that got her father so excited, but her eyes were glued to the screen the moment *she* appeared.

Women's gymnastics. A slender gymnast in a white leotard stood in front of the vault, a competitor from Romania still in her teens.

Her father was apparently less interested in this sport. He got up to go to the washroom, and since her mother was out doing the shopping, Risa was alone in the living room. Both sides of the TV fell silent as the girl raised her right hand slowly. She picked her moment with a curious flourish and started fluidly down the blue runway.

She held her torso perfectly straight as she rapidly accelerated, her arms barely swinging. She stepped hard on the springboard (Risa learned later that this was what it was called), thrust both of her hands onto the vault, and leapt.

In that moment, Risa saw snowy wings spreading from the gymnast's back.

The gymnast quickly wrapped her arms around her knees and started to rotate in a forward motion. Once. Again. And again. And then one more time.

Her feet plunged into the mat as she landed, and without taking a single step from that spot, she threw her head back, stood up tall, and flung her hands up high into the air. The venue erupted in a thunder of cheering and applause.

Her mouth hanging open, Risa watched the slow-motion replay, enthralled.

She was the only one of the girls who could jump over the six-layered vaulting box in gym class, a secret source of pride. But the gymnast in the white leotard leapt so many times higher than Risa, high enough that it seemed like she could touch the sky, all the while spinning so fast that the eye had trouble following her even in slow motion. And then she executed a perfect landing. Risa couldn't believe a human being could move like that.

The commentator's voice was hoarse with excitement as she described this technique as a "triple front flip." But the gymnast did that one rotation at the start, so in practical terms, it was a quadruple flip. The triple flip was called a "Produnova," but a quadruple flip had no name. This Romanian gymnast was the first to unveil it and to succeed at performing it on a global stage. Later on, the quadruple flip would be given her name.

But no gymnast succeeded in performing this quadruple flip again, not even at the 2044 Olympics or at the other big meets, and not even by the gymnast who gave it its name. She broke her right ankle in the leap that had so entranced Risa and retired from competition a few months later.

The name of the gymnast and the technique was "Racoviţă." This was the technique that led to Risa becoming a gymnast, the technique that, on this day when she was still a young child, she vowed she would perform herself someday.

1

"Physical full burst...?" Risa parroted back the command she had just been taught, and the F-type duel avatar in front of her raised the mouth of her face mask like she was grinning.

"Unki, before you say any BB command out loud, you gotta first think if you're someplace where it's safe to do that. If this was the real world and you were level nine, that command would've activated, and ninety-nine percent of your burst points would've vanished, you know?"

"Oh... Right." Reflexively, she slapped her hand across her mouth, but then quickly moved that hand to point at the other girl. "Mimo, I told you to quit with the 'Unki.'"

"Why? It's cute. And your avatar name's Uncia, so if I'm gonna give you a nickname, it's pretty much gotta be Unki."

"No, no, no, no. That's not what it's 'gotta be.' And it's not cute at all," Risa denied flatly. "I mean, it's true Brain Burst gave me the name Nitride Uncia. But it's up to me to decide how to pronounce it, okay? Like that chocolate-color girl we met in Setagaya Area Two the other day. You said yourself that if you pronounced it correctly, her name would be Chocolate Puppeteer, but that's not very cute, so she goes around saying she's Chocolat, in French. So I get to be Nitride You-nee-kah!"

"Well, yeah, sure. You get a certain amount of freedom there..."

The F-type avatar smiling wryly once more was Mimosa Bongo. Mimosa was the plant Acacia, and Bongo was the Artiodactyla herbivore that lived in central Africa. Just as her name would have it, her duel avatar looked something like a cow/girl, and her armor concealed spikes. But the girl inside the avatar apparently preferred to minimize the cow connection and would get into a snit if called Bongo rather than Mimosa.

"But there's gotta be limits, y'know?" Mimosa said, neatly sidestepping any mention of her own predilections. "Isn't reading U-N-C-I-A as 'youneekah' kind of a stretch?"

"Not not not a stretch!" Risa protested. "Okay, then. Try saying 'oohn-kee-ah' ten times fast."

"Oohnkeeah oohnkeeah oohnkeeah oohnkeeah oohnkeeah oohnkeeah oohnkeeah oohnkeeah oohnkeeah oohnkeeah."

"How do you pronounce U-N-C-I-A?"

"Oohnkeeah."

"Hrrngh...," Risa grumbled, vexed, and Mimosa laughed merrily.

The first part of Risa's avatar name, "Nitride," meant the chemical compound. And the "Uncia"—or "Unica" now—of the second half was a snow leopard. Like Mimosa, she was an animal-type duel avatar, but the things she could protract and retract were claws and paws featuring supple paw pads, with triangular ears and a long tail reminiscent of a wild animal of the Felidae family.

Having laughed her fill, Mimosa pet the cat ears of a now sulking Risa in a consoling fashion before turning her gaze off into the distance of the stage.

They were sitting together on top of a stony mountain rising up in Setagaya No. 1. The commercial skyscraper Carrot Tower stood in the same spot in the real world, 124 meters of tower in front of Sangenjaya Station, built at the end of the last century. It certainly could not have been said to be tall anymore, given that there were more and more next-generation super skyscrapers in the 500-meter class, the new metropolitan government building being the prime example, but it provided more than a pleasant view in the entirely residential Setagaya area.

The stage affiliation was Twilight, and the mountains of Hakone and Tanzawa, along with Mt. Fuji, were clearly outlined in the madder red of the western sky. Since there were area boundaries in the normal duel stage, they couldn't go all the way to the horizon, but someday, in the open world of the Unlimited Neutral Field, Risa wanted to run as hard as she could and catch up with the sinking sun. But the days when she could run freely in that world were still a ways off, given that she had at long last only just made it to level six and still couldn't beat a Wild-class Enemy solo, much less a Beast-class Enemy.

This thought brought her wandering mind back to reality, and she gave voice once more to the command she had just learned.

"Physical full burst… A command to accelerate your flesh-and-blood body in the real world," she murmured. "Kind of hard to believe. I mean, to think the BB program has that kind of power."

"Well, I've never actually seen anyone use it or anything. I've only heard the rumors." The Mimosa Bongo who said this with a shrug was level six, just like Risa. She was the "parent" who had given Risa the BB program and a member of the same gymnastics club in the real world, a year older than Risa. In other words, a carnivore child had come from the herbivore parent, but according to Mimosa, parent and child both being animal-types itself was relatively rare. Not to mention that both of their avatars were specialized in running and jumping. In that sense, there was a distinct family resemblance.

"…But that's the dream, right? We could run a hundred times faster in the real world," Mimosa said with a grin. "Forget the four flips of the Racoviţă—I bet we could flip five or even six times."

Risa automatically pictured it.

Of the four events in women's gymnastics, she was best at the vault, but she had yet to reach a success rate with the three flips of the Produnova that would allow her to do it at meets, much less with four flips. Mimosa's best event was floor exercises, but she was having trouble with G-level skills.

Risa was currently in grade nine and Mimosa, grade ten, so they would no doubt continue to perfect their skills. But girls as young as tenth grade could be national gymnasts with the Japan Gymnastics Association.

The selection standards were simple. Those winning the top spots at either the All-Japan Artistic Gymnastics Championships women's individual all-around held in the spring of every year or the All-Japan Artistic Gymnastics Championships individual events held in the summer were designated as national gymnasts. Risa and Mimosa had both already been selected for the national junior team, but if they were going to set their sights on 2048—a spot at the Olympics the following year—they had to make the national team this year. But they had both just barely failed to qualify for the team at the championships in the spring. Their next chance was the individual event championships in the summer, coming up in two months.

Risa's biggest and only weakness in her event was the approach run. For the vault, a gymnast had to gain speed with the approach run and hit the springboard at exactly the right angle, or they couldn't get the height they would need for the jump. But Risa was too conscious of the edge of the springboard, and her approach run speed dropped as she tried too hard to hit her mark.

But what if she could run a hundred times as fast? What if she could race down the twenty-five meters of the approach run like a leopard and spread her wings toward the sky like a bird…?

While Risa closed her eyes and imagined that moment, beside her, Mimosa said, "But, like, even if this physical full burst does actually exist, if you used up ninety-nine percent of your points, you'd definitely hit total point loss. And you could only use it the one time… I mean, that's a whole lot. You get to do this super, impossibly hard super technique just the one time, and in exchange, you don't get to be a Burst Linker anymore."

She sounded like she was telling this to herself more than to anyone else, and Risa shook her head unthinkingly.

"I dunno..."

"Huh...?" Mimosa glanced over at her.

"Even if it was just the one time," Risa said slowly. "Even if I lost everything, I feel like I'd wanna do the jump if I could fly like that."

"You mean like Racoviţă when she did that miraculous quadruple flip at the Olympics that one time and then retired right after?" Mimosa lowered her voice just the tiniest bit, and Risa opened her eyes wide.

She looked to her side, and her parent's face mask, normally so funny and kind and dependable, was tinged with a severity she'd never seen before.

"I mean, sure, Racoviţă's amazing—wait, she *was* amazing. In a time when basically no one was even doing the triple flip, she takes on the quadruple and pulls it off perfectly, sticking the landing, even... But the impact from a vault landing's the biggest of all the events. Racoviţă herself had to have known she could really hurt herself on the landing for a quadruple flip. Okay, sure, it's possible she was already having some trouble before the Olympics. But a single moment of glory in exchange for your life as a gymnast? That's not a smart deal. That's what sports is about...," Mimosa declared, trailing off to an almost whisper, and she buried her face in the knees she had her arms wrapped around.

Risa understood only too well what she was trying to say. The artistic gymnastics club at the private girls' junior high and high school they attended had been on the scene for a long time. In addition to the teacher-coach who supervised the club, the school had hired three other coaches. The head coach was a famous gymnast who had made it all the way to the Olympics, but tormented by knee trouble, she'd had to retire when she was one step away from a medal. Her constant refrain was "No injuries for athletes," and if anyone skipped out on stretching before or after practice, she would tear into them.

The word "sports" came from the Latin word "deportare," which apparently meant "to move away from sorrow," which equaled "to engage in recreation, play, enjoyment." If the original meaning was respected, then pushing your body in pursuit of fame and money and injuring yourself was a perversion of this.

But, Risa thought.

How many people in this world kept going with their sport simply because they enjoyed it? If the only reason to participate in a sport was to have fun, then people wouldn't need to compete in meets. Everyone had ambitions, ideas, desires, which was why they continued to push themselves to their limits. Risa was sure that the Romanian gymnast Racoviţă absolutely had to fly from the vault in the quadruple flip that day. She didn't know what her reasons were, but she felt like she understood just the tiniest bit that determination to do whatever it took, even if it meant the gymnast's life in exchange.

"...Mimo," Risa said, touching a hand to Mimosa Bongo's back as the other Burst Linker curled up into herself. "It's okay. I won't get hurt. One of these days, I'm going to do that quadruple flip. But it won't be the one time and then I retire. I mean, I won't beat Racoviţă like that."

After a few seconds, Mimosa slowly lifted her face and rubbed her nose. "Yeah, you better promise. Also, if you do make level nine and end up in the worst place, don't use that physical full burst."

"Listen," she said, smiling wryly. "You're the one who even told me about that command in the first place, Mimo."

"Well, that's..." Mimosa puffed her cheeks out, sulking slightly. "I figured if you knew Brain Burst was still hiding all these secrets, you'd be a bit hungrier and fight harder on this side, too."

"Huh? I thought I *was* fighting for real, though." Risa had received the BB program from Mimosa in sixth grade and had caught up with her at level six in less than three years. Even if that couldn't be called fast, she wasn't exactly dawdling, either.

As if reading her thoughts, Mimosa poked Risa in the side.

"Okay, look. The reason I stopped at level six is 'cause once you hit level seven—once you're a high-ranker—people come after you to kill you or to join you or whatever. A world of hassle, that's all. If I wanted to, I could be level seven already."

"What? Really?" Risa looked at her intently. "So then you'd just have two levels to go till nine."

The horned avatar slid over so that she was nearly falling off the edge of the roof 124 meters above the ground, but she braced herself with the exquisite balance of a gymnast and let out a heavy sigh.

"So the thing is," she started to say. "Level eight's a whole can of worms, but level nine is like ten cans of worms. There's only seven niners in the whole Accelerated World!"

"I know that," Risa replied promptly. "The Seven Kings of Pure Color. You could join 'em and be the eighth King, Mimo. But then what would you be the king of...? The cow king?"

"A bongo is not a cow!" the other girl yelped. "It's an antelope!"

"So then the goat king?"

"An antelope is not a goat! Artiodactyla, Bovidae, Bovinae!"

"So a cow, then."

"Ah..." Mimosa looked annoyed with herself for walking into that one as she cleared her throat several times, as if to change the subject. Her face grew serious again as she continued. "Well, either way, I'm good where I am. But you, Uncia—no, Risa."

When she called Risa by name, unusual for her in the Accelerated World, the grin also disappeared from Risa's face.

Mimosa reached out, clasped Risa's shoulders, and announced, as if choosing each and every word carefully, "The reason I gave you BB is because I wanted you to know that this world is so, so much bigger than you think."

"This world..." Risa frowned at her. "You mean, the Accelerated World?"

"No." She shook her head firmly. "I mean, this biiiiiiig world, the Accelerated World and real world thrown together. I mean, yeah, we're gymnasts, and we even made junior national, and we gotta live up to the expectations of the club coaches and our teammates and everyone in the organization, and more than anyone else, our families. But, like, if that's the only thing we ever think about, we'll lose sight of everything else that's out there. We've only lived, like, fifteen, sixteen years in this world, and it's full, so full of things we don't know. It's hiding all kinds of mad stupid secrets like this Brain Burst of ours. Don't… That's the thing you can't forget."

She lifted her hands off Risa's shoulders, patted those shoulders, and then laughed, embarrassed.

"Okay…" Risa slowly nodded in reply. "Got it."

"Good." Mimosa smiled. "So then, how about we get back to training hell?"

Risa looked up and saw their duel time was down to twenty seconds. Since they had accelerated during a break from gymnastics practice, when they left this stage, they would be in the school gymnasium.

"Yeah. Let's kick it in the final half." Risa closed her eyes and readied herself for the deceleration of her mind.

2

"...Hey, Mom? You really don't have to come pick me up every day. It's not that far from our house to school, after all," Risa said to her mother, who sat beside her in the driver's seat of the minivan, as she wondered how many times she'd told her that already.

From her school in Chitose-Karasuyama, it was half an hour to Sangenjaya, the station closest to her house on the Keio Line, followed by a transfer to the Tokyu-Setagaya Line. More than a few students in the gymnastics club commuted by train for over an hour, so it was pretty embarrassing to be picked up by car every day, even now that she was in grade nine.

"What are you talking about?" Her mother took her eyes off the road to glance at Risa and continued rapid-fire, "You're a candidate for the national team, okay, Rii? What would you do if you got hurt riding on a crowded train? The truth is, I'd rather you didn't ride the train in the morning, either."

"Quit it. I'm still only on the junior team," she protested in a small voice and immediately got twice the lecture in response.

"Don't worry. I just know you'll make the national team at the individual event championships in July. Didn't you hear Coach Ojima praising you to the high heavens today?"

"Ojima always says nice things. Head Coach Atoh would've been yelling at me," she muttered, quietly enough that her words were lost in the road noise, and she yanked the zipper of her tracksuit jacket all the way up to her neck. She reclined her seat a little and closed her eyes. "Sorry, Mom. Let me sleep a bit till we get home."

"That's fine. I'll drive on the slow side, then," her mother said, and she started to ease up on the accelerator.

"It's okay." Risa hurriedly shook her head. "Normal's fine. Just drive like normal."

Her mother was apparently unbothered by the time that, out of excessive concern for the sleeping Risa, she had driven about ten kilometers slower than the legal speed limit along Setagaya Street and had people honking at her.

She should just put it in automatic drive mode, Risa thought, but the AI driving seemed to make her mother anxious.

Of course, she was happy her mother had been rooting for her and her grand dream of making it to the Olympics ever since she was a child.

There weren't as many expenses in artistic gymnastics as in rhythmic gymnastics or ballet, and since she was part of her school's gymnastics club, the fees were only a thousand yen a month. But with the cost of protective gear, leotards, and similar requisites, on top of travel to meets, it still added up to a fair amount every month. After she was selected for the junior national team, she started to receive a stipend, but she could never have kept going without the support of her parents.

Lately, though, she'd felt like her mother's enthusiasm had left the realm of what was normal. Her mother would watch videos of meets from all over, uploaded onto the net, and complain about the gymnasts, saying things like "Her legs aren't quite straight," or "She's got too much meat on her." And she got incandescently furious if Risa bought snacks or junk food. She would give Risa notes about Risa's performance at practice and at meets, and recently, she was even considering making Risa quit the school gymnastics club and transfer to a more famous club. Almost like she was seeing herself in Risa.

And if that's how she sees me... Turning her body to the left in the passenger seat, Risa squeezed her eyes tightly shut.

What would her mother say when Risa wasn't able to make nationals, wasn't able to break through that wall, when she was forced to quit gymnastics? Would she reward all her hard work thus far and encourage her in her pursuit of a new objective? Or...would she toss Risa aside the way she so easily turned her back on Risa's father and kicked him out of the house after he had an affair at work and was let go by a major manufacturer?

She shuddered at the thought.

"Oh no!" Her mother's usual kind voice came immediately. "Are you a bit chilly? I'm sorry, Rii. I'll turn the temperature up."

Risa said nothing in response.

After eating a supper carefully calibrated for nutrition and calories, and then doing her daily stretches and training under her mother's watchful eye, Risa was finally able to get some time alone in the bath.

Her home in Setagaya Ward's Taishido area was a single-family home built after her mother's parents' house was torn down. She had no memory of these grandparents, though, since they passed away before she was born. Her father's parents were supposedly still alive and well, but she hadn't seen them since her parents divorced, and she was forbidden to contact them in any way.

The bathroom had been the one place where her father refused to compromise when they were building the house, and while it was a modular bath with a sink attached, it was fairly large, nonetheless. The tub was also big, and even Risa, tall for a ninth-grader, was able to extend her legs out straight.

This time when she gently massaged her legs and soaked in the warm water was the most relaxing moment in her day. Because her mother worried about accidents while she was in the bath, she wasn't allowed to take her Neurolinker off except for when she was washing herself, so that it could monitor her pulse and blood pressure. But this was still much better than being supervised by a camera. After gently kneading the knots out of her muscles, she leaned back in the tub and stretched out her legs.

An average ninth grade girl might have used this time to think about a boy she liked, but unfortunately, Risa had no such person in her life. In elementary school, a boy in her class had told her he liked her, and after she'd started at her current girls' school, a boy from another school's gymnastics club had asked her out, but she'd had absolutely no interest in either of them and simply turned them down apologetically.

Was the fact that she had no interest in romance because she was a gymnast or because she was a Burst Linker? There was an unspoken rule in the gymnastics club that romance was not allowed, but it wasn't as though some girls weren't secretly dating boys from other schools. Meanwhile, more than once in the Accelerated World, she'd seen Linkers who appeared to be a couple or heard rumors of such.

Maybe the Brain Burst program sapped the user's romantic energy, in exchange for accelerating her thoughts a thousand times. She wasn't particularly troubled by it at the moment even if that were the case, but how would she feel in the future, she wondered, as she sank down into the water up to her neck.

Many a female gymnast reached her peak around the age of twenty and retired from competition in her late twenties. The life of a gymnast would be dramatically extended if micromachine activation therapy, currently seen as the equivalent to doping, were permitted, but it would likely take another ten years for the international debate on that to reach any kind of conclusion.

Risa was fifteen now. If she had to retire in ten years, what would she do then? Set her sights on becoming a coach like her own club's coaches? Or would she leave the world of gymnastics completely for a new life?

Whatever path forward she chose, she couldn't picture a future in which she dated someone, married them, and had a kid… She also had no desire to live that future.

Mimosa had told her to look at the bigger world, but Risa

honestly didn't care about what came next, so long as she could do the Racoviță quadruple flip at the Olympics. She wanted to see the view that this Romanian girl had seen that day seven years earlier, the only person in the world to have ever seen it. That was her sole desire, and she had worked single-mindedly toward it.

Che-chee! Che-chee! Her Neurolinker alarm went off. Her blood pressure had gone past the set safe value. Standing up carefully to prevent any dizziness, she got out of the tub and sat on the bathing stool. She let down her hair, turned the shower on high, and stuck her head under the jet of water.

She wanted to wash away all of the extra things clinging to her—the weighty expectations of her mother, her own dissatisfaction and anxiety about herself. She used to be able to more or less reset all of the negative thoughts that built up over the course of the day by getting in the bath. But she'd failed to make the national team at the all-around championships in April, and as the individual event championships in July approached, she was no longer able to flip the switch on her mood with just a bath.

Still under the streaming water, she connected globally, closed her eyes, and murmured, "...Burst Link."

Her field of view was dyed blue, and the countless drops of water essentially froze in midair. From the flesh of her similarly frozen body, Risa's soul slipped out in the form of a fairylike avatar.

Her "parent" Mimosa had explained to her that the initial acceleration space of the Blue World generated by the Brain Burst program was a VR space automatically produced from the social camera feeds. But even when she accelerated in a space where there shouldn't have been any social cameras, like in the bathroom of her own house, the program recreated the real world with incredible accuracy. It was most likely using the camera in her Neurolinker, but frighteningly, it even realistically generated her own body, which was outside the reach of the camera lens.

She studied her own back carefully and had the thought that she really needed to lose another kilogram by the championships, before opening the Brain Burst matching list.

Taishido, the region where she lived, belonged to Setagaya Area No. 1. Setagaya was said to be an empty area, but her neighborhood was close to Shibuya Area No. 2, which had a thriving duel scene, so there was likely to be at least one Burst Linker on standby for a duel during the evening and night hours.

Just as she'd expected, there were eight people on the list. She selected an opponent on the same level as she was, who she'd dueled a number of times before, and challenged her. The frozen, blue world was enveloped in flames and melted into nothing as Risa's mind was carried to a new stage.

The F-type avatar with the snow leopard motif, Nitride Uncia, descended into a Factory stage, where every structure had been transformed into a mysterious manufacturing facility. The industrial park stretched out endlessly beneath the dark sky, and enormous gears, pistons, and conveyor belts moved ceaselessly—*kachank, kachank, pshhk, psshk*—while countless searchlights illuminated round spots on the bottoms of the clouds.

Risa was standing on the roof of a small factory, which was, of course, her own house, transformed. Since there was a risk of her home being cracked in the real if she stood here staring, she began to move in the direction indicated by the guide cursor in the bottom of her field of view.

As she leapt from one factory roof to another, she sliced through harmless objects with the claws of both hands to charge up her special attack gauge. The moment it was half-full, she called at the lowest possible volume, "Shape Change!"

Instantly, a white light enveloped her avatar. Her legs and arms grew sturdier, her torso more supple. Her body leaned without her willing it to, and her hands touched the roof. Now that she was in Beast Mode, the true self of an animal-type avatar, Risa increased her running speed dramatically. Without once dropping down to the road, she easily leapt across even the widest of avenues and raced through the nighttime duel stage.

If only I could run like this in the real world, too. If only I could jump like this.

This thought abruptly popped into her mind, but she quickly brushed it away and focused on running intently. At least for the length of the duel, she wanted to forget about gymnastics and her mother. Right now, all she had to do was run, carefree. Faster, farther…

But her full-throttle dash only lasted a minute or so. Just as she caught sight of the overhead Keio Inokashira Line and the large factory that was Shimokitazawa Station up ahead, the guide cursor vanished.

However, Risa hadn't missed the slight shaking of the cursor right as it was on the verge of disappearing. That distinctive movement meant your opponent was higher up than you. Risa had traveled all this way on rooftops, though, and the only building high enough for her opponent to get the drop on her was the shopping mall in front of the station, which had been redeveloped in the 2030s.

She didn't stop at the exterior wall of the mall/factory, but rather leapt up and began to climb using the ducts and pipes as footholds. In the real world, the mall was a stylish glass building, so it would have been difficult to climb the wall even in Beast Mode if it had been reproduced as is. But in the Factory stage, with its many uneven projections and protrusions, it was more like a bit of a workout for Risa.

She raced up the vertical wall at basically a run and was about to leap onto the roof of the mall when something round and shiny dropped down from above, straight toward her head. She hurriedly leapt aside to evade it, and turned to see what it was as it shot past her, brushing the end of her tail.

A massive steel hammer fifty centimeters across, with a long, thin, cylindrical handle about eighty centimeters long. She waited for an earsplitting metallic screech and a shower of orange sparks to greet her when it crashed into the duct she'd been using as a foothold a second earlier. But instead, it made an absurdly cartoonish noise, while a rainbow of star-shaped effects scattered around the area. The hammer was a hammer, certainly, but the squeaky kind, like a child's toy.

There was nothing toylike about its power, however, and the duct peeled helplessly away from the wall and plummeted to the ground. Catching sight of this in the left edge of her field of view, Risa jumped once more with another pipe as her foothold, and this time managed to make it to the roof.

"That's my Uni-Uni. You managed to doooodge that one? I thought I was attacking from totally outside your field of view, thooooough," a small girl-type avatar drawled lazily as she readjusted her grip on her hammer.

Armor in the style of a flared dress with ribbons all over. Large ribbons on her pigtail-style hair parts, too. A super-sized pendant in the shape of a comet shone on her chest, and some kind of small animal accessory was glued to her left shoulder. The duel avatar could only be described as a magical girl.

Her name was Comet Squeaker, a member of the enormous Legion Great Wall, which controlled Setagaya Area No. 1, in addition to all areas in Shibuya, Meguro, and Shinagawa. She looked adorable, but she brought more than cuteness to a fight.

"That squeaker of yours flashes when you start swinging it, Comecchi," Risa replied, still on guard as she faced this comet-blue magical girl. "Which is good and bad. It looks cool, but in a dark stage like this, it's too obvious. Not good for surprise attacks."

"Aaannh, true. But I'll never compromise! The glittering star is who I am!" Comet raised her left hand and ended this declaration with a sideways peace sign in front of her face, sending tiny stars scattering with just this small gesture.

In addition to her magical girl appearance and cute behavior, her sweet voice was breathy and high-pitched, like an anime voice actor's. She would also refer to herself with masculine pronouns, and all of this was assumed to add up to a lot of fans among boy Linkers and some pretty hostile treatment by girl Linkers. Or at least, there were more than a few people with these kinds of prejudices, who hated her in advance. But for some reason, Risa had always gotten along with her.

"I answered your question, so now you tell me," she said. "How'd you know when I was getting close to the roof when you couldn't see me?"

Comet groaned before glancing around and then nodding. "There's no Gallery and all. Sure, why not! Truth is, I fiiiiinally took my level-six bonus!"

"What?! N-now?!" Risa shouted reflexively. Comet had gone up to level six around the same time as Risa nearly three months ago.

Deciding on one of the four options displayed as a bonus when you leveled up was indeed rough, but normally, it was a matter of a week, at most, no matter how undecided you were. If you dragged it out any longer than that, you'd end up fighting with a disadvantage against opponents of the same level who had taken their bonuses, and you'd be slower to learn those new abilities—there was nothing good about it.

Risa had decided on her level-six bonus without the slightest hesitation. Except for the time she took Shape Change at level four, she had not so much as glanced at the special attacks or Enhanced Armament she was offered, and instead had diligently selected enhancements to her movement abilities. Her sole desire was to jump ever higher, and Nitride Uncia had been born to fulfill this dream.

Meanwhile, the unequivocal magical girl nature of her duel avatar was so obviously coming from Comet Squeaker's real-life personality that Risa assumed she wouldn't be the type to get stuck on what to select for her bonus.

"What was so hard to decide on that it took you three whole months?" she asked, cocking her head to one side.

"Well, the thing iiiis..." Comet stammered for a moment but then turned to her left shoulder and whispered, "Come on, you say hello, too."

The small animal that looked like a squirrel or maybe a monkey—or was it a rabbit?—and that Risa had believed all this time was merely a decorative part, blinked its large, round eyes and waved its hand adorably.

"Hallooo!" it said. "I'm Comet's pal, Borrelly! Nice to meecha, Rooo!"

"..."

Risa's brain shut down for a full two seconds. Shaking off this stupor somehow, she shifted her gaze back to Comet's face. "H-has it always been the talking kind?"

"Naaah." Comet shook her head, a somewhat complicated look on her face. "It used to be the kind that was stuck to my shoulder and sorta got in the way. For my level-six bonus, though, there was this 'option evolution one.' And I just knew it had to be this thing, right? I went back and forth on it for, like, ever, but my curiosity got the better of me, so I picked it, and—"

"Roopy! Borrelly's not an option, Roo! I'm a fun, cute, reliable friend!" The option got mad and kicked and flailed its short limbs.

"...Sorry, Comecchi. That's kind of annoying." Risa unthinkingly gave her honest opinion, and Comet nodded.

"It's okay. I get it."

"Aah! You're so mean, Roo! And after Borrelly went and told you the enemy was coming before!"

Listening to the option's violent protest, Risa finally understood why Comet had been able to so accurately target her while hiding in her blind spot. "Oh, so that's it, huh?" she said. "That option hid somewhere and told you I was climbing the wall?"

"Pretty much," Comet agreed.

"I told you, Roo, I'm not an option!!"

As the option kicked and flailed yet again, Comet grabbed its round head tightly with three fingers of her left hand. "Borrelly, shut up a second?"

"...R-roopy... Fine, Roo...," the option agreed, sounding scared, and it stopped moving once more, as though its power had been cut.

Comet sighed at length before picking up her hammer from the ground and spinning it like a top. "So there you have it," she said. "What do you wanna do? Keep dueling?"

"Ummm..." Risa blinked her eye lenses a number of times before responding. "It's, like, I'm surprised, I guess. That really cleared my head. So maybe I'm good for today. I know I challenged you, though. Sorry?"

"We're good, no worries. Pretty much anyone who sees this thing talk for the first time has that reaction. N'kay then. We'll make it a draw." Comet was about to open her Instruct menu when Risa abruptly stopped her.

"Oh, hang on, Comecchi."

"Hmm? What? You do wanna go?"

"It's not that," Risa said slowly. "Can we talk a minute?" It wasn't like they weren't friendly, but this was the first time she'd invited a Burst Linker other than Mimosa Bongo to chat in a duel stage.

The blue magical girl blinked her cute, round eye lenses in surprise before breaking out into a grin. "Yeah, of course! Let's go somewhere quiet, then."

The pair moved a kilometer or so to the east from the chaos of the area around Shimokitazawa Station to Komaba Park and sat down together on the roof of a Western-style building standing quietly in the center of the park.

Once a noble's manor in the Meiji era and now designated as an important cultural property, the Tudor-style house was more or less unchanged, despite the fact that this was a Factory stage. The buildings of the massive university campus that enclosed three sides of the park had been quite clearly turned into factories, but the noise of those didn't reach them here.

Sitting to Risa's right, Comet Squeaker glanced at the timer before asking innocently, "So what's this thing you wanna talk about, Unicchi?"

Perhaps Risa was caught off guard by this sudden question,

staring intently as she was at the animal-shaped option that was now silent on Comet's left shoulder; she blurted out the problem that had been weighing her down.

"Oh. Uh-huh… Lately, I've been scared of the vault," she said, and then thought, *Oh, crap.*

Mimosa had warned her any number of times that cracking in the real was a Burst Linker's greatest taboo. But in order to explain her slump with the vault, Risa would have to tell Comet she was a gymnast, and since there definitely weren't a lot of schools in that area with a gymnastics club, it wouldn't have been impossible for Comet to crack Risa in the real if she were so inclined. So she thought, but…

"Whaaa? Vaaault?" Comet squealed in surprise. "You mean, that guy with the faces of the Five Tiger generals on his helmet?"

"That's Ma Chao!" Risa retorted, slightly stunned at this entirely unexpected response. "And the whole face helmet thing was just in the manga!"

"Ooh, you sure know your stuff, Uni-Uni. I like Huang Zhong best of the Five Tiger Generals, maybe," the magical girl boasted, and looking at her, Risa felt foolish for being on guard against being cracked in the real.

"I'm team Zhao Yun," she replied with a wry smile. "But I don't mean that. I mean the vault. You write it with the characters for 'jump' and 'horse.' It's an artistic gymnastics event."

"Oh. Ohhhh. *That* vault! I know that thing. I've seen it!"

Just goes with the flow, huh? Risa thought, but only for a fleeting moment.

"So then, you're in gymnastics, huh, Unicchi?" Comet flashed her a smile. "Is it just the vault? You're not scared of the uneven bars or floor or the balance beam?"

"Wow, you know your stuff," Risa said, surprised.

It was one thing to know that the events in artistic gymnastics were different for men and women, but not too many people could readily list the four events in women's artistic gymnastics—floor, vault, uneven bars, and balance beam. If Comet understood that much about the sport, then Risa needed to respond to her seriously.

"No." She sat up straighter and nodded slowly. "I can do the uneven bars, the balance beam, and floor, just like usual. But the moment I'm standing on the runway for the vault, I get so nervous in a bad way."

"Hmm." Comet frowned. "You don't have a mental performance coach in your club?"

The way these words came out of her so easily, Comet was also likely on some sports team. So then why on earth was the magical girl…? Pushing aside this question, Risa nodded slightly.

"We do, but… It's kind of hard to talk to her. And I think I know the reason why I'm nervous."

"Did you get hurt on the vault before or something?"

"Uh-uh." Risa shook her head. "I'm not nervous because I'm not good at it. Vault's always been my top event. But maybe that's why. It's like I end up thinking that I absolutely have to make it, I have to get a good score there."

"Oh, yeah, I get that." Comet nodded and seemed to fall into thought, so Risa continued haltingly, half to herself.

"…The runway's super important in vault, but, like, that doesn't mean you can just run full speed. The really good people go at about seventy or eighty percent and land square on the springboard, so they can make a stable jump. But…the technique I want to do, I seriously can't make that jump running at eighty percent. Even if I can't hit a hundred percent, I need to run at, like, ninety percent and hit the springboard at the perfect moment, or I won't get enough height."

The real-world Risa's goal was to succeed in performing a triple front flip—the Produnova—in competition. While this was one flip less than her ultimate dream of the Racoviţă quadruple flip, the Produnova also had a high level of difficulty, and few gymnasts attempted it, even at the Olympics. But Risa's success rate at practice was barely 60 percent, so she very much could not use it at competition.

The individual event championships were two months away and closing in fast. Unless she pulled her success rate up to 90 percent within the next month, her coach wouldn't give her permission to do the move at the meet. So how could she balance both runway speed and accuracy on the springboard?

The answer to that was already inside of her. She wouldn't get anywhere without running, so she had to just run as hard as she could. There was no other way to do it than to focus on practicing running at 90 percent of her top speed and making sure she hit the springboard.

She knew that, but...she couldn't run. The moment she surpassed 80 percent of her top speed, her body instinctively applied a limiter. So even if she did hit the springboard right, she didn't get enough height. Which meant she was forced to open her legs wider in order to increase her spin in the second midair stage after launch, and that led to her being unable to stick her landing.

In the end, she simply lacked courage. She was not equipped with the kind of courage Racoviță had shown at the 2040 Olympics.

She realized that she was feeling even more down now, in the duel she'd started to reset her negative thinking, and a self-deprecating smile rose on her face as she moved to stand up.

But before she could, Comet Squeaker opened her mouth, after long thought. "I think there are two ways."

"Huh?" Risa stared at her, startled. "F-for what?"

"Ways to get over your fear of the runway."

"...!!" Half in disbelief, she looked intently at the face mask of the magical girl.

Large eye lenses met Risa's gaze as Comet raised a finger on her right hand. "One is to use the Physical Burst command on the big day."

"What...?!" Risa gasped. "I—I can't, not that! It uses up ninety-nine percent of your points, and there's no way I'll make it to level nine before the competition. And if I ran a hundred times normal speed in the real world, people would definitely start to wonder."

"No, no." Comet shook her head. "You're talking about Physical Full Burst, yeah, Uni-Uni? I'm talking about Physical Burst, without the Full. You can use it from level one, and it takes five burst points. The effect is that your mind stays in your physical body and only your thoughts accelerate ten times in the real world."

"Only your thoughts… Ten times…" Risa thought about it for a second and then furrowed her brow. "So then that means your own movement gets slower, right? How will that be good runway practice?"

"It's not that your movement gets slower," Comet corrected her. "It's actually that the flow of time feels one-tenth as fast. With the vault, it's barely like five seconds from start to landing, yeah? So then that experience ends up feeling like fifty seconds. Which, like, makes the whole jumping timing ten times easier."

"Oh…!" Risa finally grasped the significance of the Physical Burst command.

If her sensations were accelerated by ten, she would be able to make the minutest corrections to her timing as she hit the springboard. Meaning she would be able to land on it perfectly after running at 90 or even 100 percent.

"Wow," she murmured, impressed. "I had no idea the BB program had a command like that. I wonder why Mimo never told me."

When Risa let slip a slight complaint about her parent, Comet spoke up with unexpected words once more. "That was a kindness on Mimosa's part."

"Huh…?" Risa looked at the magical girl once more.

"Once sports people start using the Physical Burst command, they kind of have to keep using it forever. Their senses adjust to a world that's point one percent accelerated, so they can't get the timing right anymore without the command. You remember that tenth-grade batter who set a new home run record at Koshien last summer? He's a Burst Linker, too, and he used Physical Burst when he was at bat," Comet told her smoothly and out of the blue, so Risa simply opened her eyes wide, at a loss for words.

She didn't really know the rules for baseball, but she did remember this super rookie causing a huge commotion. As an athlete herself, she had sighed in admiration every time she saw him on the news. To think he was actually a Burst Linker.

But after a moment of being dazed, she abruptly realized something.

"Huh?" she said, frowning. "Hang on. They have a whole bunch of turns at bat in a baseball game, right?"

"They do," Comet agreed. "The fourth hitter has an average of four point five turns at bat in a game."

"So then, he was Physical Bursting at least once every time? Meaning he was using more than twenty points in a single game?!"

"Prob'ly…" Comet nodded, wearing an expression like she was biting her lip sadly. She lifted the squeaky hammer she'd placed on the roof and waved it lightly back and forth. With each swing, minuscule star effects danced up and faded ephemerally. "He made a real showing in the fall tournament last year, and the team even made it to Senbatsu this spring. But he wasn't in the starting lineup. Maybe he didn't have enough points. Or…"

Even Risa, who didn't know this particular Burst Linker's situation, could imagine the words that Comet didn't voice.

Or he lost all his points. That was no doubt what she was trying to say.

Risa fell silent, and Comet patted her back.

"So anyway, that's the deal," she said. "Personally, I wouldn't recommend using Physical Burst. Which brings us to the second way. This is actually the real one."

"…It's not another scary thing, is it?" Risa asked, switching gears, and the water-blue magical girl grinned.

"No risk, no return! Ain't that right, Borrelly?" The instant Comet glanced at her left shoulder, the small animal, motionless like a doll this whole time, waved its little hands.

"Oooof course, Roo!" it shouted. "You only can be as strong as you work to get!"

Risa stared at it blankly. "…So then what's the second way?"

"Simple is best!" Comet declared. "Practice in the Accelerated World."

"H-huh?!" Risa whirled her head around to look at the area and finally looked at her own avatar. "But there's no vault or springboard in the duel stage. And my duel avatar's different from my real self. Plus, to come to the stage, I have to challenge someone… And it ends in half an hour."

She listed all the problems with the idea as she thought of them, but Comet was unbothered. The option on her shoulder bounced up and down.

"You can't go saying you can't before you even try, Roo!" it cried. "If you give it a go, a path forward will open up, Roo!"

Unable to hold back, Risa brought her face close to Borrelly, opened wide the mouth normally hidden by her face mask, and displayed her sharp fangs as she murmured, "If you say any more of your 'Roo Roo,' I will eat you, Roo."

"R-roopyyyy?!" Borrelly jumped up, eyes wide and darting furtively, and when it landed on Comet's head, it began to tremble.

Its master plucked it up with her right hand and grinned once more. "No worries. We can take care of all of those issues. Although, well, we'll have to make do with some kind of substitutes for the vault and the springboard."

"Huh…?" Risa looked over at the magical girl. "You mean, you'll practice with me, Comecchi?"

"Of course!" she said, and then frowned. "Well, that's what I'd like to say. But I don't have that kind of free time, either. There's a place you can go by yourself in the Accelerated World, though."

"Wh-where…?"

"It's obvious!" Comet Squeaker leapt to her feet abruptly and pointed her squeaky hammer up straight at the sky. "The Unlimited Neutral Field! You can practice until you're half dead there. Try for a jump that's hard even with all your avatar abilities, and then run and run and jump and jump. You keep jumping till the light of the Incarnate is born inside of you, Unicchi!"

3

The next evening, while they were stretching after practice in the special gym for the artistic gymnastics club, Risa murmured to Mimosa Bongo (real name: Nozomi Inadate) next to her, "Nozo, can I ask you to hang out a bit over there after practice again today?"

Nozomi brought her head close, hair short like a boy's, and whispered, "Sure thing. But you don't usually invite me to duel, Risa."

"Oh, um, I don't mean a duel…" She felt the head coach's eyes turn on them, so she hurriedly pulled her face away. Their club took injury prevention very seriously, and they would get a harsh rebuke if they were caught slacking now just because these were cooldown stretches.

For a while, they focused on bending their torsos back without a word, and the second they felt the coach's gaze move elsewhere, they picked up their secret conversation again.

"…If not a duel, then what?" Nozomi asked. "Just chatting?"

"No, not that, either." Risa shook her head slightly.

"Geez, just tell me. You wanna raid Shibuya or Shinjuku or something?"

"Oh… Well, that's close, maybe," she replied.

Nozomi took a deep breath and was about to shout, so Risa hurriedly put a hand over her mouth.

"Mmph!" She made a muffled sound, and then when Risa removed her hand, she said, "So what already?"

"Um, it's..." Risa hesitated. "I was just hoping you'd hang out with me in the Unlimited Neutral Field."

Once again, Nozomi filled her lungs with air with twice the suction power as a moment ago. Before this could become a shriek, she blocked it off with her own hands this time.

"Mmph mmmmph! ...Th-the Unlimited Neutral Field?! Wh-what are you going to do there?!"

Risa took a second to think about how to answer Nozomi's questions, when she heard an angry roar.

"Hey, over there! If you've got the energy to chat, then you can do one more set!" the head coach yelled, and the pair pulled their heads back like snails into their shells.

Eat supper until she was 80 percent full.

Make sure to go to the washroom.

Lie down in bed, make her room a little on the humid side.

Connect to the global net via a wired connection to her home server, set a timer so that her connection was cut after two hours.

It was exactly ten PM when Risa chanted the Unlimited Burst command after doing everything Nozomi had instructed.

When she dived into the Unlimited Neutral Field for the first time in a while, it was replete with a pale, milky glow like melted pearls. The buildings on the ground were large chunks of marble reminiscent of temples. Matte-white tiles covered the roads and empty lots, and massive octahedral crystals floated all over, emitting a curious sound. The rare, high-level, holy-attribute Sacred Ground stage.

Descending from the roof of her house to the road in the form of Nitride Uncia, Risa curbed the impulse to destroy the crystals as she hurried toward Carrot Tower, where she was supposed to meet Mimosa Bongo.

The crystals in a Sacred Ground stage would not only massively charge your special attack gauge when you destroyed them but also drop random item cards in the Unlimited Neutral Field, albeit very rarely. But they made quite a loud noise when you smashed them, and this would occasionally attract Enemies in the area. Unless you could fly, it was risky to have a crystal-smashing party with only a few people.

She slipped past the group of octahedrons spinning as though beckoning her, and the moment she arrived at the front entrance to Carrot Tower, she heard Mimosa Bongo/Nozomi's voice.

"You're laaate! I've been waiting twenty minutes already!"

"If I made it to a meeting in the Unlimited Neutral Field with an error of twenty minutes, I'm doing pretty good," Risa responded as she watched Mimosa leap down from the far side of the tower.

She absorbed the entire impact with her four legs and then stood up smoothly. "...So, you make sure to do everything I told you to?"

"Of course." Risa nodded. "I set it to disconnect in two hours, just like you said."

"Good. I would've actually liked to set it to two minutes, but that totally wouldn't have been enough for what you want to do. So...should we go? Oh, wait. Before that." The serious look Mimosa Bongo wore fell away, and a somehow vulgar smile rose on her face as she patted Risa's shoulder. "We did get a Sacred Ground stage, after all. You wanna change our plans and smash some crystals?"

"Ye—N-no, no, no, no!" Risa shouted, shaking off the momentary temptation. "We came to practice the vault today! If we get tangled up with some Enemies, practice'll be the last thing on our minds!"

"Fine, okay... Still, I can't believe a lazy Linker like you would come up with the idea of gymnastics training in the Unlimited Neutral Field, Unippeh."

When her parent offered up such admiring words, Risa felt compelled to come clean. "Oh... The truth is, it wasn't my idea. I dueled Comet yesterday, and she gave me some advice."

"Whaaat?" Nozomi looked disgruntled. "That punchy little

magical girl, going and doing what she wants with a person's child..."

"Mimo, are you against me practicing here?" Risa asked with upturned eyes.

"Mmm, I'm not exactly against it." Nozomi frowned. "But I guess I'm worried, maybe."

"What do you mean...?"

Rather than immediately respond to this question, Mimosa Bongo looked up at the pearly white sky.

Following her lead, Risa turned her head back just as a flock of small birds cut across the sky far, far above. They looked like beans from the ground, but they were full-fledged Enemies. Seeing them, she was forcibly reminded that this world very much did not belong only to Burst Linkers.

"...The Unlimited Neutral Field is the real Accelerated World... My 'parent' taught me that," Nozomi said abruptly, half murmuring, and Risa gasped a little.

Nozomi hardly ever talked about her parent. Back when Risa first became a Burst Linker, she'd been curious and asked her about them any number of times. But Nozomi always dodged her questions, so at some point, Risa stopped bringing it up.

Nozomi turned her gaze back down from the sky and glanced at Risa before sitting on a marble block that was probably a flower bed in the real world. Risa sat down lightly beside her.

"...I never told you this, okay? But my parent was a gymnast, too. Not in the club at our school, though. She was in a private club..."

Nozomi named a powerful gymnastics club also in the city of Setagaya. It was the one Risa's mother had planned to transfer her to from the school club. When Risa nodded wordlessly, Nozomi picked up her explanation after a pause.

"...Her event was floor, and she was way better at it than I am. She made the junior national team in grade five, and people said she was a sure thing for the Olympics."

"Huh? So then, you mean…?" Risa said a name, and Nozomi nodded silently.

Risa had more than heard of this girl. She was a grade ahead of Risa, but Risa had seen her compete at meets any number of times. Her jumps were distinctive—she seemed to hang in the air at length, weightless—but the really astounding thing about her was her mental state. No matter how critical the meet, she was all smiles before competing and always managed to pull off the most incredible performances.

But she'd announced her retirement abruptly in grade seven and disappeared from the world of gymnastics. In the three years since, Risa had stopped hearing her name. She never dreamed that this gymnast was a Burst Linker and Mimosa Bongo's parent on top of that.

"I was a fan. No, not 'was.' I still respect her so much even now. How come you never told me she was your parent, Mimo?" Risa pushed gently, leaning forward.

"Sorry about that." A smile with a hint of sadness crossed Nozomi's face. "But if I told you, Uncia—Risa—you'd want to meet her, right?"

"Of course I would!" Risa cried. "We're both gymnasts, both Burst Linkers. And she's my parent's parent! There's a million things I want to talk to her about! To ask her about!"

"Unfortunately, you can't do that." Nozomi shook her head slightly and half whispered, "…She lost all her points and had Brain Burst forcibly uninstalled before you became a Burst Linker. That's also the reason she retired from gymnastics."

"Huh?" Risa gasped once again. "Lost all her points…? How…? Did she keep losing in duels?"

"No. But I don't know the details of what happened. She used to come to the Unlimited Neutral Field all the time. She'd dive and stay for ten hours or more of real-world time, over a year of inside time."

"…A year…," Risa repeated in a hoarse voice.

She could count on both hands the number of times she'd dived into the Unlimited Neutral Field and had always left within a day through a portal, so to her, this was an unimaginable amount of time.

"Why would she…?"

"Gymnastics practice," Nozomi replied slowly, turning her head back to the infinite sky once more. "That mental strength of hers, it came from the unfathomable hours of practice she did in the Unlimited Neutral Field. A duel avatar doesn't get tired, and it doesn't break down, either… I mean, sure, you get hungry and sleepy, but you can push past that, more or less. If you felt like it, you could keep doing the same jump for weeks, even. Plus, you can do it in places with, like, intense pressure—the top of a tower that's a hundred meters tall, or right by the nest of a huge Enemy. If you can get so you don't miss a single jump in those kinds of extreme environments, then any competition's gonna be wildly different from your usual practice spot, right? She was maybe Olympic medalist level when it came to mental strength by the time she was in grade six… But…"

Abruptly, in a gesture that was perhaps unconscious, Nozomi laid her left hand over Risa's right and squeezed it tightly.

"…But she lost something, too, in exchange for that strength. I just know it. For a while after I hit level four, I used to practice with her in the Unlimited Neutral Field. And I really did get a lot from it. The performance of your real-world body and your duel avatar are different, but I could still use the jump timing and midair sensations I'd polished here, and I got so I wouldn't get all nervous before competing. The fact that I'm here now with any chance at all of making the national team is maybe because I had that experience then. But…the Unlimited Neutral Field's dangerous. The more time you spend here, the weaker reality becomes."

Risa didn't immediately understand what she meant. But she gasped reflexively the instant she heard the words Nozomi followed this up with.

"I think that by the time she hit grade seven, her accumulated dive time was probably more than twenty years. That's nearly double the time she'd lived in the real world, you know? There's no way that's not going to affect her physical self," Nozomi said with a shake of her head. "And her memory up to the previous day would actually be hazy the day after she'd been diving for a year or whatever. But because of that, her gymnastics technique was so sharp, you would've thought she was a different person."

"Reality...gets weaker...," Risa repeated, and then she asked in a hoarse voice, "Did she lose all of her points in the Unlimited Neutral Field?"

Nozomi looked around the pearl-colored Sacred Ground stage and nodded slightly. "I think so. Like I said, I don't know what happened exactly. Three years ago, when she woke up after one of her usual long dives one day, she wasn't a Burst Linker anymore. Maybe an Enemy got her, maybe some other Burst Linkers hunted her... But she definitely wasn't a weak player, and she should've had plenty of points to spare..."

"Didn't you ask her what happened?" Risa said, frowning.

"The thing is, people who lose Brain Burst... It's like they even forget that they ever were a Burst Linker, and they completely stop talking about the Accelerated World. When I called out to her, she just looked at me like, 'Who are you?'" Nozomi cut herself off there and curled up into a ball, pressing her face against her kneecaps.

Risa gingerly placed a hand on the back of her parent, who looked so much smaller than usual.

After a minute, Nozomi started to speak again slowly, face still pressed to her knees. "She quit gymnastics right after that. Now she goes to this religious high school, and I pass her on the road sometimes, since she lives near me. But she doesn't seem to remember me... Sometimes I wonder if the Burst Linker she was isn't still here in the Unlimited Neutral Field somewhere."

"..."

Risa awkwardly rubbed the back of the curled-up Nozomi. "Mimo—Nozo. Why did you make me your child?"

Nozomi slowly lifted her face and met Risa's eyes squarely

with her emerald eye lenses, before saying something Risa didn't expect. "Maybe because you're like her. But I'll tell you right now, it's not like I wanted to replace her or anything. You're so focused on gymnastics, always on edge there… I was kinda worried. And I wanted to pay it forward to someone else, her making herself my parent. That's all."

Listening to this, Risa finally understood the reason why Nozomi had never suggested they practice in the Unlimited Neutral Field. She was probably worried that Risa would fall prisoner to this world like her own parent had.

As if sensing the direction of Risa's thinking, Nozomi abruptly brought her face in close and murmured, her voice serious, "Listen, Risa. I won't tell you not to practice over here. I used to do it all the time, too. But promise me one thing. Keep a single continuous dive to two hours, at most. That's eighty-three days and eight hours in this time. Any longer than that and your memory's gonna get confused, and your personality will change. And make sure you do normal duels, too. Not to earn points, but to have fun with the game Brain Burst."

"Have fun with the game…?" Risa said blankly, and Nozomi tugged on her cat ears with a smile.

"We don't have time to go shopping in Shibuya after school or to karaoke with friends or whatever," she said. "Because we're in it with gymnastics from morning to night. But with Brain Burst, for a mere one point eight seconds, we can spend thirty minutes in another world. We get to meet people we'd never meet in the real world. You've made new friends on this side, too, yeah?"

"Mm," she agreed as the faces of several people, starting with Comet Squeaker, popped up in the back of her mind. "Five or six."

Nozomi's smile changed to a pained expression. "That's not too many, given you're already level six, huh…? Well, whatevs. You gotta treasure them. Brain Burst's not only a tool for solving problems in the real. It's another reality, and it gives us all kinds of stuff. Don't forget that."

"...I won't." Risa nodded.

Nozomi grinned, tugged on her cat ears one more time, and then stood up. "N'kay," she said. "How about we head somewhere we can practice the vault? Around here...maybe Setagaya Park or Komazawa Park."

Nozomi listed the names of parks near Taishido, and Risa had a sudden thought.

"Oh! Right," she said. "Is that one place no good? It's kinda far, but we are in the Unlimited Neutral Field, so there aren't any walls between area boundaries or anything."

"What place are you talking about?" Nozomi asked with a frown.

"Umm, Yoyogi Gym," Risa replied.

Officially named Yoyogi National Stadium First Gymnasium, this was one of the leading indoor stadiums in the city, built for the first Tokyo Olympics in 1964—more than eighty years earlier. It had been significantly renovated for the second Tokyo Olympics in 2021, but the exterior was as it had been when it was first built. It was a place of dreams for athletes, the venue for many sports tournaments and national championships, and it was also where the All-Japan Artistic Gymnastics Championships for individual events would be held in July.

"Oh... Yoyo One, huh?" Nozomi abbreviated the name in a dubious fashion and fell briefly into thought as she looked up at the sky in the direction of Yoyogi. She finally nodded. "Well, sure, why not? But stay away from the central Shibuya area...and Yoyogi Park to the north there."

"Huh?" Risa furrowed her brow. "I get Shibuya, since there might be other Burst Linkers there, but why Yoyogi Park?"

"I'll tell you on the way," Nozomi replied, and she began running toward National Route No. 246, which passed right by Carrot Tower. Risa hurriedly chased after her.

Once they got onto 246, Mimosa Bongo sped up dramatically. The way she ran was magnificent, making it clear that she was antelope adjacent. Risa couldn't exactly allow herself to fall behind, given her status as a member of the leopard family. She widened her stride to accelerate and took her place diagonally behind Mimosa.

Apparently, a leopard-headed duel avatar by the name of Blood Leopard showed up now and again at the duel holy land, aka Akihabara Battle Ground, in the Akihabara area. Risa wanted to go up against her someday, but she didn't have the guts to go on a trip from Setagaya to the distant Akihabara at present. Once the championships were over… If she could get decent results there, she would maybe get a little more serious about Brain Burst.

While she ran, thinking thoughts like this, the Shinsencho Intersection came into view. Continuing straight down Dogenzaka would be faster, but that was the center of Shibuya, and it would be a hassle if they ran into other Burst Linkers, so they turned west at the intersection onto Yamate-dori.

They made a right turn soon after, and once they slipped through the wealthy residential area of Shoto, the figure of the national broadcaster building revealed itself ahead. The broadcast center, which was rebuilt in the 2020s for an enormous sum, had been transformed into a massive temple in the Sacred Ground stage, with a crystal, shining remarkably brightly, enshrined on its roof.

"…I bet we'd get some good loot if we smashed that," Nozomi said, slowing down slightly.

Risa felt a surge of excitement, but then shook her head vigorously. "If we do that and a huge Enemy shows up, we've messed the whole thing up! If it's still there on our way home, okay?"

"Okay, fine."

As they spoke in quiet voices, they went along the south side of the broadcast center, turned left, and now their objective came into view.

Yoyogi National Stadium First Gymnasium, a large structure with an elegant silhouette, like that of an ancient galley ship or a futuristic spaceship. It was basically the same shape in the Unlimited Neutral Field as in the real world, but the group of temples surrounding it seemed strangely natural there. They stopped for a second about three hundred meters away and carefully checked that there were no Enemies or other Burst Linkers before approaching it at half speed.

"...Now that I'm thinking about it, Mimo," Risa said abruptly, "how come you said to stay away from Yoyogi Park?"

"Oh, that. Umm... Hmm." Mimosa Bongo had said she would explain while they moved, but for some reason, she hesitated now. Risa peered over at her to see that the face mask beneath the horns had a hint of fear coloring it. "I'm just worried because you're weirdly super curious, even though you're so mousy..."

"Okay, first, I'm *not* mousy." Risa sniffed. "And I promise I'll stay away, so just tell me why."

"Fine." Nozomi sighed. "So, like, there's this dungeon that is like the triple and maximum yikes in the Accelerated World under Yoyogi Park in the Unlimited Neutral Field."

"Huh? Wait. That's weird, though?" Risa cocked her head to one side. "Didn't you tell me before that the four great dungeons in the Unlimited Neutral Field were Tokyo Dome, Tokyo Station, Tokyo Tower, and the Shinjuku Government Building?"

"I did," the other girl agreed. "But I guess they used to be the *five* great dungeons with the one under Yoyogi Park. In the first large-scale attack on it, though, a whole bunch of people ended up in Unlimited EK—basically, they couldn't escape. So they decided it was way too dangerous and sealed it off."

"Sealed it off..." Hearing this, Risa did actually want to go and take just a peek at it, but she pushed back her curiosity, because it would be grating to hear Mimosa Bongo say, "I told you!" So she simply replied, "Huh."

Even still, Nozomi got a dubious look on her face, but once they got closer to the gym, she clapped her hands, as if to shift mental gears. "Listen, Risa. The automatic disconnect safety in the real world will activate in eighty-three days on this side. You might think that's an impossibly long time, but you can't waste a second of it. You gotta jump and jump and then jump some more. Until you push past your duel avatar's performance limits... Until you touch the light of the Incarnate, okay?"

"...Comecchi mentioned this 'Incarnate' last night, too," Risa said slowly. "What is it?"

"You don't need to know yet. I'll explain properly to you one of these days, so for now, you just gotta jump!" Nozomi gave her a whop on the back, and Risa staggered onto the premises of Yoyogi National Stadium.

The enormous arena was sunk into silence, illuminated by pearly light. The nervousness she'd felt at the time of the individual All-Around Championships in April suddenly came back to life, and her breathing grew shallower. But that was all right. She had come to this place for exactly this reason, to resist this pressure and overcome it.

"...Okay, let's go," she called out, looking back, and Nozomi nodded silently.

They climbed the final slope and approached the entrance.

"...?"

As they were about to step inside the gloomy interior, Risa got the sudden feeling that someone had called out to her and stopped where she was. She looked back one more time, but there was only the tranquil, deserted world; not a thing was moving.

4

Sunday, July 21, 2047.

The spectator seating of Yoyogi National Stadium First Gymnasium was about 80 percent full for the women's finals at the 101st All-Japan Artistic Gymnastics Championships for individual events.

Risa Tsukiori entered all four events and had advanced to the finals for vault and balance beam. She'd failed to qualify in the preliminaries for floor and uneven bars, but this meet brought together specialists in each event, and she'd never managed to advance to the finals in two events before. There was one gymnast who'd advanced to the finals in three events, and four in two, but they were all on the national team.

Nozomi Inadate also broke through the preliminaries in her specialty, floor, and right about now, she was no doubt getting ready for her performance in the finals somewhere in this same venue. Even if Risa couldn't see her, she wanted them to at least give each other some last-minute encouragement on a Neurolinker voice call, but communication with other gymnasts at the stadium was prohibited.

Nozo, let's win this together and go to the Olympics next year.

She called out in her heart instead, just as the words VAULT: STANDBY flashed on the backs of her closed eyelids. The gymnast ahead of Risa was finished. From the sound of the cheering, she'd put on a fairly impressive show, but Risa was not bothered by this the way she normally would have been.

She opened her eyes and stood up.

The new leotard she'd gotten for this competition had white as its keynote color, with a design of black dots on the chest. Of all the people in the venue, Nozomi was probably the only one who would get it, but this very closely resembled Nitride Uncia's colors.

Uncia. Watch, okay? I'm gonna jump the way you do, she called out once more, this time to her own avatar, and then she came to stand at the end of the runway.

Her heart was calm. All sound receded. She didn't even pay any mind to the eyes of her mother, who would have been in the spectator seating nearby. All she saw was the twenty-five meters of the blue runway and the vault at the end of it.

In the center of her field of view, the words VAULT: BEGIN rose up and disappeared.

She held her right hand straight up, brought it down, took a breath, exhaled. And began to run.

Risa would be doing the triple front flip—the Produnova. Ever since the head coach gave her permission to do it a month ago, she had practiced it countless times and brought her success rate up. Her landing had been the tiniest bit off in the qualifiers, but since she was the only junior team member to do a triple flip, the venue had erupted in applause.

This time, she would do it perfectly.

In the now silent world, Risa ran, taking large, bouncing strides. The runway she used to think was too short felt several times longer, thanks to the many hours of special training she'd undergone in the Unlimited Neutral Field. She could get more speed. More… More.

Finally, the springboard drew near. Five steps… Four… Three. She knew before she started running that her timing was perfect. She kicked at the runway without fear.

Two more steps… One… *Now.*

She threw both arms up, and slightly bending her knees, she brought her feet down on the springboard.

Her bare feet touched the nonslip rubber covering. She clearly felt the special alloy of the coiled springs compressing beneath the board through the soles of her feet. The kinetic energy accumulated during her full-speed run changed into jumping power.

Then.

Crack! The sound and the shock raced up Risa's body to pierce the core of her mind.

The springs broke?!

By the time she instinctively understood this, her body had already been thrown ahead to the left.

The angle was too shallow. She was going to crash into the vault. She desperately threw her hands out and pushed her body up.

Somehow, she managed to get over the vault itself, but she'd only gotten half of her usual height, and she was going too fast. She lost her balance in midair. She couldn't control her axis of revolution. Lights flowed diagonally past in her field of view.

On the distant floor area, she saw Nozomi desperately shouting at her. In the spectator seating, she could clearly see her mother pressing both hands to her mouth.

Then they both disappeared, and the landing mat drew near with alarming speed.

She didn't have enough spin. She was going to land on her head. She needed to protect her head with her hands, but her elbows were numb from the impact with the vault and wouldn't bend.

If she crashed into the ground at this speed, she would definitely seriously injure her spine. In the worst case, she would never do gymnastics—no, worse. She would never move at all again.

But gymnastics, the vault, they're my everything.

But someday, I'm going to do a quadruple flip, the Racoviță. That's all I've lived for.

A black despair spread out inside of her. She could hear the sound of her future cracking and shattering.

Was she being punished? Was this payback for practicing in a place other gymnasts couldn't go, in a way they couldn't choose?

The instant this thought crossed her mind, she heard the voice from the first time she set foot in Yoyogi National Stadium First Gymnasium in the Unlimited Neutral Field. A voice inviting her to an eternal world.

The instant before her head collided with the mat, Risa shouted in a voice no one could hear.

Unlimited Burst.

Fade to black.

And then…

To be continued.

AFTERWORD

Thank you for reading *Accel World 27: The Fourth Acceleration.*

I'm sure more than a few of you recall that I wrote in my last afterword that "this volume (Volume 26) [is] delayed the most out of any previous volume," and now I have gone and updated your recollections. I also wrote, "I will be working hard this year," so why...? That is the general feeling, but I really did work hard!

The fact is, however, in 2023, the writing of short stories for every series outside of the main story overlapped with various supervisory tasks, and while I was taking on all of this work in my gloomy office, the long summer and the short autumn passed by. Before I knew it, the year's end was upon me. By the time this volume goes on sale, I believe I will have also laid out a forecast for my work in 2024, and I would very much like to make this the year I focus as much as possible on the main story.

With all of that said, a few words on the details of Volume 27. I was finally able to put into motion the players from the fourth Accelerated World, aka Dread Drive 2047, who appeared in the last scene of the previous volume. Given that I'd previously written that AA2038 was a shooter, BB2039 was a fighter, and CC2040 was a hack-and-slash, I decided to make DD the MOBA genre of game, and since the hero unit is the usual for a MOBA, the motif for the Drive Linkers is nature and superheroes.

The first out of the gate, Urocyon, does have quite the informal air to him, hmm? When I design characters, I often don't set their manner of speech, but rather leave it to how I'm feeling in the moment when I'm actually writing their dialogue. Because of this, there is occasionally overlap in speech styles. However, the fact that Urocyon's way of speaking is a little bit Niko-ish is simply a coincidence and does not mean he is her long-lost brother or some such!

Also, the top-ranked Beings that have made appearances in name only thus far all come out together, with the exception of Nyx, and this more or less concludes the debuts of all the named characters in Accel World. I do regret that I was unable to show off the student council president at the Eternal Girls' Academy junior high division, but I am certain she will play a large role in the next volume, the real start of battle.

"Leap to Infinity," the story at the end of this volume, was written as a special bonus for people who went to see *Infinite Burst*, released in theaters in 2016, and tells the tale of Risa Tsukiori/Nitride Uncia, who appeared for only a brief moment in Volume 22. I intend to have her join the main story in the next volume, so I do hope you'll continue to stick with *Accel World* as it plunges into its climax at long last!

Normally, this is where I would write about the author's recent happenings, but...this year really has been all about work! And yet the publication gets delayed and delayed again, and I've inconvenienced illustrator HIMA as well, so in 2024, I will work hard—no, I will toil relentlessly!

Reki Kawahara
A day in December 2023

HAVE YOU BEEN TURNED ON TO LIGHT NOVELS YET?

86—EIGHTY-SIX, VOL. 1–13

In truth, there is no such thing as a bloodless war. Beyond the fortified walls protecting the eighty-five Republic Sectors lies the "nonexistent" Eighty-Sixth Sector. The young men and women of this forsaken land are branded the Eighty-Six and, stripped of their humanity, pilot "unmanned" weapons into battle...

Manga adaptation available now!

WOLF & PARCHMENT, VOL. 1–10

The young man Col dreams of one day joining the holy clergy and departs on a journey from the bathhouse, Spice and Wolf. Winfiel Kingdom's prince has invited him to help correct the sins of the Church. But as his travels begin, Col discovers in his luggage a young girl with a wolf's ears and tail named Myuri, who stowed away for the ride!

Manga adaptation available now!

SOLO LEVELING, VOL. 1–8

E-rank hunter Jinwoo Sung has no money, no talent, and no prospects to speak of—and apparently, no luck, either! When he enters a hidden double dungeon one fateful day, he's abandoned by his party and left to die at the hands of some of the most horrific monsters he's ever encountered.

Comic adaptation available now!

THE SAGA OF TANYA THE EVIL, VOL. 1–13

Reborn as a destitute orphaned girl with nothing to her name but memories of a previous life, Tanya will do whatever it takes to survive, even if it means living life behind the barrel of a gun!

Manga adaptation available now!

SO I'M A SPIDER, SO WHAT?, VOL. 1–16

I used to be a normal high school girl, but in the blink of an eye, I woke up in a place I've never seen before and—and I was reborn as a spider?!

Manga adaptation available now!

OVERLORD, VOL. 1–16

When Momonga logs in one last time just to be there when the servers go dark, something happens—and suddenly, fantasy is reality. A rogues' gallery of fanatically devoted NPCs is ready to obey his every order, but the world Momonga now inhabits is not the one he remembers.

Manga adaptation available now!

VISIT YENPRESS.COM TO CHECK OUT ALL OUR TITLES AND. . .

GET YOUR YEN ON!

YEN ON

Yen Press

ACCEL WORLD, Volume 27
REKI KAWAHARA

Translation by Jocelyne Allen
Cover art by HIMA

This book is a work of fiction. Names, characters, places, and incidents are the product of the author's imagination or are used fictitiously. Any resemblance to actual events, locales, or persons, living or dead, is coincidental.

ACCEL WORLD Vol. 27
©Reki Kawahara 2024
Edited by Dengeki Bunko
First published in Japan in 2024 by KADOKAWA CORPORATION, Tokyo.
English translation rights arranged with KADOKAWA CORPORATION, Tokyo, through Tuttle-Mori Agency, Inc., Tokyo.

English translation © 2025 by Yen Press, LLC

Yen Press, LLC supports the right to free expression and the value of copyright. The purpose of copyright is to encourage writers and artists to produce the creative works that enrich our culture.

The scanning, uploading, and distribution of this book without permission is a theft of the author's intellectual property. If you would like permission to use material from the book (other than for review purposes), please contact the publisher. Thank you for your support of the author's rights.

Yen On
150 West 30th Street, 6th Floor
New York, NY 10001

Visit us at yenpress.com
facebook.com/yenpress
twitter.com/yenpress
yenpress.tumblr.com
instagram.com/yenpress

First Yen On Edition: April 2025
Edited by Yen On Editorial: Payton Campbell
Designed by Yen Press Design: Andy Swist

Yen On is an imprint of Yen Press, LLC.
The Yen On name and logo are trademarks of Yen Press, LLC.

The publisher is not responsible for websites (or their content) that are not owned by the publisher.

Library of Congress Cataloging-in-Publication Data
Names: Kawahara, Reki, author. | HIMA (Comic book artist) illustrator. | bee-pee, designer. | Allen, Jocelyne, 1974– translator.
Title: Accel World / Reki Kawahara ; illustrations, HIMA ; design, bee-pee ; translation by Jocelyne Allen.
Description: First Yen On edition. | New York, NY : Yen On, 2014–
Identifiers: LCCN 2014025099 | ISBN 9780316376730 (v. 1 : pbk.) | ISBN 9780316296366 (v. 2 : pbk.) | ISBN 9780316296373 (v. 3 : pbk.) | ISBN 9780316296380 (v. 4 : pbk.) | ISBN 9780316296397 (v. 5 : pbk.) | ISBN 9780316296403 (v. 6 : pbk.) | ISBN 9780316358194 (v. 7 : pbk.) | ISBN 9780316317610 (v. 8 : pbk.) | ISBN 9780316502702 (v. 9 : pbk.) | ISBN 9780316466059 (v. 10 : pbk.) | ISBN 9780316466066 (v. 11 : pbk.) | ISBN 9780316466073 (v. 12 : pbk.) | ISBN 9781975300067 (v. 13 : pbk.) | ISBN 9781975327231 (v. 14 : pbk.) | ISBN 9781975327255 (v. 15 : pbk.) | ISBN 9781975327279 (v. 16 : pbk.) | ISBN 9781975327293 (v. 17 : pbk.) | ISBN 9781975327316 (v. 18 : pbk.) | ISBN 9781975332181 (v. 19 : pbk.) | ISBN 9781975332716 (v. 20 : pbk.) | ISBN 9781975332730 (v. 21 : pbk.) | ISBN 9781975332778 (v. 22 : pbk.) | ISBN 9781975332754 (v. 23 : pbk.) | ISBN 9781975321338 (v. 24 : pbk.) | ISBN 9781975335083 (v. 25 : pbk.) | ISBN 9781975367848 (v. 26 : pbk.)
Subjects: CYAC: Science fiction. | Virtual reality—Fiction. | Fantasy.
Classification: LCC PZ7.K1755Kaw 2014 | DDC [Fic]—dc23
LC record available at https://lccn.loc.gov/2014025099

ISBNs: 979-8-8554-1186-7 (paperback)
979-8-8554-1187-4 (ebook)

10 9 8 7 6 5 4 3 2 1

LSC-C

Printed in the United States of America